CW01429569

Reder

Ian Smith is a writer and poet whose latest travel book "Stepping Out" (written with his wife, Alison Gelder) is available on Amazon, now. His latest collection of poems, "The Woodland Suite" is available from December 2019.
Ian lives in London.

Redemption Song

Ian Smith

Redleg Publishing

First published in Great Britain 2019 by Redleg Publishing

The right of Ian Smith to be identified as the author of this work has been asserted by him in accordance with the Copyright, Designs and Patents Act 1988.

ISBN   978-1-9993734-3-6

Redleg Publishing
7 Newall House
Harper Road
SE1 6QD
redlegpublishing@gmail.com

This book is dedicated to my wife
Alison Gelder
She is my song and my redemption.

"Won't you help to sing
These songs of freedom?
'Cause all I ever have
Redemption songs
Redemption songs
Redemption songs"

Redemption Song *by Bob Marley*

Chapter One

The body was in the middle of the path, lying under a blue fertilizer bag.

He was definitely dead.

Even discounting the large black fly walking across his open eye, death was unmistakable. Some sort of knife was buried to the hilt in the young man's throat and his hands were tied behind his back with one of those plastic strips normally used to tag cables together.

I had been walking steadily uphill for about three quarters of an hour and was singing "Redemption Song" by Bob Marley as I reached the top of the hill. Then the strange obstacle had come into view and I'd realised that it was not just a piece of refuse. A flesh coloured shape was protruding from one side of the bag as the lose plastic fluttered in the gentle breeze.

I continued to walk, the song no longer on my lips, my pace slower than before, feeling far less enthusiastic about reaching the top of the hill than I'd felt only a minute ago.

My hand was already reaching into the side pouch of my day sack for my phone as I looked down at the covered corpse. Using my right foot, I lifted the plastic sack high enough to see the body. It was of a young man whose contorted features made it difficult for me to recognise at first. He was someone who had been around only recently: a prodigal son back from his wanderings, as far as I could recall. Someone's certainly put an end to this lad's travels, I thought.

I stepped carefully away from the body and looked at my phone. I'd been speaking to the local policeman earlier this morning and knew him reasonably well. His number was on my phone, but it still took me two goes before I could press the buttons properly. This was certainly not something I was used to dealing with.

"Hello, Georges, it's John, here," he'd answered on the third ring, "Sorry, but I've just found something … that needs your attention." I couldn't really think of what to say and this was what was coming out. "I'm on the high path going towards the Chapel above the town."

He just answered "OK." and waited.

"You need to come immediately."

"Are you in trouble, John? You sound strange."

"Sorry, Georges. I have just found a dead body lying on the path. I think it is the younger son of Philip Pecheur, and he has definitely been murdered."

"Murdered? Are you sure?" Georges sounded even more shocked than I felt.

"Georges, he's dead and there's a knife buried in his throat. Please, I don't feel comfortable here. I don't think he has been here long!"

"On the top path, you say? The one that leads to the Chapel?"

"Yes, just as you come over the prow of the hill. Be careful, it's just in front of you as you come over the top."

"I understand. I'll be there in ten minutes."

I didn't want Georges to drive up here and run into the body, or, for that matter, into me.

I stood looking along the road as it sloped down from where the body and I were. The sun was not yet at full height, but the day was getting pretty warm, even on the north side of the hill. The breeze was too gentle to do much cooling, but I let it brush over me as I thought about the telephone conversation. It didn't feel real. It felt like the strangest piece of dialogue I'd ever taken part in and I almost giggled at the thought of it until I walked back and took another look at the corpse. It was definitely there, and it was unmistakably dead.

There I was, thinking "it" rather than he. Perhaps that was how I was trying to keep myself in control. Perhaps that was why I felt so detached. I thought again about who it was. He was the son of the local fertilizer dealer who had been the mayor when I first bought the house with my wife over 10 years ago. Around then, this young man had been one of the teenagers zooming around on those noisy little motorbikes we had nicknamed "sewing machines". He had disappeared from the town a few years after, but I had heard stories about him from time to time ever since. I think he'd returned to stay with the family only a few days ago.

I was still searching my brain for his name when I heard a vehicle's engine. Had it just started up or was it just emerging from the valley below? I began walking back along the path to signal to whoever it was. In this area, like most rural places, people tend to drive quickly and fearlessly around the country roads. This may have looked like a footpath, but local people actually drove their cars on it regularly. On Sundays, Mass was often held in the Chapel and the priest, as well as most of the congregation, would drive up this hill to take part. They would go up over this top, or high path to the Chapel and then down along the lower path on the way back. More than once on a Sunday I have dodged old ladies in battered old Renaults as they zoomed along this way.

The engine sound seemed to disappear as I reached the downward slope of the path. Then, a few minutes later, I heard a distinctly different engine sound as a car laboured up the path. George's pale blue Citroen emerged from the trees and pushed up towards me. I waved and stepped back towards the corpse giving him space to pull up in front of it.

He climbed out of the car, looked at me quizzically, and then stepped up to the body. He pushed the bag aside as I'd done and looked at it for a minute. Then he nodded at me again and pulled out his mobile phone and began to call the appropriate departments and people. I waited and listened.

"You phoned me immediately you discovered the body?"

I nodded.

"Did you touch anything?"

"Only moved the bag with my shoe, just as you did."

"OK!" then he continued talking on the phone.

"Did you see anyone, hear anything; anything at all?"

"Before you arrived, I'm sure I heard a vehicle below, either on the path you were on or on the lower path, but it stopped just a few minutes before I heard your car. That's all."

"You sure about that?" I nodded.

He returned to the phone and told a colleague to get to the point where the path joined the main road as soon as possible.

After the calls were made, Georges took another look at the corpse.

"This is bad." He murmured. "Really bad."

He turned and looked at me like I was someone who had spoiled his day, which, I suppose, I was.

"Do you know who this person is, sorry, was?"

"I think he is the son on Philip Pecheur. I have seen him around the last few days or so and I think I heard that he caused a stir at the bar/tabac last week, but I may have got it wrong."

"No, you heard right. God, this is bad. M. Pecheur will go mad and so will his other son." Then he looked at me again and said, "You heard a vehicle. Are you sure?"

"Well it was not long after talking to you when I heard the engine. The sound came from that sort of direction and it sounded at first like a tractor, you know. Then I thought to myself; that sounds like the old VW van we used to have. Do you remember? The old bus my wife and I had when we first bought the house?"

Georges nodded and turned to walk around the body. He looked at it in widening circles, hoping to see something useful. I had looked but not very hard. Georges then scanned the grass verge and beyond at the bushes that followed the path in a vague line. At one point he grunted, and I watched as he looked at the grass between two scrawny plants.

"Someone has walked through here recently, look."

I walked across and saw the slight indentations in the grass.

"That would probably take you down to the lower path." I said and he nodded, muttering, "damn" a few times under his breath.

We walked back to the body again and began to wait in silence.

"You are very calm, John. I wasn't sure what you were telling me when you called. I had to come because you sounded so strange."

"I don't encounter dead bodies every day." I answered. "I'm not sure it's something you can encounter without suffering some sort of shock."

"Quite, but this is strange."

6

"You're telling me it's strange. What was he doing up here with his hands tied behind his back and why was he executed like that?"

"Hands?" Cried Georges as he leaped back and then lifted the sacking up further so that he could see the body more clearly. "My God, you're right! I hadn't noticed! Executed, you say? Is that how gangs do it in England?"

I was about to answer that I had no idea when we heard what sounded like several cars labouring up the hill. Georges dashed past his car and I watched as he signalled to the new vehicles and started to direct them to various clearings just below the top of the path where the body was.

I moved along the path a bit towards the Chapel and sat down on the remnants of an old, fallen tree. I pulled out my water bottle and began to drink from it. Suddenly, I felt quite tired and very, very hungry. I hesitated as I watched the gaggle of police and officials as they began to emerge from the path below, then I pulled out a sandwich from my pack and began to munch on it.

This looked like it was going to take a while and I felt that I would not get another chance to sit down and eat for some time.

Half-way through my sandwich Georges brought up a grey man and introduced him as Inspector Limon, the man who headed up the equivalent of the CID in Lavelanet, the nearest town big enough to have such a body. He really was grey. His face seemed to be powdered grey under a mop of unruly grey hair. His suit was grey, and a dull silver tie was loose on his neck under the collar of a soft, off-white shirt. I looked down to see if he had grey shoes on and felt disappointed when I saw they were black and so highly polished they could have been made from patent leather. The name Limon rang a bell, but I could not think why.

I shook his hand and offered him a sandwich, which he declined.

"You found the body?" His voice was quiet but there was a hard edge there, like gloved steel.

"Yes," I answered, "I was on a sort of round trip. One of my walks combined with delivering a couple of letters and things."

He nodded, obviously already acquainted with the fact that I was an "eccentric invader" in his land.

"Why did you telephone Officer Dupont? Why not call the emergency number?"

I looked at him and thought about that for a second.

"I think two reasons. Firstly, I confess I'm not sure what the emergency number is here in France. I've never had call to use it before. And then, I had seen Georges, sorry, Officer Dupont earlier today and immediately thought of him, and I also have his number here, on my phone." I pulled out my mobile and waved it at M. Limon.

"You don't know the emergency number?"

"In Britain it is 999." I said. "Of course, I really should know the European equivalent, but I just couldn't think about it at the time."

"The European number is 112 and has been since the 29th of July 1991. This number applies in all countries in Europe. Britain is no exception."

I looked sheepishly at him and shrugged my apologies. Here I was, having discovered a murder victim on the hillside above the town and this person was telling me off for not knowing the correct emergency number to call. I bit back any comment and waited for his next question.

"Do you know the victim?"

"Vaguely. I know his parents and his brother socially, but he's been away from home most of the time I've been visiting or living here. I think he arrived back in town just a few days ago."

M. Limon nodded his head.

"You didn't touch anything?"

"I walked over the hill," I said, pointing out my route, "saw the blue sack and felt that it looked odd. Walked up to it and saw the top of the head sticking out, as you must have seen it, too. I lifted the bag carefully with my right foot. It was obvious that he was not alive. I could see the knife and the plastic tag on his wrists. I lowered the bag gently, stepped away and made my call. I then waited over there where everyone now is."

"You heard a sound?"

"Yes, more like a VW minibus or van but it could've been a tractor, I suppose. It came from down there," again I pointed but, this time in the direction of the lower path, "it seemed to start, then fade shortly before M. Dupont's car arrived on the scene."

"What do you know about gangland killings?"

"Absolutely nothing."

"What about estimating the time of death of murder victims?"

"Again, absolutely nothing."

He nodded, as if I'd said exactly what he had expected me to say and that he didn't believe a word of what I'd said.

"Thank you for your time. You may go now. M. Dupont has your details, I presume?"

"Of course." I nodded at Georges then turned back towards the Chapel.

"John." I heard my name and turned to look at Georges. "How are you going to get back to town?"

"I think I'll go down the 'Stations of the Cross'," I answered. I was referring to the very steep path with broken steps that went straight down the bluff of the hill from the Chapel to the edge of town. It had been closed for a few years because of the broken steps and the instability of the path, but people still scrambled down it and had effectively cleared away most of the lines of barbed wire that had been put up to prevent people from using it.

"That path's been closed for some time."

"I know, but everyone still goes down that way. The fences are all either down or have gaps in them."

Georges paused for a second, as if calculating something. "OK, but don't change your mind and walk along the low path, instead."

"Don't worry, I won't. See you later, Georges." Then, before turning away, I added, "sorry for doing this to you Georges."

"Not your fault. Can't be helped." He shrugged and turned back to the growing numbers of men in white jump suits taking photographs and measurements, talking on voice recorders and mobile phones.

I almost threw away the crust of my sandwich but stopped myself.

Contaminating the crime scene would probably not improve my relations with the local police and M. Limon. They had been worried that I would go down to the lower path and discover some vital clue or mess up evidence.

As I approached the side of the Chapel my phone bleeped. I took it out and read the text message. It was from Georges seeking my 'professional respect' and asking me not to speak to anyone about the murder and not to divulge the details to anyone.

I pondered why everyone believed that I was some sort of retired sleuth and the thought made me stop at the Chapel to say a couple of prayers before tackling the steep descent to the town.

We first discovered this small town when myself, my wife and our three children were heading south for a walking and camping holiday in the Pyrenees.

We had driven on to the ferry at Dover late on the Friday afternoon just as the rain began to fall. We'd set ourselves an optimum time for stopping and pitching our tent and, as we continued driving through the rain, it became obvious that camping was not going to be an option that night. Rather than staying at a cheap hotel, we decided to push on through the night and stop at a campsite in the morning somewhere in the sunny south.

Souillac was awash with rain and then we huddled in a café in Cahors, eating breakfast and debating what to do next. The campsite was full there, so we pressed on. It was still overcast and threatening more rain as we passed through Toulouse and by the time we arrived at Chabrassonne we were beginning to despair.

The hotel provided us with a simple answer. Stop there for the night and rest; then we could press on in the morning.

That evening, in the hotel bar we got talking to some of the locals. They told us of the local campsite, praising it, telling us how it had won several awards, but when we said we would go there the next day they all began to laugh at us. We couldn't do that. It had suffered from a terrible flash flood only a month ago and was closed for repairs.

Seeing the looks of confusion and disappointment on our faces, someone said that we didn't have to camp, anyway. We could rent one of the houses in the town instead. It turned out that we could rent a place for less than it would've cost to pitch our tents. So, we did it. We stayed there for two weeks. The kids loved it, we loved it and we had a truly uncomplicated, very relaxing and totally French holiday.

Walking around the town, we soon began to wonder at the number of empty houses. It was a place of real beauty where almost three quarters of the housing stock was medieval, with narrow streets squeezed into a squashed rectangle enclosed by three rivers. The market square was small with an ancient roof sheltering the central area, the church was hidden along a dark, narrow street and its bell rang hollow peels through the grey, stuccoed passages. But half the buildings had small cards or bits of scrap wood with "for sale" hand-written on them along with a telephone number.

What we were witnessing was the townspeople's rising dislike of old buildings and their desire for new, modern homes outside the cramped town centre. People wanted a place with a big, modern kitchen, decent bathrooms and their own garden rather than (or in addition to) one of the allotments along the banks of one of the rivers.

The house we bought dated back to the twelfth century and felt as if almost nothing had changed since it had been built. We just loved it and spent the first few years virtually camping in it each summer.

Gradually, we did things to the place. First, we put in a real bathroom and toilet and a hot water system. Then we found the money to put on a new roof. Eventually we did other bits, gradually making the place more and more comfortable without turning it into a "luxury holiday home" with modern fitted kitchen, etc. etc.

During that time our children grew up, we grew a bit older and learned to speak French in something more akin to the local accent. We even made some efforts at learning Occitan and recently I have been working harder on this amazing language. I can now speak it as well as I could speak French when we first started coming here more than ten years ago.

Two years ago, my wife became very ill. She was having black-outs and terrible headaches. She was starting to have problems with her memory and was suffering from dysphasia – she would aim to say one word and another seemingly random word would come out instead. After a series of difficult tests (she was absolutely terrified by the MRI scanner) the doctors told us she had a large and growing tumour pressing against her brain.

Drugs seemed to make it worse, her first operation almost killed her and the second left her paralysed for almost a week. Finally, they found a small cocktail of drugs that seemed to alleviate most of the symptoms while slowing down the continued growth of the tumour.

That was when we decided to move down here.

I remember discussing what the essentials were with her. The only thing we needed, apart from most of our books and music, was a cat.

During that spring we spent a week at the house making final preparations and enquiring about cats. We decided that we needed two from the same litter, preferably from a local farm. We found them on the second last day of our visit. Just a few miles out of town we visited them on a little farm nestling in the crook of a long, wooded valley. The cats were grey and brown tabbies with wide faces, pointed ears and very dense fur. The mother and the two kittens we selected all had white tips to their tails.

My wife said that the mother made her think of bobtailed cats, so we called the two kittens Rag and Tag, as the mother was the bobtail. We said we would collect them at the beginning of the summer.

I remember her disappointment when neither of the cats would sit on her lap.

"They're farm cats." I said, "What do you expect? Look at them, they're a couple of thugs – they would lose all credibility if they lolled around purring on people's laps." But I could see that she really was disappointed.

Then one day, when she was feeling particularly bad, I left her sitting in the armchair by the fire hugging a cushion while I went outside to chop some wood. About an hour later I walked back in to make some coffee and to see if she wanted anything. There she was, sitting triumphantly with Rag curled up on the cushion on her lap. They had found a formula that both could accept and enjoy. I was so pleased.

It was about that time when I became the "great detective".

Mary was going through quite a good phase. On good days we could go for reasonable walks in the surrounding hills and even when she felt bad, we were still able to go out at times and sit outside the local café and chat to people.

Mary's French had always been miles better than mine. In some ways this had been my downfall as I'd left it to her whenever I found a particular conversation difficult or an explanation convoluted. So, that balmy summer's evening we were sitting nursing our aperitifs when someone asked us what our jobs had been before we moved here. It's strange how these things work. Until then hardly anybody had asked us that and the curious ones had all been pretty good at speaking English.

I let Mary take the lead on this as I've done several types of work during my life while she had been a teacher, then a head teacher.

She found the words for her own profession without difficulty. However, trying to explain my last sort of work seemed to cause her problems and I think the dysphasia kicked in as she began to struggle for the correct words.

I had been working as an information scientist specialising in historical research and had explored a number of different types of information sources. My background had been so varied that, when I started doing this, I had all sorts of connections and lots of odd and different or unorthodox ideas to bring to the table. As a result, I had been quite a success in this field and had retired as quite a senior academic figure in my field. Something I'd never expected to be.

For Mary, trying to explain what I had been doing came out rather jumbled at first. Then she said that I had been a sort of detective. She searched for the right word and out came "forensic" and "renowned detective" again emphasising the words unintentionally. Trying to explain the sometimes private and privileged nature of my work, she used the word "security" and "secrets" and the word "official". I think she even used a French slang word which we would later translate as "hush hush", but I am not sure, as she had been losing me, as well as herself, in the explanation.

Trying to end her mess, she rounded up by saying that I had been eminent in my field and now that I had retired, I was not allowed to talk about the details of what I used to do. Of course, what she meant was that I was not capable of explaining it because of my lack of vocabulary.

It all came out wrongly and I only half-understood what had been said, so I probably gave out completely the wrong signals, too.

Afterwards Mary was so distressed by the difficulties she had encountered just speaking that I didn't dwell on what she'd said or what it might mean.

The outcome is that I am believed to have been a senior detective in a high flying but "hush hush" department in either the British police system or, possibly, the secret services. A sort of retired James Bond and Maigret, all in one. Denying it just makes it worse, so I try not to let it bother me or get in the way.

Ever since, when I have not been able to find a book, or my hat or some other thing, Mary's pointed out the missing item and has said to me, "John; how can you be such a super sleuth and still be incapable of seeing what's in front of your face!" and I've answered along the lines of, "Ah, but you would have to murder someone first and leave the book (or whatever) as evidence in order for me to see it!"

Of course, when overheard, such family banter does not help to dissipate myths.

As I left the chapel and began my descent I thought about Mary. I would have to talk the whole thing through with her when I got home.

On the way down I could see the town in glimpses through the trees. Its medieval core was like a Chinese puzzle in grey stucco and red tiles with the small square off-set from the middle, the rectangle of narrow streets and alleys enclosing it, the wider tree lined road edging around the inner part of the town then the tall outer rows of houses enclosing the whole giving it that fortified, inward looking feel so common in this area. Beyond the town the rivers cut off three sides and the opening valley formed the fourth side. Six bridges, two of which were really footbridges linked the older part of the town with the growing number of little streets lined with modern houses and gardens in the newest parts.

Almost every one of these new houses is white with a red roof and long stacks of chopped wood line at least one of their walls. Interestingly, even the houses with oil fired central heating have a wood burning stove and on winter's days the aromatic smell of burning wood drifts through the valley and can be detected as you walk down from the Chapel to the town.

At the foot of the hill I emerged from the trees and stepped through the narrow gap in the wall. Facing me was the large 19th Century church built to take the growing population of the town when it had two woollen mills, a tannery, a hat factory and various other rural industries blossoming along the sides of the rivers. The little church in town was dedicated to Mary, the Mother of God, the large church in front of me was St Joseph's and the Chapel at the top of the hill overlooking the town was the Chapel of Calvary. The steep path leading from St Joseph's to the Chapel had a series of stopping places where the Stations of the Cross had been set into the wall like little platforms with alcoves holding the bas-relief carvings showing images like "Christ falls for the third time". At Easter time people would still spend Good Friday afternoon going slowly up the path, stopping to reflect and pray at each station before reaching the Chapel of Calvary at the top (despite the damage and wire fencing).

I remember the effect the little Chapel had on us when we first entered it several years before. The walls were painted a sort of yellowish white and there were a set of huge oil paintings on the walls. Two of the Crucifixion, one of the burial of Jesus, and then His Resurrection. Three dark, dimly lit monsters on the small walls and then the Resurrection filled with an inner light that just seems to be helped along even with just a little by the candlelight. Uneven flagstones on the floor keep you a little unsteady as you walk in the semi-darkness and the whole place holds a slight chill which is the same whether it is mid-winter or the middle of summer.

Redemption song

Somehow, it just seemed to be right. It fitted with the other two churches so well and reflected the different facets of life in the town from brash and loud to sombre and silent, from hot and new to cool and ancient.

I walked across the road to the newer church and took the narrow, cobbled path between it and the river. The path sloped down towards a 19th century row of houses facing the river. One of the bridges took me from this row of houses into the old town where I passed an eighteenth-century mill that is now a flourishing local theatre and down the narrow street to my house.

Rag and Tag greeted me like a lost friend, making an odd sort of yowl out of their meows that I felt I should expect from them. We had always pursued a policy of not quite feeding them enough, partly because we hated fat cats and felt that most people over-fed their pets, and partly because they were farm raised cats and needed that edge. They were also good hunters and there was always a good reason to have two hungry cats in this neighbourhood. The problem with living in a half occupied medieval town centre close to rivers is that the rats and mice can start to make the place their own if you let them. Rag and Tag kept our house pretty free of unwanted visitors and created a no-go-zone which extended at least one house out on either side of our building.

I gave them a little bit of dried food and put the kettle on. As I was fishing out the coffee beans, grinder and filter the phone rang.

"John, it's Philip Pecheur. The police have just told me about Lucas, my son. They say you found him."

"I'm sorry, yes Philip, I did."

"They're waiting for me to go with them to view." there was a long pause, like he was choking on the words. I waited, "to view my son. Is it really him?"

A sudden doubt rose in me, but I knew it was his son. Georges would not have made a mistake in identifying him.

"Yes, Philip. I'm sorry. It's Lucas."

"O God!" was all that he said, and I waited for another period of long seconds before he said, "Who did this? Do you know? John, why would anyone do this?"

I had no explanation and wondered what to say when he continued, "We'll find him, John. You will help me. I want to know how this could have happened."

I just had time to say, "Philip." one more time into the phone before he hung up. I held the handset to my ear and listened to the ringtone, hearing the wild, disembodied voices being carried through the wires like the cries of lost souls. Then I put the thing down on its cradle and made some coffee.

So, the young man was called Lucas.

I should have remembered that. I shook my head and went to open the glass doors onto the veranda at the back of the house. I needed to sit quietly and think. I looked at the stereo and thought about putting on some music but decided I could not think of anything I wanted to play.

Birdsong echoed along the backs of the houses and through the quiet gardens below the veranda as I sipped my strong black coffee.

For some reason I started thinking about a story I had heard the night before. Charles Groussard, the man who was renovating the Chateau overlooking the town, had invited a few people to have a meal with him and see the work he had done so far on the wonderful collection of buildings he was trying to get into some sort of order.

We had finished a lovely meal and were sitting on a large raised paved area looking out across what would have been a lawn if it had been cut, weeded or maybe re-sown. Instead it was like some large open clearing or secret meadow surrounded by trees and bushes heavily laden with leaves. The light was almost green with the sun blinking off each leaf like a million uncertain pixels in an animation of a Seurat painting.

Someone told of a Summer's parish outing just before the war. There had been a small cavalcade of horses and carts which carried the parishioners along the winding roads until they had arrived at a water meadow a few miles out of town. The hills had towered around them and the grass had been wonderfully soft and long and laced with wild flowers. They had put crates of rosé and white wine in the river to chill and someone had unloaded a set of tables so that they could lay out the food. Children swam in the river and played various games with adults. Old men had sat smoking their pipes while making rude comments at the younger men's antics. Groups of women had sat together on the grass laughing at occasionally outrageous stories.

The area in front of us, we were told, reminded the storyteller of that place. Her hands were loose, wrinkled skin over stiff bones as she pointed towards the long grass. "I had my first kiss under a tree like that one there." She said and she giggled happily as we followed the finger towards the bottom of the garden.

Later, a darker story was told of the stables to the side of the house. Did we know about the shootings that had taken place there during the war? Charles seemed reluctant to explore this topic and suggested that it may have been an invention, or World War Two myth.

"I know about this," said the old lady, again. "I was working in the patisserie we now call Marie's. It was M. Thomas who owned it then, and he was a hard taskmaster, but a very nice man with hands that were so gentle it was rumoured it was not just pastries that yielded to his touch! A few of us were in the Resistance, as you know, and one of our main roles was transporting people and goods across the border; over the mountains. Before the war it'd been contraband and refugees from Franco, of course, but during those bad times we also carried guns and explosives this way and guided soldiers and airmen in the other direction. I was still young enough to think it was fun, even exciting, and couldn't understand the dread looks on some of the older people's faces."

"Sometimes we'd store the English and Americans in the stables around the side, here. Each day one of us would walk up from the town with a basket of food for them, then drop in for a talk with old Madame Groussard, your great aunt." She nodded towards Charles.

"Anyway, on the day before we planned to move one group of four young English airmen, all hell was let loose in the town. People were being arrested and doors were being banged in. Someone had talked, or perhaps someone further up the line had been captured and he'd been made to talk. I never knew what caused it, but all hell was in the wind. I was told by M. Thomas to go up and get the airmen out of the stables and as far from the area as possible, and off I dashed."

"My God, you have no idea how steep that path is up to the Chateau when you're in a hurry! I puffed and panted my way up here and I could hear lorries revving their engines, people shouting, boots stamping on the cobbles. I could not speak more than a few words in English, but they understood "Les Boches" and "quickly". I got them out of the stable and over behind the wall at the side of the building just before the soldiers arrived in a big truck. They had M. Thomas, a lady from the bar we all used to call "Pussie", but her real name was Aurélia Mouton, and a young man not much older than me, called Pierre Chatillon. He had a bad limp and I often thought that if it had not been for that he would've had the pick of the town's girls as he had such a wonderful smile and such engaging eyes. Anyway, their names are on the memorial in town, you can see them there."

"So, there we were behind the wall and people were stamping about, shouting and bashing in doors as I kept us all pressed hard against the wall wondering what to do. A clearing just like this one used to stretch out behind the stables, and I didn't want to risk running across it with these young men.

"Suddenly there was silence. I heard a strange man's voice shout something I couldn't make out and M. Thomas answered very evenly and in an amazingly quiet voice, "Fuck off!" There were some scuffles and then I heard him shout "Vive La France!" and there was a deafening roar of gunfire."

"In the silence that followed I almost smothered one of the airmen as he began to sob uncontrollably. I just pulled him to me and pushed his face into my bosom. I can still remember those tears as he shook in my arms, but I couldn't let them hear him. For them to find us after such a sacrifice would have been a terrible sin."

"We were still behind the wall when, several minutes after the truck had left, Madame Groussard came around the corner and told me it was all clear. Instead of letting us back into the stables she told me to take the young men to a farm a few miles south of here, which I did. I had to stay there for almost a week, so, I missed seeing the dead bodies and could only say my farewells at the memorial Mass with the rest of the town."

"I stopped feeling like it was all a bit of fun after that incident and M. Thomas' son was nothing like as good a baker or as good a boss!"

We all sat in the dying light of the evening, loath to put any of the lights on in the house while Charles got out some of his best Armagnac, and we all toasted the heroes of the past.

One of my tasks this morning had been to deliver a short note of thanks to Charles for the previous evening and to leave him a copy of a pre-World War One map of the area showing some details of the Chateau and the surrounding area.

As I sat listening to the birds, I heard Mary come up behind me. Her confident hands started to seek out the tension in my neck and shoulders and she asked about the day. "You look tired." She said and I told her the whole story, describing the body in as much detail as I could remember, recounting the conversations with Georges and the grey policeman.

"He sounds a bit scary." She said as she dug her thumbs into the knots in my spine, "I think you better watch out for him."

I laughed. "What do I know about executions?! Life and death can be so hard sometimes. I just wonder what it would be like to lose your child. There is nothing you can do to stop yourself from loving your children, is there?"

"No. Nothing."

I began to drift off into sleep, trying not to think about death anymore.

The word execution was still running through my mind when the phone rang again. This time it was Philip Pecheur's older son Marc.

Chapter Two

"John."

There was a long pause. I waited for several breaths then I said, "Yes, Marc."

More breathing into the phone, then, "I'm outside my father's house. Tell me, what has happened? I've been in Toulouse all day in meetings and then I come out to find several missed calls and obscure messages on my phone. No-one is available, then, I stopped at the service station and got some nonsense from that idiot Paul that something has happened to Lucas and that you are involved. What's going on?"

I stood by the phone in the fading light wondering what is going on. In my mind I could see Marc, his bulky body cramped into that Japanese sports car of his, looking across at his father's modest new house with its while walls, red roof and neatly stacked firewood.

"Marc, have you spoken to your father, yet?"

"No. I can't get a hold of him. The house looks empty, both my father's and my mother's cars are gone, and it looks deserted."

What about Diane? Have you spoken to her?"

"She is not answering her phone – neither is Jean!"

"Have the police tried to contact you?"

"Look, John, I have some missed calls from unknown numbers. People try calling me all the time. I only return calls from people I know. Are you saying Paul is telling the truth, for once? That little tick?"

"Marc, I don't know what Paul has been saying to you. You need to speak to your father, and to the police. I can't tell you anything. You must understand. It's not that I don't want to talk. You have to talk to them first. phone Georges Dupont and say I told you to call him. Tell him you don't know where your father is, and he'll help you."

"My God. Is my father OK? Is it my mother, is it Diane? What's going on."

"Your parents and sister are all OK as far as I know, Marc. Just do what I say. Do it now. Before you think of doing anything else, all right? We'll talk later."

He cut the connection and I let out a loud sigh.

As I started putting the lights on Mary came in and stood by the open door leading to the veranda.

"You did the right thing." She said.

"You think so? It felt like… I don't know. It's hard to tell people bad news, especially over the phone, but I really wanted to tell him. He sounded so frightened and confused."

"You would've caused all sorts of trouble if you had told him." Mary smiled and I nodded, turning on the lamp by her favourite armchair.

Redemption song

"I think I'll light a fire this evening. It seems like a chill is starting up. The cold air from the mountains, I suppose."

"A fire would be nice."

Later that evening I was sitting by the fire listening to some Scriabin and reading some poetry by an old friend when someone began to bang on the door.

It seems typical to me that local people never use the front doorbell. They either just walk in and call your name or they bang on the door. You can hardly ever tell what sort of person is thumping at your door or what their mood is. Once, based on the noise, I thought the police were on the verge of kicking my door down, but when I opened the door the person on the doorstep was Madame Faligan wanting to know if I would do the collection at 9.30 Mass as she was going away that weekend to visit her sister. Mme Faligan is about seventy years old and would be about five feet tall if her spine was not seriously bent. She had a short, gnarled walking stick almost as awry as she was, and she had used it to put a few new dents in my door panels.

I got up and put the light on in the narrow hall, noticing that this evening really was much cooler than last night. No-one would be sitting out in their gardens drinking by candlelight tonight. It was Marc whose heavy fist had been pounding at the door.

He just pushed past me as I opened the door, stomped down the hall and stood in the middle of the floor, waiting for me to get back into the warmth.

"Would you like something to drink?" I offered. He shook his head and stood staring out the window into the dark garden. A dark shape flitted across the wall, caught between the deep shadow and the moonlight. I realised it must be either Rag or Tag as this was their territory and they defended it with military precision.

"Sit down, Marc. You look exhausted. Have you had anything to eat?"

"No. Thanks. I'm not hungry." He sat down opposite me on the other side of the fire. I poked the logs and stooped briefly to place another piece of wood on top.

"I don't think I ever liked Lucas, you know."

"I'm sorry."

"No, no need to be. I think I loved him. You can't help loving your brother or sister, can you? But he was a bloody pain! Always getting into trouble, causing trouble and blaming everybody else but himself."

I sat and watched his face. Marc is about six feet three or four and very broadly built. His face has that sort of squashed attractive character to it that has made Gerard Depardieu rich, and he has a charm and intelligence that has made him a very successful salesman. In many ways he is the image of his father. Both are amusing, charming and both have reputations for being bullies and easily roused to violence. He seemed to be struggling to keep control, so I picked up the poker again and shoved some more wood around.

"He had a demanding father and two class acts to try to match."

"Oh, Lucas was much cleverer than Diane or I ever were, and he had a lot more artistic ability, too. I've one of his paintings on my wall and everyone always asks who painted it. He just threw everything away as if he had no use for any of it."

"He was young. Sometimes the most intelligent people do the silliest of things. From what I saw of him, he seemed to be well liked by people of his own age."

Marc just shook his head and I could see a tear glint in the corner of his eye. It was caught in the reflection of the depths of the fire and looked more like blood than anything.

"He was a thief, a pimp, a pusher, a con-man, and God knows what else. He nearly put our company into bankruptcy and almost caused my father and mother to split up, and those are just the things I can tell you about! There were times I wanted to break his scrawny little neck. He made me so angry!"

There was nothing much I could say to all of this. I just waited, wondering what he really wanted. Did he want me to tell him the circumstances of my discovery, the details I had observed? I waited, wondering what I would say.

"You discovered him." It was a statement of fact. I nodded. "How did you find him?"

"Marc. I have been told by the police not to say anything about it. Perhaps it would be wise not to ask me."

"They say he was found up on the high path to the Chapel and that you discovered 'the body' and called the police."

"Yes, that is what happened."

"He was stabbed?"

"Is that what the police said?"

"No, my father said that Lucas had been stabbed and that he had seen one of the wounds in his neck."

"You know just about as much as I do, then." I said.

"What was he doing up there? Who did this to my little brother?"

"Marc, when I found your brother there was no one else around. I waited for about ten minutes before Georges got to the scene and there was no one else nearby. I never really got to know Lucas, so I've no idea why he died or who killed him."

I wanted to be as specific as possible without actually telling Marc anything he didn't already know. Talking seemed to help him calm down a bit.

"Where are your parents and sister? Do you know?"

"Yes, mum and dad are back home. I drove them back in dad's car and then walked over here on the way back to get my own car. Dad will get mum's tomorrow."

"And Diane?"

"At home with Jean and their kids."

"How are they all taking this?"

"I don't know. Mum and Diane are like zombies. They are almost catatonic with grief, you know.

Redemption song

They hardly speak and their faces are like stone. You can feel a loss and a huge anger building up inside them. I think they blame dad or me for his death. Dad's been crying a lot. I've never seen him cry before. Never. I had to stop him from flattening that little shit, Limon, too. The sort of snide comments that he keeps slipping into his conversations are beyond belief. I'm just surprised he's managed to live this long!"

I nodded and waited. When he didn't start talking again, I asked, "Why would your mum and sister blame you or your dad? You can't be blamed for what happened."

"Oh, they say if we hadn't thrown him out, he would still be alive, so it is all our fault."

I waited. I didn't want to sound like I was interrogating him. I was just curious, but I felt uncomfortable every time I asked him another question, so I just waited. Flames flicked up around the wood and then the fire crackled and hissed as sparks flourished around a growing crack in one of the logs.

"Lucas was frightened of something. He came home to hide, but he got bored and didn't want to be told what to do by anyone. He was at my parent's home, laying around all day, making a mess. Then, a couple of nights ago he had an argument with my father and stormed off to the sports bar in one of his fits of rage. There he got drunk and tried to start a fight with anyone who even as much as looked at him. Michel phoned dad and dad phoned me. We got there just in time to stop a real fight and I knocked a little bit of sense into him. But that was it. We couldn't have this trouble anymore, so we told him he could stay in the house in town. No one is staying there at the moment as we are about to do some work on the back wall. We said he had a week and then he would have to find somewhere else to hide."

The whole story came out in quite a flat tone. I could see that Marc was very tired and that the adrenalin had stopped working in his system. He revved himself up a little bit as he finished with this statement.

"We had no choice. A bank in Carcassonne phoned me up last week and asked about a loan that was being sought under my name with the company as security. Luckily, the manager knew me, and the checks are all more effective now than they were the first time Lucas stole from us. One phone call confirmed that he was trying to ruin us again. This time I was able to stop it from happening and I put out a call to all the banks and finance companies I know to spread the word that someone was aiming to commit fraud against us. I didn't tell dad, but I told Lucas that he was history. This time I would get the police on to him. He just laughed and told me dad wouldn't let it go that far. You should have seen his face when we told him together that his time was up!"

He refocused on me, turned away to the fire then turned back and shook his head.

"Diane and mum don't know about this. They just see us reacting to Lucas getting drunk in the local bar. They just see us saying no to him once and then him being killed! He did nothing but cause us trouble when he was alive and now that he's dead...."

He shrugged his shoulders and looked both defeated and ready to lash out at the same time.

"I think it's time you got yourself home and tried to get some sleep – or at least some rest." I stood up and walked past him towards the door. "Is it wise to go and get your car now? I could give you a lift home if you want."

He just shook his head.

"No, the walk will do me good." Then, as I stood at the door getting ready to say goodnight to him, he held the upper part of my left arm in a tight grip and looked at me with something like desperation in his eyes. "You've got to help us. I can't understand what is going on in the heads of people like DuPont and Limon. They made it seem like they were doing me and my father a favour by letting us go home tonight! They almost came out and said that one of us had killed Lucas. You've got to help us find out who did this and why. We'll pay you. You know we are good for it. Money isn't really a problem. I just think dad's on the very edge at the moment. This could push him over. Whoever killed Lucas could end up killing my dad, too!"

There was no point in arguing with him in his present state. His hand was hurting me, and he looked like he was becoming more and more desperate as he talked.

I eased his hand from my arm and told him we would talk tomorrow. I was not going to argue but I was not going to agree to anything, either. I watched him shamble down the cobbled road with the wind blowing at him in gusts along the way. Little bits of paper and other detritus skipped along at his feet.

When I closed the door, I felt completely drained. It was not that late, but it felt chilly in the hallway and the quiet of the darkened evening added to the oppressive feeling that was growing in me. I was still amazed at how well I had coped with my encounter with a newly murdered corpse on a lonely path in a foreign land.

"You have always been prone to over-dramatise things, John." Mary teased me from the door to the living room. "Time to get yourself sorted and ready for bed. It looks like you're going to have a busy day, tomorrow."

"I'm not a damn detective. There's nothing I can do that will be of any help to them."

"That's not the point," she smiled at me, "Let them talk to you and give them a bit of support as the police do their job. You're a good listener and, you never know, you might hear something that helps them in the end."

I had no idea what Mary meant but I was too tired to argue. So, I went to bed.

Chapter Three

My dream was vivid and disturbing. I sat on a ladder overlooking the interior of a house. It was like one of those cutaways you see in holiday brochures where they show all of the rooms and the furniture from above, but this felt like a real place and there were real people moving about inside the rooms.

From my vantage point I could see people arguing and I recognised Marc and his father almost at blows over something. In another room Marc's mother was sitting crying on her own. Marc's wife, who had been away for a few weeks, was in one of the bedrooms making love with someone very much like Lucas, and Diane, Marc and Lucas' sister, was running around opening and slamming doors with her husband, Jean, following behind pleading with her.

As I started to go down the ladder, I noticed that Lucas was making love with the knife still buried deep in his throat. At that point his mother rushed into the room and stood by the door facing him, blocking the way so that Diane could not get through to him.

"Leave him alone, leave him alone!" Shouted the mother with her arms outstretched, but Diane pushed past saying, "Mother, I only want to help" before casually plucking the knife from Lucas' throat as if she was tidying up.

At that point Marc and his father burst in on the scene and started shouting, "See, there you are! He's always ruining everything. Look at the mess he's made!" they were pointing to the blood as it splattered everywhere from the hole in Lucas' throat.

Jean pushed in through the small group and started to pull Diane out of the room saying, "Come on. I've told you before, they're all stupid and violent. They don't merit your love. Get out while you can, or they'll suck you into their mess."

Marc shouted at them, "You're next. You deserve worse. I'll cut you both up for this!"

As I moved back up my ladder I watched as they began to disperse. It was as if they had all done their set pieces in some strange tableau-style play. However, none of them were able to leave the house.

I could hear their banging as they tried to get out, but the shutters were closed and locked against them and the doors were jammed tight and locked, too. No one seemed to notice me or my ladder as they pounded furiously on the doors and walls.

The banging continued until I woke up and put on a dressing gown to go and answer the door.

Redemption song

Georges Dupont and the grey Limon were on my doorstep. Georges was doing the thumping.

"It's just after nine AM, so I thought it would be reasonable to call on you." Limon was precise and I could see that he was not going to be turned away. The statement could have been an apology, but it was just an unrepentant statement of fact.

I turned in and said, "Thank you, I'll make some coffee. It should be ready by the time I get dressed."

They followed me through to the kitchen/dining room and I looked out of the glass doors as I filled the kettle up. It was another clear-skied day, but it was still a bit breezy. The wind would cool the skin as the sun burned it. I felt like I needed a long walk but was beginning to think that such a luxury would not be possible today.

I put coffee grounds in the jug, filled it with boiled water and set the plunger on the surface of the darkening liquid.

"I won't be more than a few minutes." I said.

They both sat at the large kitchen table ready to wait. Georges looked out into the garden and M. Limon looked around the kitchen with great interest. By the time I got back Georges was sitting, looking very uncomfortable, as Limon was checking out the large bookcase in the kitchen. It contained most, but not all of our collection of cookery books.

"You English are very renowned for your interest in food, but it's seldom matched by your skill."

"Apart from not liking the clichéd phrase which begins with, 'You English…' I should point out that I am not English. I'm Scottish and I may be called British, if you want to associate me with the rest of the people in the United Kingdom, but I'm not English. My wife is English and most of my children were born in England, so I do not object to you calling them English. That is, if you are ever privileged to meet them."

I could see Georges cringing behind Limon as I walked past them and pushed the plunger down on the coffee. I've become quite grumpy in the mornings before I've had my breakfast. I needed to get out and buy some bread, but I knew that I would have to wait and drink some coffee first and find out what these two wanted.

I sat down across from them pushing the milk and sugar at them from the centre of the table.

"What do you want to talk to me about, Monsieur Limon? International gastronomy or something more local?"

He smiled as he put two heaped spoons of sugar in his now milky coffee. I never ceased to be amazed at how institutionalised people seem to all have sweet milky tea or coffee. People in public schools, in the forces, in the ministry, in prison and those who are homeless seem to share that trait. Public services such as the police seemed to suffer from this, too.

"You had visitors yesterday?"

"I had a visitor."

"Do you want to tell me what was said?"

"It depends."

Limon looked at me quizzically, "On what?"

"On what it is you are looking for."

"And why should that be of any concern of yours? I'm conducting a murder investigation. Are you suggesting that you are planning to obstruct my enquiries?"

There was a hardness in his voice which made me dislike him even more.

"No, of course not. But what someone says to me in the privacy of my own home is, essentially, private. I have to have some reason to tell you about it."

"Nothing is private if I think it will help in my investigations."

"M. Limon. Yesterday I was told not to talk to anyone about the dead body I discovered on the path above town. I've had conversations where distressed relatives have asked me about it, and I've not told them a single thing. I have kept my word even when I knew that it would greatly increase their distress. Unless you have some better reason than the one you have given me so far, I cannot see why I should give you a blow by blow account of someone's private grief."

I sipped my black coffee and felt some measure of revival in the caffeine.

"John," Georges interjected, "We just want to know if Marc told you anything that would be of use in our investigations."

"Marc said nothing helpful unless you think that it is helpful to know that he is deeply upset by the whole thing and is worried about his father's health."

Limon snorted, "So, it's true. You are working for them."

I looked at Limon with as much scorn as I could muster before breakfast.

"I wouldn't work for them, even if they asked me to and offered to pay me. I told you before, I'm a retired academic and one-time businessman. Nothing more. You come barging in here without an appointment, make insinuations, threats and then you toss about insults and expect me to be compliant and co-operative? We Scots, as you would say, don't like being pushed around."

I stood up, "Now please leave so that I can get myself some bread and have my breakfast."

Limon seemed to be pleased that he had annoyed me to the point where I was losing my temper. Behind him I could see Georges looking sheepish and apologetic. The whole thing had been extremely silly, and I had been part of that silliness. I walked them to the door in silence and closed it gently behind them.

When I arrived back in the kitchen Mary was sitting at the table laughing lightly at me.

"You have to be bull-headed, don't you! You've not made friends with M. Limon. And yes, he is a nasty piece of work."

I just shook my head and sighed. "I couldn't be his friend any more than I could separate this milk from this coffee." I picked up the two dirty cups and took them across to the sink to clean and dry them before going out for bread.

I heard the phone ring as I was putting my shoes on, but I couldn't face answering it, so I left the caller to face the unfeasible cheeriness of my answer-phone message as I walked out the door.

The town was as lovely as ever this morning. The breeze of the night before had died down and the sky was clear. The sun cut deep shadows across the streets as I walked through the heart of the town in a diagonal from our house to the boulangerie. As I cut through the small covered market, I greeted people and others waved or called their greetings to me. Shutters were being opened and across the market square I waved as an old lady from church opened her window and shook the crumbs from her tablecloth. It was like a white and red flare caught in the morning sun. She smiled an almost toothless grin at me and, with a final flick of the cloth turned to the dark room behind her. I could see small glints of crumbs drifting down through the warming air.

There was a smell of cooking meat from the butcher's shop and the old man was pushing out a couple of old barrels he used as support for the boxes he used to display his vegetable in every day. "You're looking well today, monsieur, I have some beautiful white peaches – your favourites!" He called to me. I called back that I would be with him in a minute and turned down the narrow street that would take me out near the hotel and the boulangerie.

There are two main places where you can buy bread in town. The shop I was going to is slightly cheaper and is our preferred source of bread. It is a tiny shop with a small entrance and a little window which does not have any display in it. It looks like, and most certainly was a simple house that became a shop with the very minimum amount of adjustments. Inside, it has a small, 'L' shaped counter with glass displays and a set of shelves and baskets with different types of bread in them behind the two ladies who serve there. There are queues here from early in the morning where you can enjoy a bit of light banter, hear some gossip and be shocked by the amazing frankness displayed by the younger of the two ladies serving behind the counter.

As the only man in the midst of a large line of women I have heard some interesting details about affairs and rumours regarding the men of the town. At first it seemed that I was assumed to be too inept at French to be considered someone to worry about. The younger woman, Yvonne, would sometimes be told off by an older woman and Yvonne would say, "No harm meant." And wink at me, which would cause a flutter of giggles and other remarks. As it became clear that I understood more than they'd expected, it became a sort of accepted thing that I was either harmless or not altogether thought of as a 'man' because I was foreign.

The other shop is closer to our house and is more of a patisserie, with a wide range of very sophisticated and expensive pasties and delicacies as well as breads. As it is on one of the main shopping streets – in fact, the widest, tree lined road in town - it is very grand. Steps lead up to a tall, deco-style, chrome-framed, glass door with large display windows either side and the interior has tilled floors, large display cabinets and a cash register rather than a wooden drawer with slots used by the women in the other shop. It is a much more formal shopping experience and our tradition (one we copied from many friends in town) has been to buy morning bread in the boulangerie and buy something sweet in the afternoon from the patisserie.

This morning, I was late entering the shop and there was only one other customer there. An older woman I'd seen in church but never really spoken to. I said my good mornings and waited, looking over the bread that was left.

As the old lady left, Yvonne smiled at me and said, "You're late this morning. Finding it difficult to get out of bed, lately. Wanting someone who can give you a big push in the morning, eh?"

I smiled back, "I'm fine. It was a busy day, yesterday."

Her amusement washed from her face with a surprising speed and her tone took on a gentle solicitousness, "Of course, you found little Lucas up on the high path, didn't you? Such a shame!"

I agreed and pointed out the loaf I wanted. As she wrapped it in a thin sheet of paper she continued, "I remember him when he was a teenager, riding around on that little bike of his. He was lovely, you know. A good sense of humour and could make you feel like you were the centre of the universe. It was that family of his that messed him up."

She took my money and handed me the bread.

"What do you mean?" I asked as she turned to get the changed. She thought about it for a moment then, as she passed over the change to me, she held my hand, the coins warming up on my palm.

"I went out a couple of times with his brother, you know, and he was so full of himself, but he had no idea. He was like a charging bull, no style or thought but for himself. Lucas was the opposite. He seemed to do everything because he thought you would like it or might want it. Always trying to please you, whereas Marc wanted to have everyone, and everything, designed to please him. The whole family, apart from Lucas and his mother, are like that. They would bleed you dry and then squeeze you as if it was your fault you were now empty! I think Lucas had just had enough. He told me once they never saw anything except his failures, so he gave up trying to catch their attention with anything good and focused on the bad instead."

She suddenly realised that she was still holding my hand and said, "Ooops, sorry, you really know how to get a girl talking, don't you!" and withdrew her hand. I was about to answer when the shop door opened and of all people, Nathalie Pecheur, Lucas' mother, entered.

"Monsieur! Good morning! Philip has been trying to reach you. He says he needs to talk to you as soon as possible." She stood facing me, blocking the door, her eyes red and puffed from crying and lack of sleep, and her face held an expression that was both blank and lost at the same time. I had seen Nathalie at a mutual friend's house just a few of days before, and she had seemed so animated and happy. I supposed, on reflection, she had been pleased to have known that Lucas was home again and safe for a while.

"Madame." I touched her arm but remained formal in my address as she had been formal to me. "I'm so sorry about Lucas. I'll call Philip as soon as I get back home. Just let me know if there is anything I can do to help you."

A ghost of a smile flitted across her face as she answered, "Thank you. If you can speak to my husband soon, that would put my mind at ease, thank you." Then we passed each other with me calling back my goodbye to Yvonne.

On the way back to my house I bought half a dozen large, white-fleshed peaches and a bunch of white grapes from the shop by the market.

In the house, the answer machine beeped reproachfully at me, but I ignored it as I rinsed out the jug and set up some fresh coffee, put the fruit in the bowl on the table and fished out the bread board.

"Are you going to answer the calls?" Mary asked as I brought the cutlery to the table and found spreads in the 'fridge.

"I want some breakfast before I face anymore nonsense." I replied with a little bit of tetchiness in my voice which caused Mary's eyebrows to raise. I smiled apologetically and reached across to the machine. There were two messages on the thing. The first was from Philip, as I had expected.

"John. I need to speak to you as soon as possible. I'm on … and will be here until twelve, then I will be at home on …. Or you could try my mobile …."

The voice and message had all the signs of a businessman leaving a message for a colleague or client, but I could hear the shakiness in the voice and the struggle for control was almost physical it was so evident underneath the formal language.

The second was a brief call from Georges Dupont. "John. Please don't try to provoke M. Limon so much. He doesn't like anyone foreign. I moved here over twenty years ago and I'm still a foreigner to him! Please be more co-operative when he visits you again. He can be very dangerous and will use any excuse to make your life difficult." There was then a little scuffling noise and then he finished by saying, "I'll speak to you later." in a more formal voice.

As I ate my breakfast, I mulled over the things that had been said to me and I wondered if anyone had taken note of the vehicle sounds I had heard on the path the day before. Georges had obviously believed it to be important, but I wondered what Limon thought. Had he discounted it as the imaginings of a foreigner? I began to think of where someone from outside the area would park their car or van and how you would find out about it. Parking in town has always been a bit of a problem. The streets in the centre are pretty narrow and as you move out there are a few places to park, but people have become very protective of their spaces.

Redemption song

The only official car park in town is a small cleared site where some old buildings had been demolished about eight years ago. Instead of rebuilding on the site, the mayor at the time suggested that the town make it into a public space, so we got a bit of landscaped open ground with plants and bushes, a couple of large signs, including a map of the town, and a display board which has details of the town's history and some local information. There are a couple of toilets and three benches and about ten parking spaces with meters. The meters had been thought of as being a bit radical at the time, but people accepted that, with the number of tourists growing rapidly, they needed to do something. Everyone looked at Mary and me when they mentioned the "number of tourists growing rapidly", I seem to remember.

You can park down by the old Boulodrome, and there are a few other places that have the appearance of being good for unobtrusive parking, but most of them are actually what locals like to think as their personal parking spaces, and people take a note of any strangers parking in such spaces. Mary and I discovered this when we innocently started parking our car down by one of the old mills on the east side of town. We parked in front of an empty mill in a large cobbled triangular space bordered by tall, early nineteenth century buildings which seemed to be almost as deserted as the mill.

After a couple of days, the young man whose house we were renting knocked on our door and asked us to move the car from the space we had claimed. He explained the complex politics of where you could and could not park in the town and how people could ask permission, and everything would be alright. But we had to move the car first, apologise and then take the lead from the old lady who had been upset by the car's presence in the first place. Etiquette is a strange but heady cocktail in a town like this.

So, I wondered if anyone had noticed a VW van or bus or any other noisy old vehicle parked around town.

As I was finishing off my second cup of coffee (third of the day, so far) the doorbell rang, and I tried to remember who it was that tended to ring the bell rather than bang the door or simply open it and enter.

I strolled to the door on the third ring and opened it to find a young woman in a pale blue dress and dark glasses standing on the doorstep, unhappily glancing from side to side.

"Yes?" I asked as I looked at her. She was someone from the town and vaguely familiar to me, but I could not place her. I was going to ask her if I could help her, but she pushed passed me with a quick, "Do you mind if I come inside?"

I followed her into the kitchen where she stood, looking like a refugee from a Truffaut film – nervous, pretty, vulnerable and somehow stylish in fairly simple clothes. I was waiting for her to light up a Gauloise, and make some devastating personal statement. She surprised me by not smoking and by making the statement.

"I was with Marc when Lucas was killed, so he's not the murderer."

I waited, looking at her with even more interest.

"You must tell the police that they've got the wrong man!"

I walked into the kitchen because I had been transfixed at the threshold and invited her to sit down at the table.

"Sit down," I said, "would you like a drink? Coffee? Perhaps you would prefer some fruit juice or a soft drink?"

"No. No thank you. You must tell them that Marc didn't do it."

I walked around her and drained the last of the coffee into my cup, grateful that she was not wanting any, then I sat down across from her and beckoned her into a seat, showing her what to do by example.

As she sat, I raised my cup and said, "Hi, my name is John. Pleased to meet you…"

She stared at me for a couple of minutes. I watched and waited for the tears to trickle from behind the dark glasses, the young woman's lip trembled very slightly, then the resolve surged through her body like an electrical current and she held out her hand.

"I'm sorry, my name is Valerie Bacconnier. I used to know Lucas very well. My husband, Jean Jacques, you probably know his as JJ, was Lucas' best friend. Well, until I married JJ. Marc helped us out recently, when JJ was out of a job. I was with him in Toulouse when Lucas was murdered. With Marc, that is."

She spoke so quickly and with such a heavy local accent that I almost missed what she was saying. I could hear Mary chuckle at me from somewhere deep within the house and I focussed on everything that this young woman was saying and doing. Her hands were pulling and wrestling with one of the rush mats on the table and her eyes were hidden behind the dark glasses, but her head kept bobbing around, looking at the table, looking at me, looking at the walls and scanning the view of the garden.

I was taking a deep breath to get every word of what I wanted to ask right when the phone rang. Half with relief and half frustration I shook my head and waved her to remained seated. I picked up the phone and it was Philip Pecheur.

"John, thank God you are there! I need your help. Marc needs your help. They've arrested him. O God, Nathalie is not speaking to me and the police will not tell me what's going on."

"Has he asked for some legal help?" I asked.

"No, he is innocent. He does not need lawyers making him look guilty!"

"Slow down." I calmed my voice down and lowered the tone, "He doesn't need either himself or the police to make him look guilty; that's why he needs a lawyer. Just someone to keep things in perspective, OK?"

I could hear Philip continue to panic on the end of the line.

"Look, I have someone with me at the moment."

He jumped in, "My God, are they arresting you too? Do you want a lawyer? Is that what you are saying?"

"Calm down!" I could feel myself becoming annoyed and I was talking as much to myself as I was to Philip, "I didn't say that! I'm busy with things I can't discuss and that have nothing to do with this. Understand?"

I could hear him start to work down through the gears, "Yes."

"OK. Get onto your solicitors and tell them to send someone who understands criminal law. Explain that it's urgent and that they need to get it right, and get it done right now."

I looked across as the quiet form at the table and said, "I'll call you back in a little while and check that you have done that. OK?" He agreed and hung up before I did. I placed the receiver and looked at the young Madame Bacconnier.

"How did you know that Marc had been arrested?"

"Oh, no! Please God, no."

"What is this?" I walked around the table towards her, "You come here, telling me to go to the police and tell them that Marc couldn't be the killer because you were with him when Lucas was killed, then you try to get me to believe that his arrest is a shock? A surprise? You practically told me that Marc had been arrested!"

"I expected it to happen. He told me it would, but I didn't know it had actually happened!"

"OK. So, why should the police suspect Marc? What possible motive could he have had?"

"Marc has always been very angry with Lucas. Everyone knows that."

I waited.

"Marc was always saying that Lucas had gone too far. When he was arrested for dealing drugs it was terrible, then, when he managed to avoid being jailed over that nasty con he was running with his friends, Marc was furious, then Lucas brought the family business to the edge of ruin by borrowing to try to start up a night club and Marc said he would kill Lucas if he ever came back to Chabrassonne."

Again, it was in that heavy accent, rattled out like every word was crushing up behind the previous one, forcing its way out in a high-speed race.

"And what about you? What have you got to do with all of this?"

"Nothing. I am just a friend."

"What are you hiding?" I was looking straight at her, right into the dark lenses of her glasses and she unconsciously put her hand up to the left lens. "Who punched you in the left eye?"

She started back in her chair, ready to deny it.

"Please! You want to help Marc, yet you go around with crazy stories, hiding a black eye behind sunglasses, pleading innocence. Are you Marc's mistress? Is that it?"

"Look!" she shouted, pulling her glasses off. "JJ did this, but it was an accident. He was pointing at me and accidentally poked me in the eye. See! Right there!" and she pointed at an angry red mark at the inside corner of her eye. There were a lot of bloodshot vessels in the eye and the bottom of her eye looked like it had filled with bruised blood. I was more than half convinced it had been someone poking her in the eye that had caused it. I was not so convinced about it being an accident.

"Have you seen a doctor about it?"

"What for? What's the point?"

I held back on further comments regarding the eye and turned back to my more important question. "Are you and Marc lovers?"

She turned away and murmured, "No."

"Then what's going on?"

She put the glasses back on and turned towards me, feeling safer that her eyes were again hidden from my view.

"Lucas is the father of my daughter. JJ used to be Lucas' best friend, then, when Lucas began to get into serious crime, JJ stopped having anything to do with him. I was already married when Lucas got me pregnant. When he found out he disappeared for almost a year. Somehow, Marc got to know the truth. I think, perhaps, Lucas told him just to make him upset. Marc has felt responsible for little Sylvie ever since. I think he has always liked me, too, and he's never been lucky enough to have any children of his own, so he uses the excuse to see me from time to time as well as finding out about how Sylvie is doing. I think JJ would go absolutely crazy if he ever found out!"

"Found out about you meeting Marc or finding out who Sylvie's real father is?"

"Everything! All of it! What do you think?" She stood up shaking her head and waving her arms around like she was trying to free herself from something that was clinging onto her.

"And you would get much worse than a black eye, too!"

"God yes! I mean, no!" then she started to walk away towards the hall. "Marc thinks you can help him. He's frightened of that little prick Limon. He thinks you can solve all of his problems but all you want to do is dig up the dirt."

"Where is Sylvie, now?"

"What?" She stopped and turned back towards me. "She's at my mum's, why?"

"And where's JJ at the moment?"

"He is nursing a hangover, sitting watching the TV by the fire. Why? What are you asking me these things for?"

"Because if you don't go in now and tell the police you were with Marc yesterday, they may find it out from him and then go 'round to your home to talk to you."

"My God, no!"

"Exactly, and I don't think that Limon is highly tuned in to the sensitivities of people and their relationships. In fact, he will get off on winding up JJ while trying to squeeze all sorts of information out of him, too."

"You're right! My God I should not have wasted my time here! I should have gone straight to the police!"

I walked her to the door, but I didn't open it immediately. I held the handle and looked at her carefully as I said, "Before you go through the doors of the police department think through what you are going to say very carefully. Keep it simple, talk slowly and, please, make sure you get the basic times and details clear in your head before you start talking."

She nodded to me and left. You could see her rehearsing her story, thinking about how she would say it all, as she walked down the road.

I gently closed the door and headed for the phone.

This was a strange situation to be in. I was surprising myself and I now felt like I was drifting off from reality in some way. Stepping off into a strange world which was not so easy to make sense of.

I found myself pausing by the fruit bowl. I picked up a peach and bit into it - such a wonderful fruit.

I caught a glimpse of Mary smiling as she walked towards me.

"Prevarication can take many forms." She whispered, her lips brushing my ear, "One of the best is eating a white peach. Once you start, you can't stop…." She paused and her short breaths were warm and sensual against my ear, "and you end up smelling of peach for the rest of the day. Name one other activity you could say that about and I'll give you a prize… "

We both laughed as I drowned in the sweet scent and juices of the peach.

Chapter Four

The phone rang as I was drying my face. I picked it up on the third ring and Philip's voice boomed out at me,

"John! John? Are you there?"

"Yes, Philip. I was just about to call you back."

"Well, since we last spoke things have been getting worse. That stupid woman is going to mess everything up!"

I was about to calm him by saying that Valerie's testimony could only help when I realised Philip was not talking about her.

"Slow down, Philip. Which woman? What are you talking about?"

There was a short pause then he began again, "OK. Sorry, it's all been happening here. I've just had a blazing row with Nathalie. She accused me of being the cause of Lucas' death and was now conspiring to have Marc sent away for it! God, what a stupid woman. And now she's intent on trying to save Marc by going to the police and telling them some lie that she was with Marc all the

59

time. It's so ridiculous I just laughed in her face and she stormed out."

"So, is she on her way to the police?"

"I don't know, do I?"

"Well, has she taken her car?"

"No, it's still there, at the police station, I haven't picked it up yet. And, she's more likely to walk to the police than drive. She hates driving – only does it when she has to."

"OK Philip. I'm going to go out now and try to intercept her. I'm sure it wouldn't harm things in the long run if she did go to the police and try to protect her son, but it would be best if I could stop her now. I'll speak to you in a while."

I put the phone down and slipped my shoes on, picked up my keys and phone and left the house as quickly as possible. I knew Nathalie's most likely route to the local gendarmerie offices, and I was convinced I could reach her well before she got anywhere near her destination.

Turning left I walked briskly up the street. I was heading roughly west towards the chateau. The town is on a gentle incline heading up to the foot of the promontory where the chateau was built. Further along to the south is the outcrop with the Chapel on its top and below the Chapel, close to the church of St Joseph, is the group of modern houses where Philip and Nathalie live. The road I was walking along intersected her path just on the other side of one of the bridges leading out of the old town. I stopped on the bridge and looked down into the narrow gorge. A large swarm of midges seemed to float in and out of the shade cast by the bridge and small fish seemed to be gathered in a dark pool under these insects. I looked up from the feeding trout and saw Nathalie walking steadily up the road towards me. I waited a minute more before moving over the bridge in her direction.

"Good morning." I greeted her as we grew closer. I had always thought of her as an attractive woman. A little bit distant at times and often formal in a defensive sort of way, but her sense of humour and a playfulness always seemed to reveal itself behind those defences. Mary had always thought of her as a browbeaten woman who would blossom the moment she had the opportunity to free herself from the bulky bullies she had for a husband and son. She felt that even her daughter, Diane, tended to take part in bullying Nathalie when her father and brother were around.

Walking towards me, she looked like she had lost a lot of weight recently. If she had not been so distressed and had not been crying recently, she would have looked quite attractive. Her light brown hair had natural copper highlights which caught the morning sun and her oval face had a slight lack of symmetry which, I realised, was the origins of the impression of playfulness she projected. But her high cheekbones were well balanced by a full mouth and disarmingly large, brown eyes.

She looked as if she was going to walk past me, but I slowed down and stood in front of her and said," I have just been speaking to Valerie Bacconnier. Did you know that she was with Marc during the crucial time when poor Lucas was being attacked?"

Redemption song

That stopped her. She was about my height, but the road seemed to be steeper here and she had to look up at me from where she was standing. Her eyes looked even larger than usual and there was a pleading in them I had never seen before.

"She should be with the police right now, making a statement. I was on my way to tell you and Philip about it."

She turned from me without saying anything and stood, looking back towards her house.

In a quiet, strained voice she said, "I am not going back there."

"If you want, we could just walk around for a while and I could tell you what Valerie told me. Would that be OK?"

She nodded without turning and then she took a handkerchief out of her handbag, blew her nose and let out a large, almost silent sigh before turning to face me again.

We began to walk back across the bridge and into town. She asked me, "are Valerie and Marc having an affair?"

"No." I said. "I think Marc would like that to happen, but Valerie is not interested."

"So, why were they together? It doesn't make sense!"

"Did you know that Valerie had an affair with Lucas a few years ago?"

She slowed down and turned to look at me. There was some vague realisation coming into her face. "I think they were very close for most of their teenage years, then Lucas left, and Valerie married JJ. I always thought that was why Lucas and JJ stopped being friends."

"Lucas left when Valerie told him she was pregnant." I said. I was not intending to be so direct or so brutal, but I felt that she wanted things to be said simply and openly.

"So, Lucas is little Sylvie's father? She's <u>my</u> granddaughter?"

"So it would seem." I said, "And Marc has known about this since the beginning. I think Lucas told him as a brotherly jibe; as a way to get at Marc before he left. Anyway, that's how it looks."

"And Marc saw that as a way to involve himself with Valerie?" It was almost not a question, more a sort of statement with a hint of incredulity from someone who would never dream of doing such a thing. But she also knew her son well.

"He has been having meetings with Valerie to get updates on Sylvie's progress. I think he has a file he was keeping for Lucas, but I don't know whether this was something Lucas had asked for or even knew was being kept for him."

"A file?"

"Yes, that's my suspicion, anyway. Valerie told me about the meetings, and I think she gave him photos and other things, too."

"Has Marc been giving her money?"

"I would imagine that was part of the arrangement, too."

That little smile played on her face briefly as she said, "Marc being the big brother, taking on

Lucas' responsibilities whether he wanted Marc to or not. It was a way of trying to show up Lucas' shortcomings and punish him while he looked as if he was helping him. Marc did it all the time and it would drive Lucas mad. It was all the things Lucas didn't care about and that Marc thought were important."

"Were they things that Philip thought were important, too?"

"Oh, yes. He would win favour from his father every time!"

"Well this time, perhaps you might get something out of it."

We were entering the small square with the covered marketplace and I walked over to a bench and sat down. Nathalie sat down, too, but kept her distance from me. "What do you mean that I might get something from this?"

"You said it yourself, Sylvie is your granddaughter."

Her look became more distant and she sat quietly, looking across the empty square to the shops highlighted by the sun.

"I suppose she is all that is left of Lucas."

"When Marc is released, and other things have been sorted out, you might get him to show you Sylvie's pictures."

"I'll do it quietly. Poor Valerie, I think I will speak to her, too."

"I advised Valerie to talk to the police immediately if she wanted to keep as much of this as quiet as possible. As she told me about the meeting, I had this image of Limon barging into her house and questioning JJ about Valerie's secret meetings with Marc. I thought it best if she went there straight away and cleared it up herself."

Nathalie turned and looked at me and that little smile played across her face again, so faintly that you had to be watching for it to catch it. After a while she nodded and said, "Thank you." It was a more intimate, more informal expression than I had expected.

I nodded and asked her, "So, what are you going to do, now?"

"I think I will go and find out what is happening to Marc. My car is at the local police station. Do you think Marc will be there?"

"I have no real idea, but I suspect that Limon would have wanted him taken to Lavelanet."

"Well, it's a good job my car is close by." She stood up and I got up, too. She held out her hand and thanked me again then turned and walked away.

I stood and watched her leave the little square, heading for the police station. I turned and walked towards my house. I didn't feel like going around to Philip and I didn't want to spend much time talking to him. So, I called him on my mobile as I walked through the bars of shade and sunlight formed by the tall narrow streets as I passed them.

"Philip? I only have a couple of minutes. I've just spoken to Nathalie and she is OK. There is a witness that can prove that Marc was not in the area during the time of Lucas' murder, so Nathalie is not going to do anything silly. I think she's going to go to speak to the police and find out when they will release Marc."

Philip was relieved and almost jovial with the news. I decided not to tell him who the witness was or the story behind it. I was worried that Philip could be irrational and impulsive as well as a bully, and I didn't want to create any more problems. It would be up to Marc and Nathalie to deal with Philip. I was happier for Nathalie to be there picking Marc up. I suspected that she would manage to convince Marc to be discrete for as long as possible.

I finished talking to Philip just as I reached my front door.

The phone was ringing inside as I put the key into the lock.

I caught the call just before it went onto the answer machine.

"Dad?" came the voice of my older daughter, Judith. "How are you?"

The question was part of a longer sentence which I could hear but had not been uttered. She was saying 'How are you, I am not doing very well'.

"I'm fine Jude, how are you? You sound a bit tired."

"Oh, I could be better. I feel pretty low and I've just split up with Mike, which does not help!"

I could hear that she was on the edge of crying and felt that terrible chasm opening up when you want to help and protect someone you love and when they need your help, but you are too far away and too powerless to give it effectively.

"Well, why don't you take a few days off and come down here. You could relax and be pampered, take a few long walks, chat."

I could hear the different constraints in her life all tightening up and tying her down as she struggled to think of why she couldn't do it.

"I would really like to, but it is all a bit painful for me at the moment. I just can't face going all the way down there and I can't afford the time off work."

"I understand," I said with my heart sinking at the thought of her growing depression. "Have you seen the doctor recently? Are you still taking the pills he prescribed?"

She sighed and paused for what felt like a very long time then said, "I hate those damn things but, yes, I'm still on them. I go back next week for a review."

"What day?"

"Wednesday."

"OK, look, I am in the middle of something here at the moment, but I will try and get rid of it by the weekend and then drive up to see you. I could be in London by Tuesday morning. How does that sound?"

"Could you, dad? Tuesday?" There was a slight hesitation creeping into her voice.

"Definitely Tuesday morning. In the meantime, I will email you telling you all about the mess that's taking place here. It will be something to help you take your mind off other worries. Have you spoken to your sister or that brother of yours?"

Redemption song

"I saw Jo yesterday at lunchtime. She seems to be fine, but we all know that she is indestructible. James is somewhere in the Highlands photographing osprey or some other boring life form. I had a text from him this morning which he must have written a couple of days ago, but you know what it's like in the highlands – you're lucky to get any phone signal at all!"

I laughed with her and we talked a bit about the weather and about a couple of problems she was having at work. She is an academic and is managing a major project cataloguing and researching a collection of papers and early books that had been recently re-discovered in an early eighteenth-century house bought by her university. It was work similar to my old job and she often emailed me, asking for suggestions, using me as a sounding board. Her real problem was not with the wonderful old texts but with people.

I sat by the phone for some time after she had rung off.

Mary came into the room and said, "That was Judith, wasn't it?" Mary never called her Jude. I nodded and looked up to see her looking very concerned.

"I will go up now and be with her."

"Mary!" I started to protest.

"No, it will be OK. I will look after her while you see what you can do here. You don't really need me to be around you all the time, you know. Judith really needs the help."

I nodded and stood up to go towards her. "I'll miss you. I always miss you when you're not here.

It's like a chunk of my life has been carved out of me when you're gone."

"Well keep yourself busy and you won't even notice I've gone!"

Later on, as I started to put some things together for my lunch I wondered at the silence in the house. There was an emptiness you only get when you are on your own. Even a house full of people sleeping contains a distinctive presence of life. As I put the bread on the wooden board I looked up. I had noticed a movement in the corner of my eye.

A large, pale blue butterfly danced on the light breeze as it entered through the open window. I watched as it moved around the room bobbing and fluttering along. It checked out various bits of furniture, a light fitment and even a little rug on the floor before moving further into the house. It drifted through the living room as I followed it. Keeping up its gentle bump and flit, it explored that room and moved out into the hall. Touching the mirror and the coat stand, it seemed to hesitate before moving into the front room. The stove attracted it for a minute as did the stereo and the small table with drinks. It ignored most of the books before drifting to the window looking out on the street. I opened the window just as it moved back into the room. I opened the other window and watched as it danced from chair to chair, then onto the stove one last time. With a great flourish it danced right past my face and left through the open window. An upward draught from the hot street caused it to disappear immediately as it was swept up and away from the house.

I closed the windows and walked back to the bread feeling the house emptier than ever before.

After lunch I took a cup of coffee through to the study and checked my emails. Jude had sent me a more detailed outline of the problems she was facing and, after reading it through twice, I sent her a quick note suggesting some possible solutions that struck me as being both potentially useful and unlikely to have been tried before by her or her team. I then made a few comments about how some of her colleagues seemed to be behaving. One of the odd things about working in the academic world is the amount of politics you have to deal with. Jude is not a political person, but if you point her in the best direction, she usually manages to plough her way through the intrigue and game playing.

I then sent her some 'photos I had found in an old box of albums and loose snaps. I had scanned them in the previous week and so I added a note of where and when they had been taken. One of them was of myself, Mary and Jude when she was just old enough to walk. It was before James was born and the photo had been taken on the beach in a place called Cavaliere on the Corniche des Maures. It's a place we've visit intermittently and one of those magical sites that never leave you. It was of me sitting on a beach towel, still wet from the sea, Mary is under a large parasol with the sand carved out like a low recliner so that she can read, and Jude is running away from us towards the camera, which I had set up on a tripod with the timer switch on. Behind us you can see part of the small cove with its golden sand shot through with little mirrors of mica and the sun haze making the rising cliffs look further away than they really were.

I included a little story about Mary and I when we were at that very spot in the spring earlier this year. Mary had wanted to go back there so much, and the spring is always a good time to go with fewer people around and the weather much milder and cooler than the summer. Mary was also feeling low from her illness and depressed because of the result of the recent elections that had resulted in the formation of a coalition government in Britain. So, we had needed the break and we were standing, holding hands and looking out from the cove towards the Île du Levant when a young woman walked up to us and asked us in broken English if Mary had known a woman called Nadine Colbert.

Everyone in our family knows the story about how we discovered Cavaliere. Mary's sister, Jean, had been going to go on a French exchange with a girl called Nadine she had been writing to for more than a year. Sadly, at the last minute, Jean had contracted chicken pox and had not been able to go. Their parents had paid for the trip and everything had been arranged, so Mary, who was just a year younger than Jean, went instead.

Although it was difficult, and Nadine had been resentful of the last-minute change, Mary had found the experience wonderful and had spent two weeks in a truly French home and environment, living in Nadine's grandparent's holiday villa there in Cavaliere.

The holiday when we had taken the photo with little Jude had been our first of many visits there. But both Jean and Mary had lost touch with Nadine immediately after the school exchange and they had always wondered what had happened to Nadine and her family.

The young lady standing in front of us that spring day earlier this year was a taller, prettier version of Nadine, and Mary asked, in French, if she was Nadine's daughter. The girl nodded and began to explain that her mother still talked of the summer when she had met Mary. We went to a small hotel near the beach and drank coffee while talking about our families.

Apparently, Nadine's parents had been on the verge of divorce at the time of the holiday and immediately after that summer the final arguments had taken place. The parents had divorced and there had followed a traumatic two years spent moving to different parts of France, dealing with arguments and legal wrangles. It was no wonder that contact with Nadine had been lost.

The young woman told us that last year her family, including her mother, Nadine, had been on holiday in Cavaliere and had heard of our regular visits. The place is small enough for there to be a mini-gossip factory, and when a French-speaking British couple take the time to get to know people and talk affectionately about a family that no longer frequents the place, the story stays in peoples' minds.

Ian Smith

Halfway through their holiday, someone pointed us out to Nadine's daughter, Josephine. Nadine and Josephine had tried to visit us at our hotel that afternoon, but sadly they had missed us by only a matter of hours. Mary had not been well enough and the weather had been too hot for her, and we had ended up leaving much earlier than planned.

So, there we were, a year later, on a short spring visit and Josephine was on holiday, too, staying with a friend. Her stroll on the beach yielded something more than the shells she had been looking for, and we had sat, chatting for quite a long time that day.

I attached a photo of Josephine, Mary and myself taken by the waitress at the hotel that day. We were both struck by how Nadine and Mary had chosen Josephine as the name for one of their daughters. I included an apology for not telling the story earlier and copied the email to our own Jo and James. I also said we had an open invitation to visit the home of Nadine and her family who were now located in a very nice suburb of Paris.

I sat looking at the photos for some time before sending the email off to the "kids".

I also thought, "Mary, look after little Jude, please. Take good care of her."

I got an email immediately from Jo saying thanks and an "I am out of the office" message from James as he was in the Highlands of Scotland. Another piece of junk email arrived in my inbox trying to get me to divulge all my bank details just as the phone rang.

Redemption song

I picked up the receiver on the study extension and grunted a 'hello' as I clicked the junk email into the recycle bin.

"John, it is Georges, here. Hello?"

Georges' voice was distorted by what sounded like the noise of an engine running, "Yes, Georges, what can I do for you?"

"Look, Limon is on his way from Lavelanet to see you. I am following in my car. He's furious. He thinks you set up him up somehow and have tripped him up with Valerie Bacconnier. He's looking for blood. Your blood!"

"OK Georges. I was thinking about going down to the Bar Tabac and having a small beer. I will take my mobile with me. phone me if he tries to smash in my door. If he wants to shout at me and threaten me, I think I would prefer a few witnesses. Does that sound right to you?"

"Well you better get on your way, my friend, we are going through Le Peyrat at speed. Take care."

"You too." I said and put the phone down.

I didn't hurry as I wanted to make sure all the windows were closed, and the shutters secure before leaving. As I was turning the corner leaving my street I was sure that I could hear tires screeching on warm roads, but I didn't turn to look back and strolled quietly to the bar where I sat down at a small, outside table with a glass of icy bier blonde. A gentle breeze was growing, making the little paper napkin under my beer wriggle from time to time. The sky had some fairly large clouds moving in from the west and the warmth of the day was being tempered by the cooler air brushing my face, and the shadows travelling across roofs and along streets. As summer moves on we quite often have warm, sunny mornings followed by a period of showers during the early afternoon and then a warm evening with a cooling breeze. We always admired the way that the rain seemed to come during the period when all the shops are closed.

On the street I watched a mother walking with a small daughter on one hand a smaller son on the other. On one of her shoulders hung a large shopping basket with long handles, and I could see a couple of medium sized loaves of bread poking out beside the end of a bunch of celery and what might have been a frisée lettuce. The children were singing something that was just beyond my hearing. All three seemed to be in a little world of their own, sealed in a bubble or with an impenetrable aura around them. Strangely, it was their bubble being burst that alerted me to the arrival of Limon.

I realised afterwards that they must have heard them marching down the narrow road from my street, and it had sounded like some jackbooted Nazi hoard marching towards them. The woman looked slightly startled and held onto the children's hands a bit tighter as she picked up the pace and moved them further up the street, glancing back only once before I heard his voice.

There were four of them. Limon and two of his men, followed by Georges. I was expecting all three police from Lavelanet to have boots on, but they seemed to have ordinary shoes on their feet. Limon was still in a combination of greys while his companions had chosen suits of a dark blue and an ugly shade of green. Blue was the tallest and thinnest of them and Green was so wide it made him look shorter than the others, but when I looked again at him he was a good couple of inches taller than Limon or Georges.

"There you are!" Limon's face was red, which made a stark contrast with his soft greys. "You are coming with me, now!"

"Monsieur Limon, good afternoon. What brings you to Chabrassone?"

"Get the car." He said with a slight nod to Blue who turned and tramped back towards my house. "You, get up!"

"I'm sorry?" I said, slowly picking my glass up, "What exactly do you want from me?"

"Answers. I want answers. I don't want you to keep any more secrets from me."

As he spoke, he moved closer and closer to me until he was almost spitting in my face, our noses only inches apart.

"I have told you everything I know, Monsieur Limon, and what's more, I have told everyone who has spoken to me to tell you everything, too!"

"No, you have not!" He was now leaning over me with his hands planted on my table.

"Yes, I have!" I answered, firmly, not ready to put my glass down on the unsteady table.

By now the bulk of M. Green was at my side and Georges was hovering to one side looking like he was going to melt into the cracks between the paving stones from fear and embarrassment.

"What's going on here?" Michel Martin, the bar owner's voice emerged behind me. "Harassing my customers? Maybe I should call the police. Some real police."

"Keep out of this, Martin." Growled Limon.

"Monsieur Limon," Michel stressed the Monsieur, "This is my Bar. Are you making an arrest on my premises?"

"I just want to have a quiet word with this gentleman." Limon stressed the quiet, making it sound like it would be anything but quiet.

"Is this agreeable to you?" Michel asked me.

"Well I would like to finish my beer first, but I have no objection to helping the police. In fact, I have gone out of my way to give them every co-operation!" I was still looking at Limon and I put emphasis on the words helping and every.

I could see that Limon was getting more of a grip on himself. "Perhaps Monsieur Limon would like a beer or a coffee. I think he is under a lot of pressure, today." Michel said, "I have a table here you could sit at with your friends."

The car screeched into the road less than a hundred metres from the Bar and I looked around to see the tall man driving slightly hunched in the vehicle.

"Go wait in the car." Limon almost growled at the Green policeman, then he slipped into the seat next to me without moving his gaze from my face. A coffee appeared before Limon and I had not heard Michel either leave or return.

Georges stood around for a couple of minutes, agonising whether to sit or walk away. "Sit down, for God's sake!" snapped Limon then he picked up his coffee, gulped at it as if it was some cold beer, then looked around him as if he was seeing the place for the first time.

"I am still not sure if you are clever or stupid. Are you too stupid to be frightened or have you the bravery that comes from some knowledge I don't have?"

"Perhaps it is because I am a foreigner. Perhaps I am too detached. After all, I'm the one who found the body, but that doesn't give me any special knowledge in its self, does it?"

"This should be a simple enough case. The people around here are not particularly clever. We hardly have a crime wave on our hands, yet your involvement in a simple case seems to be turning it into a 'murder mystery' rather than the usual 'open and shut case'."

"Not my fault. By the way, have you found anything about the Volkswagen van? Or is that classified information?"

I could see Georges itching to say something, but I focused on Limon. It was clear that Georges' best strategy would be to keep quiet and take orders. Limon shook his head then picked up his cup and drained it in another couple of slurps.

"No VW vans registered to anyone in this town. Can you believe it? Not a single person! There are a couple of people with VW cars but most people in the area would rather walk than own one."

"Are you saying that I didn't hear a VW van, or that I was mistaken in my interpretation of the sound?"

"I'm saying that I checked it out and it's a dead end."

"Only if the killer was from around here, or if I got the vehicle sound wrong."

"You're just wasting my time, aren't you? You want me to waste my time, here! What's your vested interest in having someone from outside as the killer? Who are you protecting?"

"Is that an accusation, Monsieur Limon? Are you accusing me of lying to protect the murderer? Because if you are, I want you to arrest me now! Arrest me now or take back what you just said."

I was furious with this irritating man.

Mary always warned me that my temper and bloody-mindedness would get me into trouble eventually, and here I was, sticking my neck out as if I knew something about the law in France, or even knew my rights! But I was seriously pissed off with this idiot and for that few seconds, sitting facing him down, I didn't care a damn about what was going to happen.

"I merely observe that I do not know what you are up to." His words were slow and measured as he stood up, "But I will find out and we will continue our conversation at a later date."

He walked away and climbed into the car without looking back. M. Green stared at me as the car went past, but Limon looked forward, his face set hard and, no doubt, his fists clenched in rage.

"Idiot!" I thought to myself, then I realised I had also uttered the word out loud. I turned around to see that Georges was still there. Michel appeared at my side and clapped me on the shoulder, "Phew, that little bastard is a poisonous toad! Here, let me get you another, and he took my glass away. Georges sat for another few minutes until Michel had placed the new drink in front of me and retired to his place within the Bar.

"I don't know whether it was wiser to face him down here or go with him!" He said to me, quietly.

"I have no idea what that man's problem is, but he should see a doctor about it rather than spend his time trying to piss down other people's legs!"

Unexpectedly, this made Georges laugh and he continued, "Inspector Limon comes from a troubled family. He has a great dislike for the people of this town and now, I am afraid his dislike extends to you, too."

"Well he made that clear to me on our first meeting. Tell me, did he really check up on VW vans?"

"That's part of the issue. He drew a line around the town and got one of his minions to do a check of everyone within the perimeter. I have no additional facilities to extend the check directly, but I will do my own search as soon as I can."

"Can I make a suggestion?"

"By all means."

"Are we really looking for someone local? Lucas hardly knew most of the people here anymore. I've been told that he had been hiding from someone and was already frightened when he turned up here.

George shook his head, "Limon says that we only have the word of Lucas' family for that. They could have got together and concocted that story amongst themselves."

I asked, "Do you believe that?"

Georges shrugged, "It doesn't matter what I believe! To Limon, it proves that the whole family were in on it – there is a history between the Limon and Pecheur families – something that makes the whole thing impossible!"

"Well, do you know where Lucas was, just before he came here? What was he doing, how was he making his living?"

"Oh, we know a lot about what Lucas was doing. He was making a living as some sort of petty criminal linked to one or more gangs on the Med. He lived in Toulon but was involved in half a dozen little scams between there and Cannes – right along the coast."

"Really?"

"Why are you so surprised? Yes, that's where he operated recently."

I shrugged my shoulders, "Oh, I thought when you said the Med that it would be Perpignan or Narbonne. You know, a bit closer to home."

"Much richer pickings along the coast from Toulon."

"Yes," I said, "I can imagine. I know some of that coast well."

"Really?" Georges seemed to perk his ears up at that. "What's your connection with that part of the coast."

"We used to holiday there a lot. It's where I took Mary in April this year."

"Of course." He said and seemed to sink back into a vaguely morose mood again.

"Another thing I meant to ask you." I said, trying to pull him back into the conversation. "Do you still get those notes from Madame Binoche?"

"Yes, of course! And from a couple of other busybodies. Every week. Why?" Then he looked at me and smiled. "Of course, something I can check up without M. Limon breathing down my neck, asking questions. Thanks."

"You would have gotten around to it eventually." I said.

"No, I would not! Limon is driving me mad and I'm not even being allowed to do my own job! I'll go and check on that now. You never know, I might have something useful to say to Limon, after all."

"Well don't mention I had anything to do with you looking." I said as I stood up.

"Don't worry. That would be the kiss of death to any good idea at the moment!"

"Nice to know I can help. Good luck."

I shook hands with him as he left and then carried my empty glass into the dark interior of the Bar.

I offered to pay for my drinks and Michel waved the money away.

"You be careful," He said to me, "That man's not just full of shit. He leaves it wherever he goes!"

"I'll try to be as careful as possible." Then I looked around me and discovered that we were quite alone in the Bar. "Tell me, Michel, was there a bit of trouble with Lucas here a few nights ago?"

82

"Yes. You heard?"

"Just that he got into a fight and that Philip and Marc took him home and read the riot act to him."

"That was about it. He came in at about eight thirty and didn't look drunk, but after a couple he really was much drunker than I would have liked. He was sitting in that corner there, smoking and finishing his drink and he was full of these little ticks, you know, and twitches. It looked like he was possibly even talking to himself. At first, I thought he was on a mobile phone, but he was just sitting there. Mumbling to himself and making jerking movements. Then he said something to someone who was sitting across there."

His finger moved from the furthest corner of the bar to a place close to the way out.

"I didn't get what was said as I was half talking to a couple of people here at the bar. His voice caused me to break away from the conversation and check him out closer. As I watched he got up, steadied himself with a hand on the back of the chair, then he came across to me. He had just enough to pay for his drinks, mumbled something that might have been 'good night' to me and stumbled towards the door. I was glad that he was going, but then, just as he came up next to the guy at the door, he let fling with a reasonable right hand that caught the guy on the cheek. Glasses went flying off the table and I was around the counter before anyone could get another swing in."

"Anne was on the phone to Philip before I was on them. She said later that she was about to call him anyway, because she was worried about Lucas' state. Anyway, I sort of hustled Lucas with one arm, pinning his arms to his sides and told the other guy to get out. When he protested that he had not started it, I just told him that that was fine and now I was finishing it, so he could go home straight away. He was furious but he left and then, a few minutes later, Philip and Marc arrived and bundled Lucas into their car, both taking turns to apologise to me, promising to pay for anything that had been broken."

" Funnily enough, nothing had been broken! Even the glasses that landed on the floor had not broken, so it was more of a nothing incident, really."

"Who did Lucas punch? Do you know?"

"Of course, it was that that hard-faced bastard JJ that Lucas used to hang around with. I don't blame Lucas personally. I have been tempted to put a couple of fists in that one's face a few times, but don't let Anne hear me say that. She would just get worried in case I ever did!"

"Why would you want to do that?" I was interested to hear what Michel was going to say."

"That bastard is a wife beater. He used to hit girls when he was a kid, he tried to be a bully and succeeded in bullying Lucas for a while. I know because my daughter went to school with them. She's still good friends with Valerie, JJ's poor wife, and the stories I have heard! If anyone deserved being bumped off around here, I think he would be one of those at the top of my list!"

I chatted a bit more with Michel about other things like weather and food and families, then I left wishing him and Anne all the best.

On the way home I took a detour past the old Pecheur family house – the place Lucas was staying in just before he was killed.

I suppose I half expected there to be police tape around it and people in white coats searching for clues in the dust on the windowsills, but there was no one there. It was now well into the time of day when everyone has their afternoon rest. The streets were quiet and even the birds seemed to be elsewhere at the moment.

The quiet and the change of direction caused me to keep walking. I took the grand tour around the old town, working my way through the streets until I came to the old church.

I stopped there and pushed open the ancient, bulky door and stepped into the musty stone smell, with its slight overtones of candle wax and incense. The light was very poor, and the place held a slight chill to it that seemed to reach right back into the middle ages.

I genuflected and blessed myself at the beginning of the aisle, then walked up to the front pew. Kneeling in front of the altar, which seemed to be permanently kept lit by one window or another high up in the walls of the building, I began praying.

I prayed for my daughters and son and for my beloved wife. I also prayed for the people in this town, especially those who had been touched by this tragic death. I prayed for Lucas, too and then I said another prayer. One for the fool who thought it was a good idea to take someone else's life. He needed forgiving but he also needed to be found.

So, I prayed for that, too - for someone to find the person who had killed Lucas.

Chapter Five

I spent some time praying and thinking in the church then I walked up past the town hall and Chabrassonne's only hotel, heading towards the little boulangerie. I was thinking about something to eat but I was not really thinking clearly.

The shop had just re-opened and a couple of older housewives were already inside chatting and selecting the evening's bread and pastries. I stood outside half thinking about food and mulling over the incidents of the past day and a half. One of the women leaving the shop brought me out of my reverie and I wished her a good afternoon as I let her past before making my way through the narrow door.

Yvonne was counting out change into a very elderly woman's hand. When the old lady turned, she looked straight at me and said, "Well, well. So, it takes an Englishman to show some backbone in this town, now, does it?"

Instinctively, I replied with, "Actually, I'm Scottish, Madame." And she laughed, "That will explain it, then! Good afternoon." And off through the door she went, her basket full, her skirts rustling across the threshold.

I turned to Yvonne and asked, "What was that all about?"

"It seems that you have won favour with a number of the older members of our little town by standing up to that nasty little bully from Lavelanet!"

"Oh!" I sighed, "This place is just one big swamp filled with gossip. I have an argument with a policeman in a bar a couple of hours ago and it is all over town like that." I clicked my fingers. "How can people ever keep secrets in a place like this?"

"You can't!" Yvonne grinned one of her cheekiest grins, "Nothing gets past me. But don't worry, I can be discreet when required." And she gave me a little wink before leaning forward and asking me what I wanted.

Sometimes she could be a completely disarming flirt and it seemed to take me a long time to work out what I was going to buy. In the end I bought a small loaf and a couple of pain au chocolat. As she was putting the sweet pastries in a bag, I asked her why people didn't like Limon. Was it because he was a policeman from another town, because he was a particularly unpleasant person or what?

"The Limon family has a history in this area," she replied, "you need to speak to someone like Madame Clerembourg to get the full details, but it has something to do with the war. There are still lots of rivalries and accusations flying between the

Limons and the Pecheurs that date from that time. It's just like a sort of old family feud to most of us, now. But for the older people it is something pretty serious."

"That was Madame Clerembourg I spoke to a minute ago?"

"Yes, she lives down by the old mill. You know?"

"Yes, I know where it is. I once parked down there when I first came to Chabrassonne."

"Oh dear!"

"Yes. The old lady .."

"Madame Ducloy."

"That's her, yes. Madame Ducloy wrote me down in her little book and reported me to Georges."

"I think she has reported everyone in the town for parking almost anywhere. But she did manage to push through the decision to have the car park in the town centre. See, even busybodies have their uses."

I picked up my bread and pan au chocolat and said, "But do they all keep notes in little books?"

"For some things." She smiled, "Just let me know when you want to be entered into mine."

"That's certainly something to think about." I said as I left the shop.

Yvonne's flirting and gossip completely distracted me, leaving me deep in thought as I wandered back across town. It was not until I was standing outside the old Pecheur family home that I realised I had been heading for it again. I stood looking at the house, wondering what I was trying to work out when my mobile phone began ringing. After fumbling for it and juggling shopping I answered the call.

"John, it's Nathalie Pecheur."

"Yes, Nathalie, what can I do for you?"

"I have just been hearing about how you stood up to M. Limon. I wanted to thank you and ask you if I could give you the number of our solicitor. If Limon tries to attack you again you can call him, and he will deal with the wretched man for you."

"Well, thank you Nathalie but that will not be necessary."

"Please, for my peace of mind. You have been such a help and I would not want you to fall foul of Limon while trying to help us."

"Nathalie, by all means give me your solicitor's details, but I can't use him. It would be a bad idea. Trust me."

"I don't understand?"

"Limon attacked me, as you say, because he wants to get at your family, and he connects me with you. He can't harm me because he is mistaken. I'm just an individual. I am not working for you or Philip. Anyway, what could you pay me to do? If I suddenly wheeled in your solicitor, it would be like proving that I was working for you and he would feel justified to attack me more."

"Are you saying you are not on our side?"

"It's not as simple as that, Nathalie. Caring about you and offering my support is one thing. But taking sides?"

I could hear her struggling with what I was trying to tell her.

"Look," I said, "I was going to say I don't take sides but that is wrong, too. If I could be described as being on someone's side, I would say that I'm on Lucas' side. If anyone deserves representation and a friend at the moment, I feel it should be Lucas. Don't you?"

"Why, yes. Of course!"

"Well let's leave it at that. The feud which appears to be taking place between the Limons and the Pecheurs or between the old guard of Chabrassonne and the Limons is getting in the way of finding out the truth. I'm standing outside your old family home at the moment and I'm wondering what the police have been up to. For example, there's no police tape sealing the place. Have the police examined it already?"

"I don't know if they have done very much there, John. Lucas was found on the high path not in the house. After all, you found him!"

"Yes, but how did he get there? He was staying in this house, wasn't he?"

She was silent for a few seconds. "What are you trying to say?"

"If you want to do something with that solicitor of yours, perhaps you could get him to pester the police. Get him to ask where the investigation is going, how far have they got with investigating the people Lucas was running away from, has the pathologist established the 'when', the 'how' and the 'where' of the murder? Things like that. Get him to do some of the pushing, OK?"

"Yes, of course. Do you think that will help?"

"Well, you want to know what happened, you want to have them catch who was responsible, don't you? You want them to stop harassing your family? Get them to investigate the murder. Perhaps you can get your solicitor to threaten to take the story to the media. Get him to speak to the people above Limon."

"I see. Yes, John, that sounds like a good idea."

"Good. I'm going home now to make my evening meal and sit down for a while. It's been a busy day." I wished her goodbye and pocketed the phone.

From behind me a small voice said, "Excuse me, monsieur."

I turned to see a young, very frail looking girl. Her blond hair was so light it was almost white, and her skin was so pail it was almost translucent. She was very thin and her high cheek bones made her eyes look almost oriental and gave her slightly wide, thin mouth a look of tending towards a permanent smile. She had huge, hoop earrings and wore a threadbare T shirt with a faded "Mario du Lavandou" sign on it in pink, pale blue jeans and espadrille sandals on her feet. She had a large shoulder bag with handwritten slogans, comments, names and other graffiti scrawled all over it.

She could have been anything from sixteen to twenty-six years old, as far as I could tell, but I suspected she was on the older end of that scale. She brought up an almost bony, but still elegant hand up to brush back her hair from her eyes, and

I could see that the first two fingers were nicotine stained. "When she said, "Excuse me," again I expected her to ask me for some money, but that did not seem right. I had never encountered anyone begging on the streets in Chabrassonne before.

"Monsieur, I could not help overhearing. Do you know Lew, I mean Lucas Pecheur?"

I looked at her, trying to think if I had ever seen her before in Chabrassonne, and wondered at the fact that the T shirt she was wearing was from Le Lavandou, which is a resort on the Mediterranean near Toulon. I know the place and have passed through it several times.

"Are you looking for Lucas?"

She seemed to brighten at this question. "Yes. He told me to come here but there is no answer and I was not sure where to go next. Do you know where he is?"

I quickly debated what to do. Should I just tell her that he is dead and that she should go to the police? Probably that would be the most advisable approach to take. If I was kind, I could even take her there. I could send her to the Pecheurs and let them handle it?

"Have you tried phoning him?" I asked.

She shrugged her shoulders, pulled a phone out of her bag and waved it at me. It was well worn, covered in plastic jewels and other things. "No charge, no credit, no calls." Then she put it away again, asking, "Have you seen him?"

She looked disarmingly frail, but I sensed that there was a toughness in there. Throwing her straight into the wolves' den would be hard, but she would cope. I looked at her and thought that I was just too tired, hungry and fed up to have to cope with it all so I said to her, "Yes, I know where he is, but you can't see him at the moment. I'm on my way home, "I waved my packages from the boulangerie and continued, "Do you want something to eat, then I'll tell you what's been happening here."

She looked a bit warily at me, but shrugged her shoulders. Hunger. and possibly exhaustion. seemed to be fairly strong factors in her decision-making, and she trotted beside me like a little puppy, hardly capable of walking in a straight line or with even steps. When we reached my door she almost tripped up, yelped, "Ooops!" and then asked me if this was where I lived. I opened the door with my key and said that it was.

I took her straight through to the kitchen and suggested she sit at the table and I offered her some fruit juice from the 'fridge as I began to rummage around for inspiration amongst its shelves. As she slurped at a large glass of mango juice, I considered the bowl of pasta sauce and meatballs I had been planning to put away in the freezer for the last couple of days.

"How about spaghetti with tomato sauce and meat balls?"

"OK by me." She said, still concentrating on the juice.

"The meat balls are pork, any objections?"

"What are you saying?" She snapped back, "Do I look Jewish?"

94

"Just wanted to know if you liked pork or not."

"I eat anything!" Then, "Have you any more of this?"

I passed her the carton of juice and told her to finish it, then I pulled out a couple of pans, started the water to boil and began to gently heat up the sauce. I poured myself some sparkling mineral water and stood by the stove drinking it and looking at her.

"My name's John, by the way. What's yours?"

"My name is Charline Jacquin, but everyone calls me Charli."

"Hello Charli," I raised my glass, "Have you known Lucas long?"

"Yeh!" she cocked her head at me, "I've known him for almost two years. He's never mentioned anyone called John, though. How do you know him?"

"I've lived here on and off for almost ten years. I watched Lucas grow up. I know his parents, brother and sister, too." I really just wanted to tell her that he was dead but the food was going to be ready quite soon and I felt she needed at least one meal inside her before anything else happened, so I played for time and a tried to fish for any information I could.

"How did you meet?"

"I was working in Mario's and he came in to have his hair cut. He was just nice – not like most of the people you would get in there. ' Mario's for international intercoiffure, haute coiffure Française, Dames et Messieurs, Grande Parfumerie' and so on… There are two types of people who go there.

Redemption song

The tourists – and most of them couldn't tell a good hair salon from a butcher's shop, but they want to be pampered on holiday, which is fair enough. Then there are the locals – regulars who should know better but come because they believe the rubbish in the ads just as much as the tourists do!"

"So why did Lucas have his hair cut there?"

"He did it so that he could chat me up! Can you imagine that?"

Funnily enough, I could. But I could just as easily see Lucas telling her that was the reason once he discovered her distain for the place.

"You're not working in the salon now?"

"No, I stopped a couple of months after meeting Lew. He travelled along the coast on a regular basis and I travelled with him. It was a lot of fun most of the time – anyway, Lew made it fun. But the last couple of months have been a bit harder."

As I put the pasta into the boiling water she suddenly stood up, as if a lightning bold had shot through her. "Have you got any cigarettes?" she asked me.

"No. I don't smoke. No one does in this household. The shop 'round the corner should still be open."

"Fine." She started to sink back down onto her seat then she stood up again, rocking the table in front of her and the chair at her read. "Look, do you have some money I can borrow. Lew owes me and as soon as we connect, he'll pay you back."

I pulled out my wallet and gave Charli a ten Euro note. "Is this enough?"

"Yeh. No, well sort of. Maybe twenty would be better."

I looked in my wallet and pulled out another ten for her. I walked her to the door and took the lock off the latch. Then I pointed her to the shop and came back to tend the food. By the time she was back I had grated some strong hard cheese and opened a bottle of strong, dark red wine, set the table, drained the pasta and tossed it in a little extra virgin olive oil. A small envelope of tobacco smoke clung to her as she brushed past and dropped down onto her seat. Despite this, I was grateful she had not wandered back into the house while she was still smoking.

I stood opposite her and created two little mountains of spaghetti on our plates then divided the sauce between us. It made a sizeable meal and as I passed her a plate, I wondered just how much she would be able to eat.

I shouldn't have worried. Her table manners were pretty rudimentary, and she ate with gusto, at great speed and with even more noise than she had managed to produce while she was drinking the fruit juice. She also slurped the wine down at an alarming rate.

The impression I had was of someone who had not seen many meals for quite some time.

"How did you get here?" I asked, half expecting her to say that she had walked all the way from Le Lavandou.

Redemption song

Mainly hitched but I took a couple of buses first, then I walked from a horrible little place called Laroque something or other."

"Laroque Dolmes is about sixteen kilometres from here."

"Yeh. A bloody long way! Don't think I have ever walked that far in my life before, but no one would stop for me on that road. They just went zooming past. Some even beeped their horn at me!"

"How long did it take you?"

"Well I started from St Raphael and although it would have been relatively easy to get to Marseilles by hitching from there, I took a bus, then another bus to get there. Then it was hitching along more of the coast and up to Carcassonne and then a couple of rides took me as far as that Laroque place and all transport just dried up on me!"

I wondered at the need to get the buses and thought that it might have been because she wanted to avoid familiar faces along that bit of the coast. Sadly, her caution had not stopped someone from finding Lucas and killing him before his girl could arrive on the scene.

She waited for me to finish then asked if it was OK to smoke. I pointed to the door leading onto the veranda. "I'll find you an ashtray," I said. "Do you want some coffee brought out?"

"White, three sugars." Then as she got out through the doors, I heard a belated, "Please."

She was sitting at the end of the veranda enshrouded in a dull grey cloud of smoke when I arrived with the coffee.

"Thanks for the food. I really needed that!"

I sat down opposite her and picked up my coffee. In the fading light I could see that her face was showing more anxiety than earlier. She had spent the time during the meal focusing on food and eating, then she had spent a bit of time feeding her prodigious nicotine habit and now she was getting down to something like reality again, and she was beginning to see something unpleasant moving towards her. I think she had spent a lot of her life dealing with such things.

"You have something to tell me about Lew, don't you?"

I nodded and drank a few little sips of my coffee.

"I'm sorry, Charli."

"He's dead. Right?"

"Someone killed him."

She was shaking and the smoke from her cigarette began forming jagged zigzags next to her as the shaking took hold.

"The fucking bastards! They didn't have to do it! They just did not have to do it. Oh God, my poor Lew. My poor, poor Lew." Then she began to sob. Her cries seemed to rip through her in waves and my heart felt like it was tearing apart as I sat there. I wanted to go around to her and comfort her. She looked so much like a fragile child in utter despair and agony. I put the cup down and began to get up and she said, through her hands, "No! I'll be alright in a minute. Just let me be for a minute, will you?"

I walked off the veranda with my coffee, fished out a heavy glass and poured a measure of Armagnac into it and quietly placed it beside her as she sat, rocking quieter now.

Back in the kitchen I put the radio on and tuned it to a jazz station. The quiet rolling tones of sax, and the rippling tension of the bass line, took some of the tension out of the air. From nowhere appeared the two little muscular brothers Rag and Tag, and they performed their set of figure of eights around my legs as I fished out their dried food and replenished their water bowl. I had not seen them for more than a day, but they seemed as content and independent as usual as they settled down to some crunchy treats.

After a while Charli came in and immediately dropped down next to the cats, stroking and chatting to them in her odd, childlike voice. She even picked up one of them, Rag I think, and he let her hold him and cuddle him for what seemed to me to be a remarkably long period of time before muscling his way down from her arms.

"You have been honoured." I said. "He never lets anyone hold or stroke him."

A weak smile passed across her face and she sat down beside me at the table.

"How did he die? Do you know?"

I nodded. I thought about what I should say. I had been thinking about these very questions ever since she introduced herself to me. The truth seemed the best course to take.

"I found him. I was walking on a quiet path up above the town and found him lying dead in the middle of the path."

"My God. Just like that?" and she half waved and clicked her fingers at the same time.

"Someone had left him there, partly covered with a plastic sack."

"How had they killed him?"

I looked at her and she stared straight back at me with a growing determination and I answered her, "Someone had stabbed him in the throat, just here." I pointed at the place in my throat where I had seen the knife buried.

She nodded and turned away from me just a little.

"You know who did it, don't you?"

"I don't know. I don't really know."

"Are you frightened of what they might do to you?"

"Of course I'm bloody frightened! My boyfriend has just been murdered!"

"I meant, are you too frightened to say who you think it might have been."

"OK. OK. Yeh. I think I am. I don't know. Sorry, it's all just such a fucking shock, you know. I thought he was safe. I KNEW he was fucking safe!" She stamped her foot on the floor and she seemed to shudder again as if she was about to start crying again, but she took a deep breath instead and looked back at me. "I've an idea but what can I do? I mean, these are nasty, horrible people. They're used to hurting anyone they like. They pay policemen all along the coast so that they'll look the other way. What could I say or do that would make any difference? It would be like pinning a target on myself!"

Her sense of rage and frustration was taking her outside her grief. It was animating her and depressing her in turns. I decided to interrupt the emotional turmoil.

"Does one of these people drive a VW van of some sort?"

She started as if I had poked her with my finger. "What colour?"

"I don't know. I'm sure you can tell me the colour. The important thing is that one's connected with this, and the police will soon be able to connect a particular van with the murder. From that, they'll be able to connect a person to the van. Some clues might help."

Further realisation came into her and she sat back a bit. "Hold on. I can't go to the police. I can't. There are things Lew and I did. The police would do me for those and I'm wanted for a couple of minor offences in Nîmes before I went down to the coast. I skipped town and they'll do me for those, too. I can't go to the police. They won't listen to me – all they'll do is rub their hands with glee and put me in jail."

Similar thoughts had passed through my mind even when I was looking at her in front of the Pecheur house. Her whole being seemed to cry out that she was someone who'd been hunted all her life. It wasn't a matter of whether she could cope with facing the police or not; it was a matter of should she have to cope with it, or should she be allowed to slip away? It was difficult to know which was worse. The lessons that prison can dish out or the lessons that always seem to be taught to people like her on the streets.

"I'm not asking you to speak to anyone. I just want to know a bit more. Perhaps what you can tell me will help."

I knew then that I was about to get her version of the story. Her whole body-language said that she was going to tell me. But before she could even say that she was ready to tell me, someone began banging on my front door and she jumped out of the chair, already looking around for an escape route. I grabbed her upper arm and pulled her into my study, picking her bag up on the way. "Sit down here and keep quiet." I whispered then I closed the door on her and looked down the hall towards the noise.

"OK, OK! What are you trying to do? Knock the door in?"

On the dresser just inside the kitchen there was an old fashioned marble rolling pin set on a wooden stand. I always thought it looked like an ancient scroll, but it was great for rolling out pastry. I picked it up and walked towards the door.

"Who is it?" I called as I approached the door. The only answer was a steady thumping on the big old door.

As I swung it open a young man slightly larger than me with tousled hair, unshaven face and wild eyes rushed at me grabbing my lapels and projecting me backwards. I tried to swing him around as I was unable to push back effectively, but his grip was strong and built on a furious rage. Spittle flew from his mouth as he shouted abuse at me and slammed me against the wall. I could smell drink on his breath and his denim shirt and trousers smelled of car oil and sweat.

The thought of hitting him on the back of the head with the rolling pin flashed through my mind, but the fact that his face was about three inches away from mine stopped me. I also thought that it would either make him more determined to hit me or do more damage to him (and me) than was sensible. Although it was all happening very rapidly, I also felt a sense of detachment, which seemed to slow everything down into a dream-like state. I whacked him as hard as I could in the lower part of his back and he just crumpled at my feet letting out a sort of muffled groan.

Looking at the open door I could see an old couple, who had obviously been passing at the time of the initial rush, standing staring in at us. Keeping the rolling pin at my side I walked to the door and closed it, waving my free hand at them and saying, "It's all right. No problem! Good evening."

They nodded in astonishment at me and then the door was shut.

I walked back and put the rolling pin back on its stand then strode across to the freezer where I took out a small bag of frozen peas which had not yet been opened. I brought it back into the hall and helped the young man up.

"Here, press this against your back. The pain will subside in a while." He limped with me into the kitchen and I got him to sit at the table. I then walked back to the study and checked that Charli was OK. I wanted her to know that everything was under control. She was sitting at my desk with her hands clasped tight between her knees, her face even paler than before. I told her I would be a couple of minutes and that she should just sit and wait for me.

Back in the kitchen I checked the kettle and switched it on.

"Let me make you some coffee and you can tell me why you attacked me in my own home." My voice was remarkably steady but inside I felt very shaky. Presumably the adrenalin was still coursing through me. I tried to steady my hands as I made us both a cup of instant coffee – his white and sweet, mine strong and black.

"What did you hit me with?"

"Never mind that," I said, not wanting to explain and certainly not wanting to have a debate about the use of weapons, and such, "What did you think you were going to do? Beat me up? Drag me out and run me over with your van?" I had noticed an old, battered white Renault van as I had closed the door and suspected it was his.

He shook his head, tried to sit up to take his coffee and winced a little bit.

"My name is Jean Jacques Bacconnier."

"I know who you are!" I had worked out that this was JJ. I could recall seeing him in the garage at the bottom end of town and, although I had used the place a few times over the years, I'd never needed to have any contact with him. He was one of those mechanics behind the scenes, with Jules Guillamot, the owner, fronting the shop.

"Well, I wanted to know why my wife came to see you today and why she went to the police."

"So, you thought the best way to find out was to come and beat me up?"

"I was not going to hurt you! I was angry and worried."

"OK. We won't argue about what you intended. But you pushed into my house, shouted abuse at me, slammed me against the wall. Why not just ask your wife? Why me? And if you wanted to speak to me, you could've knocked on my door, then you could have asked me if I had a few minutes ,and then perhaps you might have got some answers."

"My wife has gone. She has taken little Sylvie and disappeared. I thought she might have come back here."

"Until this morning I had never spoken to your wife before. As it is, she was quite rude to me, too. She didn't go as far as physical abuse, but when she left, I didn't think she had much intention of coming back here."

"So, what did you talk about? Why did she come here?"

"I think you should ask her that when you see her."

"Was it about Lucas? Did she tell you anything about her and Lucas?"

"See," I said, "This is what it all comes back to in the end. Everyone seems to think that I have something to do with what happened to Lucas, or that I can find out what happened to him." I paused and looked at him, closely, "I never knew Lucas, hardly saw him when he lived here. I just happened to be the one who discovered his body."

I said the last bit in a quieter, softer tone. Trying to calm things down a bit as I had been running on that adrenalin and I was beginning to feel that our conflict was becoming pretty pointless.

"Did you see Lucas during his latest visit? You had been good friends at one time, hadn't you?"

He shook his head.

"I never saw him, no."

I let that lie hang in the air for a minute, unchallenged.

He had turned away from me as he answered my question then turned back to shrug and add, "Except for the other night in the bar. I was sitting near the door and I could see him getting drunk. I thought that nothing had changed. He was still the arrogant, drunken clown he'd always been, and I think I must have sneered at him when Monsieur Martin told him that he shouldn't have another drink. Then, as he staggered past me, he punched me in the face! I couldn't believe it! And then M. Martin told <u>me</u> to clear off, as if <u>I was the one who had started it</u>!"

I watched him run through the various emotions held in his story, his face illustrating each one in turn. He was one of those people with what used to be called a finely chiselled face. Each feature seemed slightly exaggerated in a sharp, angled way, from the chin and strong nose to the high cheek bones and brow. The black hair and deeply tanned skin accentuated everything, and he would have been more classically handsome if the whole face had been just a bit more symmetrical.

He had put the peas down on the table and they were in danger of leaving a damp stain on the wood, so I picked them up and threw them in the bin, then took a couple of squares of kitchen towel to wipe the surface dry.

He looked around him as if he was seeing the place for the first time and then he said, "I thought you had someone with you. I could hear you and I thought you were talking with a woman!"

"You must have remarkable hearing."

He looked sheepishly at me and said that he had lifted the flap on the letter box to look in, and that was how he could hear inside the house. I nodded and walked out of the kitchen and asked Charli to come through. She looked a bit apprehensive, but I felt she put on a good front. I introduced her as a friend of my son's, who had dropped by to catch up on the news and drop off some books she had borrowed from James. They shook hands and greeted each other quite formally.

I was about to send him on his way when it occurred to me that it might be useful to get one more thing out of him.

"Have the police been 'round to see you, yet?"

"No, why should they. I have not had anything to do with Lucas for years."

"I would have thought they needed to check everyone out and eliminate various people from their enquiries. After all, the last time you saw

Lucas he hit you. It was a public incident and you were very angry with him. A short time later he's found dead."

JJ began to protest, and I raised my hand to him, "Wait. I didn't say you had anything to do with it. I'm sure you have a perfect alibi. But the police need to check everything out in such a case. They always do."

He looked even more sombre now and he nodded without speaking.

I finished by suggesting that he should expect them to visit him sometime soon. "They can be a bit rough you know." I said, "Don't let them make you angry. Try to keep that temper of yours in check."

Again, the ghost of that sheepish smile flitted across his face and I could see how he would act violently towards people and expect them to forgive him soon after. For him, none of the violence and raging tempers were that bad; they flashed past him and then they were gone. He expected it to be like that for everyone else, too.

He actually said he was sorry, too. Then he winced a bit as he stood up.

"One of these days you'll have to tell me how you did that! God it hurts!"

"Have long soak in a bath and take some Ibuprophen. It will take the swelling down as well as kill the pain. And don't drink much alcohol for a couple of days." I said. I amazed myself by sounding so authoritative when I really was nothing of the kind. I'd just said the first thing that had come into my mind

"Yes, but.." he shook his head.

"Trade secret." I said in order to stop him asking again about how I had managed to hit him so hard.

After he left, Charli asked me about the incident, and I explained who he was and about his relationship with Lucas. She admitted she had heard the name but did not know a great deal about him.

When she asked about how I had subdued JJ I said, with sleight of hand. She didn't understand at first so I explained that conjurers could distract you so that you never noticed what they really had in their hands. In times of conflict and sudden violence, people either don't see anything useful or make up things, convincing themselves that they have seen something they had not seen. I had the rolling pin in my hand, but he had not expected me to have anything, so it went unnoticed. I put it away immediately, so by the time he was able to make any sense of the world around him it was gone, so he filled in the gaps himself. I wondered about the old couple outside, though. They must have watched the whole incident. Did they see the rolling pin? Did they make sense of it all?

It was getting late and the day had been pretty exhausting. I could see that Charli was beginning to become agitated, so I asked her if she had a place to stay. She had been expecting to stay with Lucas but that was not now an option. I told her that there was a spare bedroom she could use and took her up to one of the rooms our girls usually used. It was next to the first-floor bathroom, and its window looked out over the gardens to the back of the house. I pulled out a fitted sheet, some pillowcases and then fished out a duvet and put a clean cover on that, too.

She opted to have a bath and go to bed, so I walked back downstairs and washed the dishes in the kitchen. I then popped through to the study and checked out my emails. There was quite a happy one from Jude, which made me feel a bit better. Jo had been 'round to see her and they had spent some time talking about the 'photos I had sent. Mary was now watching out for them and I knew she was doing a good job. I just missed her so much when she was not here, and I sat by the light of the computer screen thinking about times we had enjoyed together on the coast, walking high over the rugged paths above the sea and lying, floating in the gentle, clear waters of a quiet cove with the sun beating down, and our children diving off the floating platform tethered a few hundred metres away. I could see the complex patterns of light and colour dancing across the water's surface and then James bursting through the scene from below in an eruption of water, arms and goggles.

Eventually I wrote a couple of short and amusing emails in response the messages and walked out onto the veranda. A fox was making its strange asthmatic coughing sounds in the distance. The unsettling noise seemed to be perfect for this particular night. A bark that was not a bark; summer that was no longer fully summer; a violent presence had arrived and did not want to go away.

The idea that a death is the end of someone is not really true. Lucas was still alive in the actions, thoughts and emotions of the people here. The momentum of his life was still pushing through the community like a truck whose breaks no longer worked, ploughing through a field of corn.

I wondered whether I should be looking in the direction he had come from or in the direction he had gone.

Chapter Six

That night I took some time to get to sleep. I read a bit of a book on the American Civil war. It was really just about the battle at Gettysburg and focused on the key characters, and I was warming to a few, including Burford. The geography of the place fascinated me, and I was making a mental note that I should do a bit of research on the area when I realised that I was dozing. I had been lying on my side in bed with my left arm supporting me as I read the book. This freed my right arm to turn pages and, if I was writing, to use my pen.

My arm had started to go to sleep and I sat up with a start, pins and needles jangling up to my shoulder and down to my wrist. Slightly dopey, I got up out of bed and walked to the window. I had not closed the shutters and could see across the dark gardens to the backs of the other houses on the next street. Everything was dark, the foxes had been quiet for some time and there was very little noise apart from a strong breeze blowing in varied strengths of gusts. The lights from the next street outlined the roofs of the houses and some distant light held the hill beyond in dark relief. No stars. The night was being dampened down with clouds moving silently across the landscape.

Below me I heard the sound of something moving through the bushes. It could have been one of the cats or a fox. I watched for a while but could not see any movement. There was not enough light. At one point I caught a flicker of light with the corner of my eye but when I turned to look there was nothing. It could have been an optical illusion – a flaw in the window glass bouncing back light from my own bedside lamp.

I went quietly to the toilet and returned to bed.

Later on in the night, the rain woke me. I heard this rushing, hissing sound approaching from the direction of the mountains. I lay waiting as the sound approached and almost felt the cold, hard pounding of water as it passed over the house. Rain drumming on the roof, the water droplets pounding every leaf and every pebble in the garden. I thought about the BBQ in the garden and how I had been meaning to close its lid for the last few days. Too late now. I heard something rush through the gardens in the rain. It was loud enough to be heard over the water's din. Whatever it was, it did not like being rained on. I smiled and drifted back into sleep with the comforting sound of being safe and dry in a storm easing some of the tension out of me.

One of my dreams stuck with me well into the morning. It was about a place I was familiar with when dreaming. It featured a mountainous area and a city which varied in size depending on the dream. This time it was a vast city that had spread from a wide plain into the hills and then nudged its way into the mountain range. I was sitting at a huge picture window looking down across the city towards the plain and I knew that the mountains were looming up behind me. In the distance I could see lots of movement and there was a faint noise bubbling up from the streets below.

I stood and the huge windows just opened up for me. I think I had expected them to slide open or slide up into the wall, but the window split at an invisible seam and opened out onto a large wooden balcony that I had not realised was there. The land dropped sharply from me and I could hear the noise of crowds. They were all charging up the hill, shouting and waving their arms in the air. They began flooding past my house and on up to the mountain and I managed to be able to follow their progress around to the back of the house without really moving much.

Above me were the great jagged mountains, much like the Pyrenees, with bare, cracked rock sides and snow covering the sharp peaks. But below this was a large sloped grass hill with a set of huge walls in a long sequence. They cut people off from access to the mountains but there were gaps like tall slender slits between each section of wall. A terrible crush was taking place as more and more people flooded up the hill to encounter the walls. Only one or two people at a time could squeeze through the gaps and mayhem was ensuing.

Redemption song

Behind me I felt a great, bright flash of light and a sudden searing heat and I turned around to see a mushroom cloud build up out of the centre of the city.

"My God, they have actually done it!" I said out loud and walked back into the room. I could see the textbook wall of wind and debris expand out across the city with one edge heading towards me. From behind me I heard Mary say, "You better shut the windows and fix the shutters, John." And I struggled to get these simple tasks done. The speed of the wind was picking up now and I had very little time left. I kept shouting, "Get in the cellar, Mary! Hurry, you'll be safe there!" But as I tried to push and crowd her out of the room the more solid and immobile she became. I was at my wit's end, pleading with her to let me save her when she turned her face towards me and smiled that patient, drawn smile she had when she was suffering from her terrible headaches. It was like she was focusing all of her energy into just making the smile form on her lips, in her eyes, across her face, then the wind struck, and everything was gone.

I woke up with a start and it was a bright clear, early morning. Birds were singing, a small cloud was slowly drifting across a sky pale blue with early sunshine. I looked at my clock – it was half past six. Although not particularly early for me, I was feeling the effects of a stressful couple of days and a night of broken sleep. The dream was like a strange companion walking beside me, letting me see the difference between it and the real world and I welcomed it, wondering how long it would stay with me, today.

I took a little while at my ablutions but was still downstairs before seven.

Yesterday's bread never seems to be much cop and I thought about using it to make something, so I put the loaf to one side and looked at the pain au chocolats. They seemed OK, so I put them on a plate and set up the coffee machine, filled the kettle, left the hot chocolate and a couple of coffee bowls next to the kettle and put my shoes on. I wrote a short note saying I was getting bread and propped it up in front of the kettle then I left the house, locking it after me.

The streets were still damp from the night's rain, but it felt more like they had been well scrubbed than they had been rained on, and the smell was not so much of damp dust as of wet stone. It was the difference between the summer and its companion seasons of spring and autumn. The whole sense of place caused me to want to prolong the trip to the shop, so I took a route around the outer edge of the old town, saying good morning to people as I encountered them, looking at the world waking up, watching people heading off to work and off to the shops.

When I eventually arrived at the boulangerie there was a little chatty queue jutting out of the door onto the street. At this time of the morning there were always a range of people waiting to buy their morning bread. A couple of young mothers were there, one with a small child balanced on her hip; next to them was an old man with a crumpled face topped off with an ancient cap. In his mouth he held an odd-looking pipe which seemed too long and straight in the stem, and the bowl looked like it was too large. When he put his hand up to move the pipe around, I could see that they were gnarled with age and as gnarled and grey as badly sculpted granite. Two elderly women were standing with their backs straight and their appearance was as effortlessly formal and stylish as they could make it. A young couple stood behind them chatting closely. They could hardly keep their hands off each other, and I could see tolerant and affectionate glances coming from the old ladies. Next to them and immediately in front of me was the unmistakable bulk of Marc Pecheur.

I could not remember the last time I had seen Marc buying anything in the Boulangerie, or any other shop for that matter. I imagined that such tasks were left to the women of the household. However, today Marc was there, queuing up to buy his own bread.

"Good morning, Marc."

He jerked with surprise, as if he was still half asleep, and looked around at me. His face was drawn and pale and the shadows under his eyes were more pronounced, like dark sacks. He nodded and hardly moved his mouth as he wished me good morning.

"How are you doing?" I asked, "You looked tired."

"OK." He nodded again, as if seeing me for the first time. "Just getting some bread. I was going to pop in and see you on the way back. Ask if you could come to the office and speak with my father later this morning."

"I would like to do that." I said, thinking that Marc wanted to actually say something to me in private first. He looked slightly embarrassed, which was something unusual for Marc. It was as if he had a guilty secret to tell me. "Perhaps, if you don't have your car with you, we could walk back together once I get my bread?"

He nodded again and just turned away from me, not wanting to talk.

I stood patiently and moved with the queue, listening to Yvonne's light banter as we edged into the shop towards the counter. It was warmer inside and I gradually noticed that this morning was not as warm as it had been. The rain of the night before had brought a cooler band of air with it, and although the sun was coming up on a clear sky, it was fresher than previous mornings.

Marc bought his bread with a couple of light jibes from Yvonne about being the one to do the shopping. She seemed to be pulling her punches not for his benefit, but out of respect for his mother and perhaps his wife, who was still not around. I wondered what the story was with Marc and his wife. The rumour was that she had left him, but he had resolutely claimed that she was just visiting a friend.

I bought my bread. I had thought about having croissants but decided against it. They seemed too rich and buttery for today; I already had the pain au chocolats, and I was hankering for some sort of simplicity that the bread seemed to offer. Yvonne flirted and hinted at knowing about my encounter with JJ, but again she was restrained, and I was beginning to feel that some sort of change was in the air, but could not work out what it was.

Outside on the narrow pavement, Marc was standing like a schoolboy waiting to be seen by the headmaster. I walked up to him and his bulky figure looked like it was sheltering the bread in his arms like it was a fragile baby. We walked in silence past the corner with the hotel and cut through the central cluster of medieval houses that made up the heart of the town. There were few people around and we wished those that passed us good morning as we headed up through the market square, past the opening shops. I stopped to buy a local paper, but Marc stayed outside as I chatted to the shopkeeper and tucked the paper under my arm.

"Do you want to come in for a coffee?" I offered. I was reluctant to do this but felt he desperately needed to talk to me in private. He leapt at the offer and I silently cursed myself for letting my sympathies dominate me so much, and I was not sure what to say when he encountered Charli. So, we walked for a short while to my house in silence and I unlocked the door.

Charli was not around, so I picked up the note as I reached the kitchen table and put the bread and paper down on its surface. I then moved towards the kettle to start making coffee. Marc sat down quite heavily in one of the kitchen chairs and placed his bread in front of him.

We were silent as I started the hot water dripping through the filter into my coffee jug. Filter coffee has always felt more like a proper morning ritual for me than the cafetière à piston, and I did it almost automatically when I was needing time to think. With two cups in my hands I walked back to the table and slid his across to him indicating the milk and sugar.

"How did they treat you?" I asked, referring to the police.

He was silent for a moment and then sighed. "They were deeply unpleasant."

I thought the sentence was strange, coming from him, but I waited. "They harassed me, trying to get me to admit that I'd killed my own brother – and this was less than a day after his death! I was just beginning to feel the shock of it all when they started on me, and they kept showing me photographs of Lucas, there on the path! Black and white 'photos at first, which seemed so cold and clinical, and then colour ones that were almost unreal. I didn't know what to say. You know me John, at heart I'm a salesman, I live by what I say to people, but I had no words for them. That bastard Limon was just so, so.. I don't know, he just kept on making statements that were designed to make me upset and angry, and there was nothing inside me, nothing!"

I listened and watched Marc carefully. He was someone I had known socially for quite some time, and yet this felt like the first time he had talked to me in such an unguarded way. I felt like an intruder on some sort of very private conversation, but what he was saying was very much directed at me.

"What sort of things?"

"Well, you know? He was trying to get me to say that I hated Lucas and had always wanted to get rid of him. That he was a thorn in my side. He even talked about the prodigal son and how I was the older brother, angry and wanting to have him thrown out. Then they started on about where I'd been on the day Lucas died. They had done their homework and knew where I was, but they still persisted that I was really here; that I had arranged an alibi so that I could do away with Lucas! It was terrible! He was my brother. He annoyed me and sometimes frightened me. He was an idiot and almost ruined the business – you know about that. But he was my brother. It was madness!"

"Did you tell them about Valerie?"

He looked up at me but I could not tell what he was thinking, then he said, "No. Not at first. I didn't want to drag her and the baby into it. I thought that at least that would be safe. But they were on me like a pack of wolves, snapping away at me with facts. Making them look like I had lied to hide the fact that I had killed Lucas. Then they all left the room and I waited for what seemed like hours. Finally, Limon came in and started trying to suggest that I had gotten rid of Lucas because he had discovered my affair with Valerie. So, I told him that I had been with Valerie but that we had not, nor had we ever been lovers. He got me then.

I was really angry with him, and he just laughed back at me and told me that I could go."

"Was your mother there to meet you?"

"Yes, thanks. She told me that you had advised her to go there. How did you know?" He looked genuinely confused. It all seemed a bit strange. As if it was not all quite right, but I didn't want to try teasing it out at that point, so I just said, "Valerie came to see me. I think she had some crazy idea that I had been responsible for your arrest, but she was just frightened and worried, mainly about her daughter and JJ. So, I advised her to go to the police before they decided to come to her. Then I saw your mother a short time after Valerie headed off to the police and suggested that she could get to you in time to bring you home. I think she wanted to do that herself."

"Thank you." Marc was silent for a few minutes then be blurted out, "I think Louise has left me."

There was a long silence. I had not expected this.

"Everyone keeps pointing at me and whispering behind my back. They all seem to know, but I don't know anything. Her parents won't tell me where she is, and she's not been in touch with me, and then Limon kept saying that Lucas was not the only one I was responsible for getting rid of. At first it did not even dawn on me what he meant, then I realised, and I thought, 'My God, is that what people think?' and I didn't know what to do. Can you find her for me? Please John, I need to know that at least she is OK!"

"Marc, what do you expect me to do?"

"Well, you helped find that girl last year. The one who ran away."

"That was different." I said, "It was not very difficult to help. You know the family. They're not very bright and didn't know what to do. I just helped them through the system, acted as their advocate, did a bit of research and made a few calls. She was a child, and we already knew where she was heading."

"Yes, but.."

"We were lucky!" I interrupted.

He looked hurt and deflated.

"Marc. Do you have any idea where she went?" He shook his head and looked at me like a little child in a man's body. "Why do you think she left you?"

"It was after Lucas came home. We had been arguing and she made some comments about him which made me very angry." He stopped and I looked at him with as stern a look as I could muster without feeling like an old fraud. "She said that if he wanted to. If he put his mind to it, he could run the business much better than I ever could. She called me an over-inflated salesman and I hit her. Just once! But I hit her all the same, and then she stormed out without taking any of her clothes or anything. She just picked up her handbag and her coat, walked out the door and drove away."

"You didn't try to stop her?"

"What could I do? I swear I had never raised my hand to her before. She just got under my skin too far. After I had done it, there was just this emptiness between us. You know? An emptiness… and then she just walked out. I didn't know what to do. I waited up all night, then I called her parents the next day. She was not there according to them. I went over in the afternoon and tried to speak to them, but they wouldn't even open the door, so I came home and waited. Then I told everyone that she was away for a few days and all this started happening."

It was only the beginning of the morning. I was only halfway through my first cup of coffee and suddenly I felt tired; as if a whole day had passed.

"OK Marc. Give me their address and number and I will see what I can find out." He was so relieved he fumbled out a piece of paper from his pocket and passed it to me with grateful fingers. He had already written out their names and address, their home phone number and both parent's mobile numbers. He had even written Louise's full name with both surnames, her telephone number and car registration number. I felt almost surprised that they were not in a brown envelope with candid photos of her and a sheaf of money!

I stood up as a signal for Marc to get up and leave. As he stood, the toilet upstairs flushed. He looked at me and was about to ask.

"A friend of my son's arrived last night. I am putting her up for a day or two. He was supposed to meet her here, but he's been delayed somewhere in the north of Scotland and we can't get in touch with him."

Marc just nodded. He was preoccupied with his own thoughts and this was more than enough information for him to process at the same time. As I walked him to the door, I felt that he had told me more in our short meeting than he had told me in almost all of our other conversations put together. I was still pondering on this, wondering if it was really true, when he said, "So, can you come around to the office about half past ten this morning?"

"I'll be there, Marc." I shook his hand and he turned to walk out the door, then he turned back and asked,

"Did JJ really come here yesterday?"

"News travels fast, here, doesn't it? Yes, he was here."

I could see that he wanted to ask more but he just did more of his nodding and left.

Charli was coming down the stairs as I walked towards the kitchen.

"Good morning!" she said to me, looking like a little girl, like one of my daughters. I greeted her and told her that the coffee was probably still fresh enough, or she could have chocolate, if she preferred. "Mmm, chocolate! Lovely!" she grinned.

She went straight to making her chocolate, using the pan I had on the stove to heat the milk. With her back to me she said, "I heard voices, so I thought it best to wait a while before I came down."

I understood the question behind the statement and told her it was Marc, Lucas' brother and some of what had been said. I asked her if she had ever met Marc and she told me she had not. She had never been to Chabrassonne before.

"How did you know where to go?" I asked and she said, lightly, that Lucas had drawn her a sketch map of the town and how to find the house. She pulled out the map and showed me. It was a roughly scribbled set of lines with a couple of street names and three arrows; one pointing to the chateau for reference and the other two pointing to Lucas' houses. The writing was almost illegible, but you could read "Chateau", "Parents' house", "Holiday house" and a couple of street names.

"It's a little bit confusing." She said as she sat down at the table with the chocolate, "The place is a sort of box filled with lots of streets and I came in at the wrong end and found the wrong bridge so I wandered around for a bit before I ended up on the right street."

I understood what she was saying. For such a small place it did hold the capacity for confusion. I explained that it had been rebuilt in medieval times after a flood had destroyed the town. It was built in a way that made it easier to defend and was in a good position between the confluence of three rivers. What had caused it to flood had been the damming of the main river up-stream to create a lake below the castle at Puivert. The first dam had been built badly and it had burst, causing a terrible flood. She looked a bit concerned about that until I explained that this had happened almost a thousand years before. Now, the rivers all seemed a little tame in the summer months but in winter they could flow around the town in deep, dark turbulent streams that brought home their strength and danger.

We ate bread with lots of butter and some really good apricot conserve made by a neighbour. I watched as she dipped her bread into her chocolate and asked her where she originally came from.

"I was brought up by my aunt in Nîmes." She said.

"What about your parents?"

"My mother died when I was three. I don't really know anything about my father. My aunt looked after me, but I was never really part of the family. I felt like an outsider all the time. My cousins bullied me and my uncle, especially, took their side every time! I swear, even the teachers looked at me like I didn't belong, so as soon as I could, I left."

"You said you had some ''problems' in Nîmes before you left?" I emphasised the problems but left it to her to tell me what they were.

"You could say that!" she said, and half giggled at the thought of it. "I had been caught shop-lifting a couple of times. I swear, my cousin Jean put me up to it. He was awful, I think now he wanted to, you know… but he was always trying to get me to do things, and I stole some CDs from a music shop and some makeup for myself. Then I tried stealing some clothes from a little boutique which had some wonderful little dresses and they caught me! There was a terrible scene at home and then I went out and stole some jeans from another shop and when I put them on the next day my uncle said they were going to tell the police. He tried to lock me in my room, but I got Jean to unlock the door while everyone was downstairs shouting at each other while my uncle was calling the police."

She looked sheepishly at me then said, "I stole some money from my uncle."

I raised my eyebrows at her, and she laughed. "His jacket was on this stand in the hall. Everyone was in the dining room arguing and I got Jean to go in, too, then I went over and stole my uncle's wallet and left the house. I was at the bottom of the road when the police car turned the corner heading for the house. I took the first bus I could get on and travelled around Nîmes until I worked out what to do. I got a local bus to Pouix, then I walked across country paths to Pont du Gard where I could get a bus to Avignon. I stayed there three days, hardly spending any money and sleeping on benches and in parks during the day and wandering around at night. Luckily it was summer! Then I took another bus down to Marseilles, but that was so scary! Ugh!"

I listened and watched her as she acted out her story for me, waving her bread, dipping and munching it, tearing another piece hungrily, drinking and talking. She was so lively and nervous that it put me on edge. It was like an electric current was running through her as she talked.

"And then to Mario's in Le Lavandou?"

She became more guarded. I think there were lots of things she did not want to tell me about her experiences, and I did not want to press her on them.

"Eventually. I've been a waitress and a chamber maid and all sorts of other things, too!"

"And then you met Lucas."

Her face clouded a little, she said yes and was quiet for a while.

"Have you thought about who might have caught up with Lucas?"

She kept her eyes on me, looking straight at me and asked, "What will happen to me?"

I shrugged. "No one knows you are here, right?" She nodded. "Tell me the truth. Did Lucas tell anyone he was on his way here? Apart from you, of course."

"Lew told me he wanted to move on. I was to meet him here then we would go north."

"Did you tell anyone you were heading here?"

"I swear, no one knew I was coming. He wanted to keep it a secret. He said he did not want a trail from me to him, or him to me."

"Well, no one knows who you are. Tell me what you think might have happened and give me any information you think will really help and then go. I can give you a lift somewhere and then you can get a train or a bus from there."

"Really? You would do that?"

I smiled, thinking how silly this all was. She was possibly a major witness even though she did not know anything about the murder itself. But she was extremely vulnerable. Someone like Limon would not protect her. He would just waste her evidence and treat her like a criminal. To me she seemed too young to be condemned out of hand. I shuddered to think what might happen to her when she went north, but her chances were as good there as anywhere. I really wanted to at least give her an opportunity.

"Just remember that my son's name is James."

She repeated it a few times with my help. I knew that James was not an easy name for the French to pronounce in anything other than a French way and that for her to pronounce it well would suggest, at least, that she was telling the truth if she was challenged.

"Now tell me, who was the guy in the Volkswagen."

She told me more than that. She described how Lew, as she insisted on calling him, had been doing odd jobs for a small gang of criminals based on the Mediterranean coast mainly from Le Lavandou to St Raphael, but sometimes as far as Nice or even Cannes. He seemed to move up and down the coast, staying for a while in one seaside town then another. Then he would spend a few days moving back and forth from one to the other carrying various packages before stopping again and spending time slowly moving around. Mostly they had rooms in apartments over shops or above nightclubs. Sometimes they would stay in a villa near the coast for a few days, then back on the road. Whenever possible, she would make something for them to eat and they would pretend to be living in their overnight stop like a married couple and other times they would be out all night partying or dining in some really good restaurants. To hear her describe it, the period with Lew must have been very exciting at times and at other times dreadfully boring.

There were some characters she started to know who seemed to be friends of Lew's and others that were deeply unpleasant to him, but who played their part as Lew played his. One of these characters was a young burly man called Michel. Everyone called him Mitch and he seemed to have known Lew before they came down to the coast. Apparently, they had both been involved in some sort of confidence scam where they would drive around the more rural parts of France near the Pyrenees, stopping in places long enough to con their way into a few old people's homes, mainly while pretending to be police officers. They apparently had fake IDs that fooled most old people. They would steal what they could from a few old suckers then move on. When things started to get a bit hot for them, they decided to quit. This guy Mitch drove Lew down to the coast and they split up.

Once Lew was established with this gang, Mitch turned up and tried to weasel his way into the gang, too. Lew didn't really like him and tried to get him to leave, but eventually Mitch was given the chance to do work for the gang and they would eventually see each other from time to time. He always drove an old VW minibus with a cream body and sickly green panels on the sides.

I asked if she knew what Mitch did, but she was not sure. She thought he did some of the rough stuff and some debt collecting. According to her, Mitch always carried a gun and a knife. He was an

Ian Smith

ugly man with a dark complexion who insisted on
dyeing his hair very pale blond. He had a face that
looked to her like an ape's, with heavy features
and a long thin nose that seemed to have been
squashed flat into his face. He had little neck
between his big, ugly head and his large but
rounded shoulders, and his arms seemed to be far
too long for the rest of him.

I asked if she knew what Lew had been
carrying and she admitted it had been things like
drugs, money and stolen goods such as jewellery.
She said that they would steal it in one place and
fence it in another. It didn't seem to me to be a big
enough area for it to make that much difference,
but what did I know?

The final thing she shared with me was that
Lew had been stealing small amounts from the
gang for several months. Firstly, it was to pay for
things he wanted for himself and her. Then he had
stolen to give himself what he called some 'seed
money'.

When they started to show awareness of his
petty pilfering, Lew waited as long as he could and
then stole the maximum amount of cash that he
could get a hold of.

"Not drugs - just cash?"

"Of course," she said, "You can only realise the
value of drugs when you sell them – and you can't
do much of that before someone gets to know
about it. Then they either want some of the action
or all of it, including your share!"

That sounded convincing. I wondered if he had
brought the money here with him. He may even

have hidden it in the house not far from here. They might even have forced or tricked the money out of him before killing him. But I wondered if the money was actually in her big bag under her meagre collection of clothes and other personal effects.

"And you were to meet him here with the money." I said it as a statement and she jumped up so suddenly it surprised me, even when I thought that she would do that. She almost left there and then but I stopped her saying I didn't want it. I didn't want any of it. I was thinking that she would need every penny of it to keep her even vaguely safe.

"I meant what I said. I don't want to play games. I'm going to have to go out in a little while and I think you should keep yourself to yourself while I was out. Don't answer the door and don't answer the phone. Just wait and I will give you a lift either this afternoon or tomorrow morning."

Strangely, she asked me if she could go out onto the balcony and smoke. I said that of course she could, and I handed her the paper. "Read this. Tell me what they have to say about Lucas. I'm just going upstairs to the bathroom."

As I walked up the stairs, I heard her open the doors and go out onto the veranda.

I contemplated searching her bag but put the idea to one side. This really was not my problem. I was tying myself up into everybody else's problems and I was beginning to feel like it was becoming too much to handle. I thought about Mary and wished that she was here. I put out a silent prayer to her, calling her back to me, but I knew that she was looking after our children. I wanted to be back in London, too, making sure that they were all right. They were clever, competent, and mature people, but it is the parents' lot to worry and offer protection.

Which led me onto Lucas and Charli. There was a toughness under the skin that always looked like a contradiction when you could also see the vulnerability that lay alongside it. How much of Charli's life had she spent being abused? Had she ever stopped being abused? Is that the factor she and Lucas had in common, or did they just share the same desire for self-destruction? That was me being unnecessarily cynical. It seemed to me that they had both shared a strong desire to survive, despite their actions. Streetwise enough to survive, intelligent enough to have little victories, too immature or limited in focus and not enough knowledge to see beyond the short-term dreams they shared. "Let's get enough money to get out of here and make a new life." Which led my thoughts back to what was in her bag. I decided to not risk searching it. Her best chance was for me to give her a lift out of here and if she thought I was trying to trick her or steal from her she would run like a frightened rabbit.

I finished in the toilet and washed myself.

Back downstairs, I asked Charli if she knew the name of the gang. She did. They were called Les Gamins. I said, are you sure and she nodded. Les Gamins is argot or slang for a kid or perhaps street urchin. I always associated it with playful banter where you would say that your child was a little gamin, which was the equivalent of saying something like she or he was a cheeky little monkey. I thanked her and returned to the kitchen where I picked up the phone and called Georges.

He picked up on the first ring and was brusque and defensive. He demanded that I stop trying to get him into trouble. He wanted to know if there was something that I knew and was not telling him. I said, "Georges, did you check out that old lady's notebook? I bet you found a cream and green VW bus was in Chabrassonne around the time of the murder."

"How did you know?"

"I have just been in touch with a friend of mine on the coast. He says that Lucas used to hang around with a couple of people who did a lot of travelling conning old ladies out of their savings whilst pretending to be policemen. They drove around in that VW van. Then Lucas and the driver of the van, an ape like thug called Mitch or Michel, went to the coast and joined a gang there called Les Gamins. Rumour has it that Lucas disappeared with some of the gang's funds."

"Why in hell's name didn't you tell me this sooner!" He shouted at me down the phone.

I took a slow breath and then said, "Georges. I learned of this a minute ago and called you straight away."

"Who told you this? What is their connection with all of this?"

"Calm down! My connection is on the coast and he told me in strictest confidence. You know how these things work. I am just a member of the public – and a foreigner, too. No-one wants to admit to telling me anything. He texted me and told me to delete the text immediately. Job done. I thought I was giving you some assistance. I didn't think you were the sort to shoot the messenger."

Georges was silent for a little while and I was beginning to wonder if he was still there when he said, "OK John. You told me nothing. This conversation did not happen. I'll see what I can do with this, but I want you to back off now. Don't interfere anymore, don't beat up innocent people and don't pick any more fights with my superiors."

"I have done none of those things, George and I don't intend to start doing them now." He snorted quite eloquently and hung up on me.

Charli was standing in the doorway when I turned.

"I have to go out and speak to Lucas' father and brother. Is there anything else you can tell me? Anything you want to pass on to them indirectly?"

"Nothing." She said. "It says in the paper that Lew's brother had been arrested on suspicion of being Lew's murderer. Is that true?"

"Of course it is. It's in the paper, isn't it?"

"But why arrest his brother?"

"Because his father had too good an alibi and the officer in charge has a strong dislike of the Pecheurs."

"I read that a policeman called Limon was in charge of the case. Lew told me about a policeman with that name. He was constantly being harassed by him when he was a teenager.

His bike was stopped every day by this man, and he was searched so often it became a routine. His friends even had jokes about it – but not Lew and Limon. They hated each other."

I thought about this. She had told me something no one had bothered to mention. Limon knew Lucas well, yet he had approached me on the first day acting as if the dead body was that of a stranger. I didn't want to build this into anything. Limon was capable of acting in all sorts of unpleasant and stupid ways as far as I could see. Maybe he thought that his approach was "professional" and "dispassionate" or perhaps he was trying to hide his secret joy in encountering a tragedy centred around the Pecheurs. I put the thoughts to one side.

"Remember, don't answer the door or the phone. If you want to, use the computer but do not tell anyone where you are and use your own email account, not mine. Here is my mobile number. Call me if anything happens, if you remember anything else that might be important or if you begin to worry and need to talk. You know where the food and drink are. If you play music, don't play it loudly, OK?"

She said she understood, and I went out of the house, locking it as if I was leaving it empty. There was a set of keys she could use to get out if she wanted to, but I hoped she would stay out of sight and keep reasonably quiet.

Time to meet with les Pecheurs; father and son.

Chapter Seven

The offices of Pecheur, Pere et Fils, were on the road to Lavelanet, at the beginning of a nineteenth century row of buildings lining the route leading out of town. The whole row was built of a dull grey stone and although Philip had cleaned up his building considerably, it was still not the most attractive place in town. Next to the offices was an empty plot that the Pecheurs used as a car park for themselves and their guests.

There had been some controversy about this land when I first started coming to Chabrassonne. A tall wooden building had been on the site. It had once been a hat factory, which seemed to have been one of the industries common in this area up until the nineteen fifties. After the factory closed it was left abandoned and Philip had tried to buy it to build offices on. However, the then mayor and some of his cronies did not want Philip to own the land nor to build on it. So, Philip was blocked from doing anything and the building next door continued to crumble.

Redemption song

Finally, Philip went into politics and became the Mayor – something that his father had been, but it was not a role that really suited Philip, from what I heard. Ironically, being mayor did not solve Philip's problems. He bought the wooden Victorian property next door and shortly after that a mysterious fire destroyed the old building and damaged his offices, too. Some people said that Philip did it deliberately. Others claimed that Marc was told to do it and he screwed it up. And some said that one of Philip's enemies did it to damage him economically and politically. After quite a long legal dogfight, he managed to get his insurance company to pay up, and he transformed his offices from drab to modern and comfortable, but still hidden within a dull building. The cleared site of the old factory remained a bit of an eyesore, but it was a convenient parking lot for Philip.

It took me less than ten minutes to walk to the offices. As I passed the parking lot, I could see both Pecheurs' cars plus a few others that were presumably driven by staff or clients.

The receptionist on the ground floor greeted me with a very genuine and warm smile. I thought how lucky the Pecheurs were to have found such a good receptionist, and then I took time out to look around the reception area. There were a couple of framed advertisements looking like they were the original artwork. There were a couple of awards for marketing, one for quality management, a couple of industry awards and a special plaque from the local farming Co-op for services rendered to the local economy over the past fifty years. I was just reading the last one when the receptionist caught my attention and asked me to go straight up to the boardroom. I knew where that was. It was a large room on the first floor with tall windows on two sides looking out onto the road and onto the empty lot. From these windows you could look across the south edge of the town and see the mountains edging up over the local hills.

Philip and Marc were sitting at the big, blond wood table as I entered the room. They both got up at the same time and walked over to greet me. I shook hands with them and let them lead me to the table. There was a large flask of fresh coffee and I agreed to a cup of it as we sat down. Marc did the coffee as his father looked out of the window then looked back at me.

"It has been a harrowing couple of days!" He said. His voice was even but a bit weaker than I was used to hearing from him. "My son's death and the way the police have dealt with the situation… I don't know what to make of it all. And I hear that you've been harassed and attacked as a result of all of this too. I must apologise. This all seems so much more complicated than I would have ever expected."

"I would say that virtually everything that has happened has been out of your control, Philip. What is there to apologise for?"

He waved his arms vaguely and said thank you, and that I was very kind, but he was not really listening to me. It was obvious that he was preoccupied with something and was not his usual focussed self.

Marc took over from his father and said, "We followed your advice and went on the offensive. You were right. Limon had made no real efforts to check up on who might have wanted to kill my brother or why. Dupont, our local policeman – of course you know Georges – has informed our solicitors that there are some links between Lucas and organised crime in the Mediterranean coastal towns. I don't know if he means Marseilles or what, but it sounds terrible. Of course, we want to get to the truth and find his killer but to think that my brother was involved with such people. The publicity could be very bad for our business."

I waited, watching Marc become more forceful and witnessing Philip wince at some of the phrases Marc was using.

"We knew he was in with a bad crowd, of course. He was always in trouble here in Chabrassonne when he was younger, but…"

"Yes," I interrupted, "I was meaning to ask you about that."

"About what?"

"Well it seems that Lucas was arrested quite a lot and stopped frequently by the police as a teenager."

"This is true. He was a cause of great distress to his family."

"And who did most of the arresting?"

"The local police, of course."

"But who in particular? Was it Georges? He is relatively new to the area and I thought he worked out of Lavelanet for the first few years after he moved down here."

"I'm not sure." Marc was not so bullish as he had been just a few minutes before.

"Limon!" Philip spat out the name. "That's what you're looking for, isn't it? It was Limon who did most of the arresting!"

Marc was not certain which direction the discussion was going. He wanted to join in but had started off saying the wrong thing.

"That little bastard was based here, then. It was before his promotion. He took great delight in rubbing our noses in the fact that our youngest son was a criminal."

I looked at Philip and could see the pain in his eyes, but I wanted to keep on with this. "Yes, but Lucas didn't start off that way, did he?"

"What do you mean?" Marc jumped in. I kept looking at Philip.

"It was only after a long campaign of harassment that Lucas started to act badly. From what I hear, they used to joke about how often Limon brought Lucas into the police station. They used to say to Limon, 'Why don't you just propose to him. Then you could have him whenever you wanted him.' They also used to say, 'Here comes Limon again I wonder who he has in his car this time!'"

At the first comment, I thought Philip would get up and hit me, but by the second he was deflated. Marc was angry but he just could not see how to vent that anger. He wanted to punch me in the face and at the same time he wanted to turn everything around and stop me from going on.

"The Pecheurs and the Limons have some family feud going on between them – it's behind what happened to Marc yesterday and it was one of the things that Lucas suffered from when he was a teenager. I suspect that he tried to handle it himself because every time he went to either of you for help you told him to "be a man" or "stop being such a coward" so he tried to handle it, and you didn't even notice. No matter how brave he was you never gave him the credit or backup. That was when he decided to act the way he did. It got him a lot more attention, and he found that it was actually more fun, too."

It was interesting to see both of them struggling in their different ways to deny it or come to terms with it.

"Limon should never have been on this case in the first place. He's too heavily involved in the people and could not possibly take a dispassionate view of the whole thing. Have you told your lawyers about the feud and about the victimisation that Lucas suffered at the hands of Limon?"

Philip said that they knew about Limon's attitude towards the Pecheurs, but that the official line was that Limon could deal with it professionally. They'd not talked about Limon's past behaviour with the lawyers. I told them to bring the lawyers up to speed immediately.

"Limon has been holding back the investigation and there must be a record a mile long showing

Limon's attitude towards Lucas. It was a dangerously warped attitude which should have been investigated a long time ago. It's the sort of unbalanced attitude that can often lead to violence."

"My God, that's true." Marc had immediately seen an opportunity to attack and had grabbed it. He now had something that he was comfortable with and everything else we had said just re-assembled itself around that new idea. "I see what you are saying now." He got up and started to walk out of the room turning briefly to say he was going to call the lawyers immediately. When he was out of the room Philip seemed to slump even more on his chair.

"I understand what you have been saying."

I waited as he struggled to put the words together.

"The age difference didn't help. And Lucas was such a weedy boy compared to Marc. Why even Diane was stronger. And he was a very clever, artistic person. He just didn't fit in, always seemed to be whining."

"He was much younger than either of them. We often forget what children are like once they grow up." I said.

"I suppose. But I wanted to toughen him up. Make him strong!"

"Marc and Diane just took advantage of that to bully their little brother."

Philip shook his head, "They loved him. They still do. But children can be cruel."

"Adults, too, Philip. By the time Marc was being harassed by Limon, Marc was well into his twenties."

"He was working for me and just saw Lucas as freeloading while he did all the work. But yes, I can see it now. It's terrible to think of it, poor Lucas!" Philip turned and stared out of the window, his mind running through some of the scenes from his family's past.

"Well, the least we can do is remember him in a better light. With a bit more love."

He turned back and looked at me with painfully sad eyes, "I will always remember him with love, John. He was my son!"

I took my leave shortly after and as I began to walk back into town, I took out my mobile and phoned Nathalie, Lucas' mother. It took her a little while to answer the phone but when she did, she seemed genuinely happy to hear from me – she had been on her way out of the house when she heard the phone ring. I asked her if she could spare me a few minutes and when she told me she was coming into town to do some shopping I invited her to my house for some coffee. I agreed to meet her in half an hour and dropped into the Patisserie for some fancy cakes. It was more on my way home than the Boulangerie and I did not want to handle any more of Yvonne's banter this morning.

I unlocked the door and went straight through to the kitchen. Charli was outside on a recliner in the sun, her thin dress pulled almost up to her hips, some cheap sunglasses covering her eyes.

The ashtray next to her was full and a glass of fruit juice next to it was attracting a few flies. I picked the glass up and walked into the kitchen. Cleared up the dishes from the morning and started cleaning them. Charli had not lifted a finger to clean or tidy anything.

After cleaning the dishes, I filled the kettle and prepared the cafetière, took out the pastries and put them on a plate. I then covered them with a light, muslin cloth and walked back to Charli. I called her name lightly and she sat up with a start, making a little yelping noise as she rose. I stifled a small laugh and told her that Lucas' mother was about to arrive. As if I had timed it deliberately that way, the doorbell rang. Nathalie had actually remembered to press the button rather than pound the door!

This sent Charli into a panic and I tried to calm her before going to get Nathalie. "Remember, she knows nothing about you. Just pretend you know James, my son, be polite for a couple of minutes and then take your leave. OK?"

I heard her agree as I walked quickly down the hall to the door.

Back in the kitchen I started the coffee and asked if Nathalie would like to sit there or in the more formal lounge. She opted for the kitchen – it was more homely. I had introduced her to Charli and the two sat down at the table. Both remarked on the lovely pastries I revealed from under the cloth. With coffee in cups and pastries on plates and in mouths, I said that I had been talking to Philip and Marc. Charli made to get up and leave when Nathalie put her hand on the girl's arm and told her there was no need to go.

I was more tactful and gentler, but I gave the same analysis as before, telling her how I feared that Lucas had been affected by Limon's victimisation and by the hard, uncompromising stance of Lucas' brother and father.

"And you do not include me in any of this?" She demanded. Her face was full of hurt and conflicting feelings seemed to pass across it like clouds over a hill. "Do you think I didn't notice or that I didn't bother to do anything to help him?"

"I didn't say that, Nathalie. I don't think Lucas needed to or tried to prove his bravery or manliness to you. He was suffering to win favour or respect from his father and brother, not from you. Likewise, I don't think you had any power over the others to change what was going on."

Nathalie was very close to tears. She was deeply distressed but handling it well, considering. Charli had tears in the corners of her eyes and looked ready to run at any moment.

"I felt that you needed to know this, or at least have it confirmed, and to tell you that Philip and Marc have discussed this with me, too." Nathalie looked at me and I added, "Philip feels real, deep guilt, Marc feels like he needs to have some revenge, so I pointed him towards Limon and told him that he should explain things to the family lawyers."

"He won't do anything silly like go after Limon, personally?"

"There are lots of reasons why he wouldn't do that. Don't worry."

"What is your point in all of this?" she wanted to know.

"Lucas deserves better than what has happened so far. Two families feuding, evidence ignored, people being bullied and threatened, rumours, lies. And in the middle of it, the attitude is that Lucas was just some petty criminal who got what he should have expected."

Nathalie was listening and tears were rolling down her face and dripping onto the table. Charlie was silently sobbing with a hankie stuffed in her mouth with both her hands.

"It's not an attitude I share." I was going to say more but words became less and less appropriate, so I waited in silence and drank some coffee. The pastries were lovely, too. In a few minutes Nathalie took out a hankie, wiped her eyes and blew her nose.

"What shall I do?"

"It's up to you. While other people are trying to put together the story that led to Lucas' death, I would suggest that you see if you can find out a little more about his life. I feel that the more you know, the more it will help you deal with his death. It won't lessen the pain, but it'll strengthen you." I had some experience of death and knew this to be true for me, and I hoped it would be true for both of them, too.

Nathalie was just saying that I was right when the phone rang. I excused myself and walked out of the room. I heard a sentence from Nathalie which lifted my spirits as I closed the door, "Before Lucas died, he told me that he had found someone called Charline. From his description I would have said you are very like her."

It was Georges on the phone. He just wanted to let me know that my lead had been useful, and that Limon was heading my way filled with a wild fury. Now, he said, would be a good time to leave the house.

I walked out of the study and paused by the kitchen door. The two women seemed to be deep in conversation so I went back to the study and called up the British consulate offices in Carcassonne and asked to speak to a man I had met a couple of times at parties in the old city over the last couple of years. I had kept his card in my index file, and that was now in my hand.

When he came on to the phone, I told him very briefly about finding a dead body and some of the things that had passed since. I explained that I had been publicly threatened once by the officer in charge of the case and that I had just been warned that he was coming for me. I then said that if I was taken to the police station, I would refuse to speak any French and demand that I have a translator and proper representation. He agreed with me that I could do that, and I asked him if he would be the person to call for help once I was under arrest. He said that he was not the person, but he told me who was and gave me a direct number. He promised to brief the man immediately and offered to get him to start on the road immediately. I said it was not necessary – you never know, it might not come to it, but I would appreciate a speedy response if one were needed.

I just had time to nip in and tell the women I was going to be arrested and that they should stay there for the moment. I left the house and was just locking the front door when the car screeched to a halt. Rather than have my keys on me, I pushed them back through the letter box and turned to the men who were rushing out of all four doors of the car. I raised my hands up as two of them grabbed me and slammed me against the door, then turned me and slammed my face forward against the door as they put the handcuffs on me. The metal bit into my wrists and pain jerked up my arms and into my shoulders as they manhandled me into the back of the car. Blood from a cut on my forehead trickled down into the corner of my eye making it difficult for me to see. One of the men gave me a hard punch in my stomach which hurt badly at first then subsided into a pain much like muscle cramps. I received a few more blows from fists and elbows, but they were not as vicious as the first one. Through my troubled vision I could make out the figure of the ape with the green suit from yesterday. He had wanted to punch me then, too.

It took almost half an hour to reach the station in Lavalenet. My arms were almost asleep, and my hands were swollen and painful as a result of the reduced circulation. As they dragged me out of the car a wave of nausea came over me, presumably as a result of the punch I had received earlier, and I threw up on the Green man and part of the inside of the car. The green man hit me, this time on the side of the face and I spun around and lost my balance, hitting the ground with my left shoulder and rolling almost onto my back. The pain in my shoulder, arms and hands seemed to cancel out the pain in my stomach and head, but now I felt dizzy as well as nauseous. They picked me up roughly and dragged me through a door and along several dark, unpleasant smelling corridors. They did one final act of slamming me face forward into a door as they undid the handcuffs, then they spun me 'round and pushed me backwards into a small cell. I fell hard, my arms not good enough to break the fall and my head too dizzy and disoriented to allow me to react properly. The back of my head banged hard on the stone floor and the sickening pain nearly caused me to pass out. I rolled on my side and enjoyed the silent, smooth coldness of the dull stone on my cheek and waited for the pain level to reduce and the spinning in my head to stop.

I gradually got up and sat on the narrow wooden shelf that would have been a bed if there had been any mattress or bedding in the room.

Amazingly, they had not taken anything from me, they had not cautioned me or said anything to me except for some simple abusive statements. I pulled out the card with the new number written on it and my phone. I called the number and told the man, whose name was Charles Patron, where I was. My words were not too distinct, I explained because I had been beaten up. No, I had not been cautioned and I did not know what I was doing there. Finally, I said that I would not speak any

French and would only speak English until he got there.

I put the phone and card away and lay down on the shelf, trying to stop the spinning in my head and focus out some of the pain. I moved my arms around and tried to get some circulation into them, then I had to sit up and finally stand to allow myself room to move them about. My shoulder was now hurting badly, and it was swollen and tender.

After a few minutes of trying to stand up I sat down again. It felt like being drunk or trying to come out from under an anaesthetic. I was starting to hear a ringing in my ears, and I had to stop moving around to check the sound out in case it was a fire alarm. Then I thought to myself that the idea was silly, the noise was definitely somewhere in my head. Waves of nausea started to wash over me and I had that feeling as if I was falling backwards, even although I knew I was perfectly still. I lay down again, feeling sweat break out on my brow and almost immediately after the sweat, I began to shiver. The shivering seemed to overtake my whole body. Was I cold? It was certainly a cold cell and I was in very light clothing, but this was silly.

With my teeth clattering together uncontrollably and my body shaking painfully I tried to rouse myself from the foetal position I had moved into. I sat up and hugged my body, shivering and making little "uuuh" noises as I tried to gain control. Gradually it reduced to an occasional spasm and I wondered if it was my willpower or if I was just moving through from one phase to another.

I was now definitely cold, and I was beginning to suspect that I had just gone through the effects of another bout of adrenalin working its way through my system. The dizziness and ringing made me wonder about concussion – I had banged my head badly on the floor. Slowly, I began to take stock.

Firstly, I checked the time - it was one forty. I had met Nathalie at around twelve and the bovver boys had arrived around quarter to one. I checked my phone and saw that I had called Charles Patron at one twenty-three. He would be here in about an hour to an hour and a half, so I should expect to see him some time after three o' clock.

I was shivering lightly now, and I was certain that this was as a result of the cold rather than anything else. I had a short-sleeved shirt and a pair of light, cotton trousers. I was wearing sports sandals on bare feet. When I breathed out, I looked and could see little clouds of condensation forming each time I exhaled. I tucked my shirt into my trousers and slipped my hands through the front of my shirt, tucking them into my armpits. Slowly, I got up and looked around the cell. The door was made of wood and metal with a small spy hole and no door handle or keyhole on my side. Very high up on the wall facing the door was a small, arched and barred window. I was not aware of going up or down any stairs, but Lavelanet was much closer into the mountains than Chabrassonne, so the police station could have been built into a hill, making the window high on my side of the building but almost ground level at its entrance. I sensed that it looked out onto an alley or courtyard because no direct sunlight reached the window, but I could see a patch of blue up there. The room was dark, damp and cold.

I focused on the promise of sunlight high up in the sky and started to move around the cell. Once I was moving, I felt slightly better. All the aches and pains were in their places and the dizziness was becoming less of a problem. As my hands warmed, they became pretty painful, then they gradually settled down again. I looked under the bed-shelf and found nothing; there was a small metal hand basin with one tap and a sign above it telling me not to piss in the sink. Below this was another sign telling me that the water was not for drinking. Under the little sink was a dirty blue plastic bucket with a white handle. As I moved forward to look inside, I felt a swelling of nausea rise in me again, but this time it was due to the smell that grew as my face drew closer to the thing.

The stink lingered in my senses as I staggered away from the bucket and the sink.

There was nothing else in the room. The floor was covered in cheap, dark linoleum tiles, the walls were tiled in a dirty green colour up to my waist then a paler coloured plaster covered the walls and ceiling. A single, unlit bulb was set in a recessed socket in the middle of the ceiling. I reckoned that even with a chair or a table I would not have been able to reach the bulb. So, the room was much taller than it was wide.

The plaster on the walls and even the tiles, were covered with simple graffiti. It was mainly names, some obscene statements and drawings and a few better crafted images including a butterfly and a lion. I wondered if Lucas had ever been locked up in this cell. I suspected that it was unlikely as most of his harassment had taken place in and around Chabrassonne when Limon was stationed there.

It was now well after two o'clock and I was beginning to feel very weary and quite hungry. I had not had much to eat and had lost some of it en route to this cell. I was beginning to wonder when Limon would make his appearance. Would he burst in and abuse me or pretend that it was all a mistake and take me up to his office to ply me with coffee, warmth and probing questions? I was not even clear about what he really wanted from me.

To me, his aggression didn't make sense. I was, at best, a minor witness for the prosecution who could talk about where I found the body, when I found it and that I had only a vague idea of who it was at the time. I knew the deceased's family and some of the people that the deceased knew, too. It was this silly conviction that I was a detective or something that seemed to fire him up. He could easily have done a check on me to find out who I really was – a simple ex-businessman and more recently, ex-academic. I was an expert in research and was able to make useful intuitive leaps and see links between information streams that people never seemed to be able to put together themselves. I had been a pretty good manager, too.

I had been pacing up and down the cell, growing more vigorous in my steps than I had intended as I sank deeper in to thought. However, the exercise was becoming too much for me, so I sat down carefully on the bed and continued my thoughts.

They jumped away from my predicament and began to focus on my daughter, Jude. I was going to drive up and see her soon, regardless of what was going on here. Perhaps I should have just driven up yesterday instead of staying here in order to mix myself up in someone else's affairs. I pulled my hands out from under my arms and plunged them together between my legs as I sat and drummed my feet on the floor.

I was gently rocking and thinking about how Mary was currently up there looking out for the children when the door burst open. My heart leapt and I tried my best to not jump up but, rather, slowly lift my head up to see who it was. Limon strode in with two of his louts just behind him.

"Right! Up you get. Stop wasting my time sitting around in here, just look at you!" If he had not been in such a position of immediate power his scowling face might have been laughable to study. However, in my present state I felt disinclined to laugh in his face. I did not get up. Instead I looked at him, turned to his two friends and said in English, "I'm sorry, you must speak English as I cannot talk to you in French. Do you understand?"

Redemption song

Limon took two quick steps towards me and slapped me in the face. It was a hard slap which took my breath away and left the whole of the left side of my face stinging. The ringing in my ears increased from a low jangle to a loud clanging. "Stop pissing me off! I know that you speak extremely good French. Get up!"

I shook my head to clear it and saw him draw back from hitting me again. Instead, he motioned with his head to his two henchmen and they stepped forward and grabbed me by my arms and proceeded to bundle me out of the room. They had some definite skill, which I might have admired if I had been watching them from afar. They managed to walk me steadily along two corridors and up one curved set of stairs without missing a step or slowing down behind Limon. But on the way they were able to bang me against every hard surface and sharp corner we passed. I was beginning to wonder at their complete lack of concern regarding my bruises and cuts. Why did they think that they were immune, that they were free to beat people up whenever they wanted to? It didn't make sense.

I was bruised and dazed when they finally thrust me into a small, brightly lit room containing a small table and two chairs. Limon sat down on one and the two thugs dropped me on the other one. They closed the door and stood, side by side in front of it as if they were guards. Indeed, I thought to myself, I suppose they are.

I let out a sigh and tried my best to sit up. It was a lot warmer in here and I was willing to accept any good sign, even something as small as that. I placed my now bruised hand on top of my right pocket and felt my mobile phone. I thought to myself, I hope they didn't break it. Then I thought that such a thing was impossible. It was my old, very basic, but indestructible, Nokia. I wondered how they had managed to bruise my hand, too? Then a sudden thought sparked brightly into my mind. I put my damaged hand into my pocket and pressed two buttons on the phone – one to open the line and the other to redial the last number.

Limon leaned towards me and said, "I have been checking up on you!"

I sat silently, not acknowledging his words.

"You are nothing but a washed out old academic! You have no connections! You have never been involved in any sort of police matters. You do not even have any driving offences against you! You are a nobody!"

Well, I thought, at least he has got it through his thick skull that I am just an ordinary person. I was a bit annoyed by the suggestion that I was a "washed out, old" person. I had chosen to retire at the time when I was doing very well in my chosen subject and when I had built a bloody good department as well. I thought all of this in what seemed like a fraction of a second then had to stifle the word "idiot" before I spoke it out loud.

"I just want to show you that I can do what I like to you. I can stop you and find a hundred faults with your car, book you for speeding, I can test you and find you over the legal alcohol limit, I could even find drugs and pornography in your car and house. Do you understand?"

"Would you mind repeating that in English?"

He casually leant over the table and slapped me again.

"I told you! I'm not stupid. You can speak French!"

"Is this how you used to treat Lucas when he was a teenager?" I said this in English and his reaction was quite spectacular. He suddenly stood up and hit me again, propelling me to the floor.

"That little Pecheur shit deserved everything he got." He must have signalled to the two thugs because they picked me up and plonked me back on the chair. Limon dusted himself down and moved back to his seat.

"Beating me up doesn't solve Lucas' murder!"

It was then that he began to laugh, and I felt that this man really was on the edge of madness.

"Solve the murder? Who gives a fuck about that? Do you think I care who killed the little cunt? He should never have come back here. If I had known sooner that he was in Chabrassone, I would have had him picked up! I would have arrested him!"

He had been so worked up he had not realised that I had spoken to him in English. He suddenly stood up and walked away from me towards the opposite wall. He put his hands behind his back and stood erect, like a parody of an army officer.

"What sort of feud do you have with the Pecheurs?" Again, this was in English but this time he did not respond. I noticed the clock above his head for the first time. It was ten to three and I wondered where Mr Patron was.

"In a short while I will put you back in that cell and I will leave you there for a while. While you are there, I want you to think about what I have said. Perhaps you might decide to go back to England and stay with your family for a while. A few months away from here and you might decide to sell up and move back to England permanently." He turned around and looked at me with complete confidence. "The last thing you want right now is to try and challenge me. There are things I can do to you that will make my earlier threats seem like the good old days."

"There's a solicitor out there, sent by the Pecheurs, I believe. You might want to advise him that you were treated well. I might even allow you to clean yourself up before you leave."

He sat down and motioned for the two men to take me away. I stood up and looked down at Limon and said, "Do you know what depresses me most about this whole thing?"

He signalled for the men to stop while I spoke. He said "No, what depresses you the most?"

I answered, "What depresses me most is that you were one of the people directly responsible for ruining that young man's life but, in the end, I believe you didn't kill him!"

Limon just shrugged as if he didn't care either way. "And, so what is your point?"

"Apart from going out of your way to prove something that I have known for some time, I don't see why you suddenly decided to have me arrested and beaten up."

He shook his head and actually sneered at me, "I did it to show you that I can. You were acting under false pretences and causing me trouble. So, when I discovered that you were nothing, a nobody, it gave me the green light!"

"I kept telling you I was just a retired academic, but you wouldn't listen!" I shook my head and turned to walk out, and he called to me as I passed through the door, "So what have you known for some time?"

I shook my head again. I didn't feel like telling him that I had known, from the first time that I had met him, that he was an incompetent fool. I now knew that he was also a stupid bully, but I just walked away wondering when Mr Patron would get here and if he had heard any of the conversation with the phone in my pocket.

They did not even touch me on the way back to the cell and I walked into the little room without hitting a single surface with any part of my body except my feet. Then I sat down on the shelf and felt very, very tired.

Chapter Eight

Despite the bruises and bumps; despite the cold and the lack of comfort; once in the cell I lay down on the bed shelf and fell asleep. It was like switching out the light. One second I was lying there and then I was unconscious. It took me a little while to pull myself out of the deep dark place I was wallowing in when they came for me. I heard the door open and voices, but I was sitting up and rubbing my eyes before I really made sense of where I was.

A stranger's voice, in English, said, "Good grief. How are you? Let me give you a hand there!" and I stood up from the bench, blinking at the light from the corridor.

"Mr Patron, I presume."

"Absolutely. Presume away. Let's get you out of this stupid little place." Then in spotless French he turned on the people blocking the door and said, "make way, let us through at once!" and we were moving along the now empty corridor. I tried to walk as steadily as I could and nearly fell over

only once before we reached the front door. Then
we were out onto the steps of the police station
where Mr Patron led me to a large black Mercedes
saloon.

Once I was safely in the passenger seat,
Patron trotted around to the other door and slipped
behind the wheel.

"Quite the most interesting day I have had in a
long time!" He started the car and set off down the
road before turning to me and saying, "Let me
introduce myself. Charles Patron." He held out his
hand and I shook it saying how pleased I was to
meet him. The comfort of the seat I was in seemed
almost sinful it felt so good, and the warmth was
so welcoming that I turned to face the front and
settled deeper into the seat before I looked at the
time. It was half past five, the roads were wet with
afternoon rain and the sky was clearing to let the
strong sun warm up the early evening air.

"Can I suggest you turn off your phone?" He
said and I made a noise like Oops as I pulled the
phone out and switched it off.

"Interesting trick. I was quite close when the
phone rang. I stopped immediately and switched
the thing on and heard it all quite clearly. Luckily, I
had my trusty little Dictaphone handy, too. So,
after the first couple of sentences I got it all on
record. Fascinating! Of course, it presented us
with a neat little problem. Inspector Limon may be
a vicious, arrogant creep, but he has some friends
in the local hierarchy, too. Talk about stepping on
a hornet's nest! The usual form in this country is
that investigations are run by the local magistrate

– police are the instrument of the state and all that, but in some rural areas, especially where the Gendarmes are in control, the magistrate has been known to be more hands off. You seem to have encountered a bit of a legal Jurassic Park, here. Ought to be different now, though. Limon is unlikely to be attacking you again."

"I have been trying to mind my business all week and he has just gone out of his way to make life difficult for me."

Mr Patron looked at me with a slightly amused expression on his face. "I would say that having you arrested and systematically beaten up by a set of thugs was more than making your life difficult."

"Yes, but that was only today. He has been threatening and abusing me all week, telling me what I think, who I am and what I should do, and he has failed to grasp even the basics of the truth."

"From what he said to you this afternoon, he isn't interested in the truth."

"I know. Are you taking me back to Chabrassonne?"

"Only if you want to go back. Wouldn't blame you if you decided to hop it. You can sue him from England, you know. No need to do it from here."

"I have some people waiting for me, hopefully, back at my house. I was planning to go back to London after the weekend. I won't go any earlier to fit in with the plans of a bastard like Limon."

"You won't have to worry about 'Old Citron'. He will have his hands full for a while."

"What did you call him?"

Redemption song

"Sorry, someone said that his nickname was Citron – quite simple, really…Limon/Citron. But not as obvious when looking at it purely from a French point of view." Charles looked at me quizzically.

"It's odd. I was just trying to remember where I had heard it before. I don't think it was in connection with my friend, the policeman. What exactly happened after you took my call?"

"Interesting," he said as he turned the car down a minor road heading for Chabrassonne. "I made a couple of calls back to the office and then drove as fast as I could to Lavelanet. At the old cop shop I waltzed in and asked for the top man – my office had already set the ball rolling. I said I was here to represent you in the matter of police brutality and that if he wanted a copy of the evidence as it currently stood, I could let my Dictaphone talk to his Dictaphone. We both listened to what had been said, he identified the police officer and sent for him. Should have seen his face when his boss played the tape to him! Ha! Not so much a lemon as a raspberry! Anyway, informal apologies from the boss, a few papers signed, and I was collecting you from the little cupboard you were being held in. Damn cold in there! How did you manage to sleep?"

"It's been a tiring sort of day."

He laughed as we slipped through a lovely little village called Sainte Colombe. The bunting from the summer fair was still up over the street and I saw a friend I sometimes played chess with as he came out of the Boulangerie with the evening bread.

For some reason this image sparked my memory and I said, "Why would Limon have the same nickname as a French resistance fighter? Is it some sort of ironical joke?"

"Worse than Irony, I would say. If you are talking about the chap called Citron he was not a Resistance man. He was a collaborator. I know because he got his nickname from an English airman."

I sat up, "Are you sure?"

"Absolutely. Odd we should be talking about this. I read about it in a newspaper article not long ago in Carcassonne. There was a famous trial after the war when Citron got off Scot-free after being tried for executing some resistance fighters. He had records proving he had sent them off to a so-called "work camp" in Germany, but the local people claimed that he had shot them. It was up here somewhere. Might even have been your town."

"I see. And how did he get the nickname?"

"the story in the paper said that a young girl was leading a small group of allied lads through the town in question when they had to nip behind a wall to dodge a patrol of a group called the Milice, or something. They then watched from their hideout as this chap marched his men through the town. One of the airmen said, 'who was the sourpuss at the front of the men?' and she said something that the airmen couldn't understand but ended with the man's name - Limon. Then one of the English lads who knew a few words of French said, you mean 'citron', and everyone laughed as he explained the connection between the French and English names for a lemon and at the irony of calling him a sourpusses in the first place ." Patron slowed down as he said the last bit. "This Citron was a local administrator and a bit of a right-wing fanatic. Fiercely patriotic, but just as fiercely anti-communist. It was one of the things that saved him, really. He was also a devout Catholic, but I wouldn't hold that against him."

"I might. I'm a Catholic myself but I sometimes wonder what it means when someone calls themselves devout."

"I know what you mean." We were already in Chabrassonne and I guided Charles Patron to my house.

"Would you like to come in for a coffee?" I asked.

"Rather not, if you don't mind. I'll have to spend a bit of time with you tomorrow. Need to get a few things down and work out what has to be done, but I think we've caused enough mayhem for one day, don't you?"

I smiled at him and he put the car into gear and swiftly drifted down the road and turned out of sight.

I looked back at my house and walked up to the door. It opened before I could raise my hand to ring the doorbell. There was quite a little gathering in front of me. They were all at the doorway and I wondered if they were going to let me in. Everyone was asking questions and making remarks when someone said, "Why don't we just let him into his own house!" and they all laughed and seemed to draw me in through the door and down to my kitchen where there were welcome smells of coffee and something else, possibly soup, cooking on the stove. I sat down and someone placed a cup of coffee in front of me and everyone seemed to sit down like an audience, on the other side of the table.

Silence gradually passed through the kitchen as I slurped some of the coffee. The kitchen clock said five past six. I had only been away from my house for about five hours, but it seemed like I had been away for weeks. Everything looked fresh and clean, yet old and familiar. It was comfortable and it was warm.

Across from me sat Nathalie and Charli. Next to them was Valerie with a little girl on her knee, presumably her daughter Sylvie, and there was Philip, too. He was sitting uncomfortably at the end, as if he was not sure how to deal with being in such a large group of women. Well it was not as many as it had felt like when I had been greeted at my own front door. There was almost a party atmosphere, and everyone seemed to be sitting there waiting with great anticipation, so I said, "Thank you for the coffee," raising the cup into the air, "What's in the pot?" I looked meaningfully towards the stove. Nathalie said, "I brought over some soup."

"It smells wonderful. Might I have some?"

"Of course!" she leapt up and swiftly served me a big bowl of soup and some fresh bread.

Redemption song

Philip could not contain himself any longer, "What did they do to you? You look like you have been in the wars!" and everyone was talking again, commenting on how long I had been in custody, how they had never seen anything like it, how I must be in terrible pain, and I just concentrated on getting a few spoonful's of soup inside me before I said anything else.

I then gave them a potted history of the last five hours. They laughed at the recorded admissions and gasped as I described some of the brutality. It was agreed that I probably had concussion and should be seen by a doctor immediately. I ate and protested at the same time, but it was no good. As I was arguing, Philip was outside in the hall calling out his family doctor, insisting that he come immediately. As he sat down again, he asked me if I had a camera.

"Of course." I said, "digital or film?"

"Both, I would say." He answered. "Where do you keep them?"

"In my study, on the small table to the right of the fireplace."

He got up and to fetch them as the doorbell rang and he went off to fetch the doctor. Philip cleared the kitchen of everyone but me, the doctor and himself, then he said, "Doctor, this man has just come back from a brief visit to the police station in Lavelanet. You are a witness to his current state. Before you examine him, do you mind if we get some photographs that you can swear to as being accurate?"

The doctor was astounded, and I was a bit surprised.

"Of course," said the doctor, "We must do this at once." Which surprised me even more. I agreed to a couple of photos with the 35m camera and the digital one as I stood by the bare wall at one end of the kitchen. I then took off my shirt and dropped my trousers and several other pictures were taken of me as a whole, back front, sides and close-ups were done of bits of me, too.

I then pulled up my trousers and put my shirt on. I was surprised to see several bruises on my body as I took off, then put on my clothes. When you are in the middle of something like the incident I had faced, you spend your time concentrating on getting through it. You do not consider the blows individually. Thinking of a boxing film I once saw as a child, I joked that at least they left my face unmarked and Philip looked at me strangely. The doctor asked me to sit down while he examined me properly. I then remembered the times I had hit doors and walls with my face and when I had been slapped by Limon.

"Perhaps I should look in the mirror, Mmm?" I said and Philip nodded at me.

The doctor was very thorough and agreed that I might be suffering from mild concussion. He wanted me to go into hospital for observation, but I refused. He also told me that I had several severe bruises and probably needed to have some X rays to be sure that I had not suffered from minor cracks or fractures. I assured him that I would report to the local hospital in Limoux the next day.

He made me take tome strong painkillers and then he left after placing a small parcel of different drugs in my hands.

Everyone came back into the kitchen and passed around the digital camera to choruses of OO and Ahh at the pictures of my injuries.

I went back to consuming more soup and commented that it seemed pointless to have sent all the women out just to show them the pictures afterwards.

Philip went away to my study to print out a copy of each digital picture and to save copies onto a CD. He also took out the film from the camera and promised me that he would have the pictures developed first thing in the morning.

I had a chance to look at the pictures before people left. I confess that I am not someone who studies photographs of myself. I have seen others do it; looking for imperfections; checking that the photograph does them justice, and so on. But I did take care to look at myself in these pictures. I had a black eye as a result of the split eyebrow and Limon's blows. I had scratches on my face and my lower lip and part of my chin seemed to be very puffed up. There was a nasty lump and cut on the back of my head and my shoulder was swollen to about twice the size of the other one.

My body had a spattering of large and small bruises resulting from fists and elbows as well as from door jambs and other hard and pointed places.

It felt strange saying goodbye to people at the door with Charli standing beside me. As they began to leave, I felt a tension in her. It was as if she was making an effort to stand still, or like a child who was desperate to go to the toilet. I closed the door and she almost dashed back to the kitchen. I locked the door and walked back to her. She was already outside with a lit cigarette in her hand, and I wondered if the cause of her action was simply a result of the overwhelmingly powerful nicotine addiction she seemed to have.

A light breeze was blowing down from the direction of the mountains, but it was very mild. The chill that seemed to have set in my bones earlier in the day had gone and, although I was suffering from lots of different aches and pains, I did not have that nausea I had been troubled with earlier.

"Would you mind if I stayed a bit longer here?" She was looking away from me, projecting clouds of smoke across the silent, darkening gardens.

"Not a problem for me. What about your plans to escape to the north?"

"I think they are on hold for a while."

"What about the person who killed Lucas?" I had to ask this question directly. I wanted to be clear about what she was thinking of.

"I don't think it was anyone from here. And if it was, they wouldn't be interested in me."

I walked up and leaned on the veranda beside her, wincing as I put weight on my swollen shoulder.

"I think it was Mitch." She said. "I think he either wanted the money or wanted to prove himself to Les Gamins. He must have caught Lew unexpectedly. He probably got him just as he was waking up – it always took Lew an hour or more to really waken up, you know. He was a night person, really. At night he was so alive." She was very tense, and I could see she was working hard at keeping herself under control.

"Hopefully they will catch up with him quite soon. You heard me speak to Georges this morning about Mitch. With any luck, the events of this afternoon will have helped speed things up."

She turned and looked at me, "Did you let this happen to you in order to speed up the investigations?" She seemed quite shocked.

I laughed. "I had no control over what was going to happen. I did think that perhaps Limon had been responsible for Lucas' death, and in a way, he actually was, but Limon had other things on his mind. I think he is not a well man!"

Again, Charli seemed to be looking at me with unbelieving eyes, "You feel sorry for that pig?"

"Not exactly sorry. Partly I feel relieved that he was not Lucas' murderer because, if he had been, I might have been in more danger than I actually was. I feel that the whole thing was out of control almost from the beginning and that Limon was at the heart of the chaos, but I'm still not certain why. Whatever the malaise is here, it seems to me that Lucas was just one of the victims."

She turned away from me and blew some more smoke at the hills.

"Why have you decided you want to stay here for a while longer?"

Charli took her time answering. I watched a dragon fly move across the garden, its electric blue body as rigid as steel. It turned with mechanical precision in one direction, then another and it dipped onto the panes of glass that made up the roof of my small greenhouse a couple of times before moving on. Suddenly it decided to be elsewhere and rose up quickly to a height where the breeze could propel it over our heads and off to one of the nearby stretches of water.

"I have been talking to Nathalie all afternoon. She has been telling me about Lew's childhood and I have been telling her about my past year with him. Lew really loved her, you know, but he could never get close to her. There was always some sort of barrier there. I think, together, we can get to know Lew better than either of us could when he was alive! Isn't that crazy?"

"Nathalie's a good person. I like her a lot. I'm glad you and she have started to get to know each other."

"Did you do it deliberately? Were you planning to put us together?" Somehow, it seemed very important for Charli to know but I didn't really have an answer.

"I'm not sure," I shrugged, "I was not going to reveal your relationship with Lucas unless you wanted her to know, but I felt that it would be good for her to know. I also suspected that Nathalie had a closer relationship with Lucas than she had enjoyed with any of the rest of her family. In the end I think she made the connections without any help from me - so it was really up to the two of you to decide what you wanted to do."

She had finished her cigarette and was listening to me with her arms crossed and her head cocked to one side, then she stepped forward and gave me a little hug which quite surprised me.

"Thanks," she said and then she moved past me and into the kitchen. I followed her and said that I needed to quickly check my emails and then I was planning to have a long soak in the bath. She followed me into the study and picked up a photograph album that I did not recognise, which was on my desk, next to the keyboard of my computer.

"Do you mind if I listen to the radio?" She asked.

"Of course not. What's the book?"

She smiled, "Nathalie brought this over along with the soup. I want to spend a little time with Lew as a boy."

I smiled back at her and sat down gently in my office chair.

I had two emails from my kids. One was from James telling me that he was almost back in circulation. He was in Ullapool, which was a huge distance away from me and a great distance from his sisters. I had thought that he was in the Grampians, but he was much further north and west.

His email told me that he was about to head back south and that he had some wonderful photographs. Being the modest young man that he is, he described his latest trip as "another great success" and I believed him. Mary and I loved his photographs and we had some of them displayed on various walls around the house. He said that he had replied to his sisters' emails and had told them of his estimated time of arrival.

I emailed saying that he would get there before me as I expected to be there by Monday or Tuesday. I also told him that I was living in "interesting times" and how I had discovered Lucas' body on the path. I wondered if he had ever encountered Lucas as they were close to the same age.

I was in the middle of trying to construct a response to Jude's latest email when the system bleeped and there was an answer from James. It said,

"Hi dad, just about to head off to the pub so caught your email just in time. Lucas Pecheur? It rang a bell then I remembered that our paths crossed a couple of times. I remember him when they had those funny art classes up at the Chateau not long after we started going to Chabrassonne. He was one of the few locals there and I think we were the only boys. He was really shy but a bloody good draughtsman. Impressed me, anyway. Didn't get to know him though, because I fell in love with that blond girl from Nantes who was staying in one of those Gites in Puivert. Remember, I pestered you to take us to the lake there instead of the Plan d'eau in Chabrassonne so that I could meet her!

Redemption song

Which leads me to the other time I crossed paths with Lucas. We were actually at the Plan d'eau the next year, I think, and he was there as part of a little crowd of local kids. We made friends with them and played a few silly games in the water and out, but he was always on the edge and at one point I remember him being picked up by his brother because he had not gone back home for lunch or something. His brother just drove up to the gate and shouted to Lucas and I remember watching as Lucas trotted reluctantly across to the car. His brother got out, cuffed him across the head and literally threw him into the car shouting at him. All the other French kids just muttered about how much of a shit his brother was and how bad it was for poor Lucas, etc. In fact, I think they called him Luke or Luis, something like that.

You say he was murdered? Was it the brother? Weren't you and mum friendly with the Pecheurs, Lucas' parents?

Anyway, off to the pub Love Jim"

I tried to remember if Mary and I had been at the Plan d'Eau at the time of the incident. James was probably old enough to have been there on his own, but if Jo had been there too, I think we might have been somewhere in the background. I just couldn't remember such an incident.

I wrote, re-wrote and then wrote again until I had a simple email for Jude which added to my thoughts regarding her project at work and gave her some more personal thoughts and words of support. She was still emotionally fragile and, although I had encouraged her to think about talking to Mary, she seemed reluctant. So, I told her how much we all loved her, and I suggested a few good books I had recently enjoyed, pointed her towards a couple of friends she had not seen for a while and reminded her that I was still on target for coming up to London at the beginning of the following week.

I was looking forward to the visit more than I had been and I wondered if it was because of the violence I had encountered today. Strangely, I felt quite detached from what had happened. It was not so much unreal as not related to anything real, despite the cuts and bruises. I kept wondering if Limon had been behaving like that for some time or if he had started acting in that way only recently.

I checked through my other emails and sent off a couple of short replies to the more pressing ones. When I stood up, I felt a little bit wobbly. I found Charli in the kitchen sitting at the table studying old photographs and listening to a station called Sky Rock, which had been a favourite of my children for some years – I think that Jo still listened to it from time to time on-line. A French rap artist was doing what sounded like a live session, Charli had a big glass of fruit juice and ice next to her and one of the cats, I think it was Rag, actually on her lap!

I went to get a glass of malt whisky and asked her if she wanted anything. She said she was fine, and I told her to help herself if she changed her mind. I then said that I would be going down to Carcassonne for a couple of hours the next day and asked if she wanted to come with me. She said she would think about it. Finally, I told her I was going for my bath now and she said it was about time! As I was about to leave the room I stopped and thought for a moment.

"The photographs in the album." I started, "are they all of Lucas?"

"Basically." Charli nodded, "They sometimes have other people in them, but every picture has Lucas in it somewhere."

"What sort of age range?"

"From a baby right up to his teens."

"Nathalie brought it for you to see?"

"Of course."

"Does Philip know about you and Lucas?"

"Good heavens, no! We decided there was no point, not a good idea!"

"But Valerie knows?"

"Yes, she's lovely. I can see why Lucas liked her. And Sylvie has her father's eyes and his mouth, too!"

I nodded and walked heavily up the stairs wondering if Philip had noticed the album on my desk. Perhaps he didn't recognise it? I wondered what that might mean as I sorted out towels, started running the bath and generally prepared things for my soak.

I put on a CD of Scriabin's Sonatas and submerged myself in hot water and complex piano music. As the music drifted from the 3rd to the 4th sonata and then through to the 7th and 9th the music became more unsettling and demanding. It helped me work my way through the events of today and acted as a form of therapy. Occasionally

I would slip up out of the deep water and take a sip or two of the smoky spirit and then sink back into the heat.

After the music stopped, I lay quietly for a while listening to vague sounds in the house and outside. I wanted to put the whole business of the day out of my mind, but I kept coming back to images of Lucas as a young lad and I thought of the contrasts between his life and that of my son's.

James had studied ecology at university and, although he had done well in his studies, he had excelled in the photographs he had taken during his field trips. During his last two years as a student he was earning more from his wildlife photographs than most graduates were earning in full time jobs, and now he seems to spend most of his time somewhere wild and often wet, capturing exquisite images of the most beautiful, most endangered or most exotic wildlife in existence. He seems to be able to hold that wonderful contrast that young people can embody where he expects everything to be perfect and go his way, and at the same time he cannot believe how lucky he is to be allowed to do the things he loves the most and actually get paid for it, too.

His teenage years had been pretty up and down with the usual struggles to get him to do schoolwork, come home from friend's houses, try to stop him from getting drunk, from experimenting with too many drugs, from getting someone pregnant or contracting some awful sexually transmitted infection. We struggled, he bobbed and sailed through the problems, and has ended up as the one we both worry about most (when he is in some war-torn country photographing butterflies amidst the bullets) and worry about the least (when he is anywhere more civilised).

Compared to Lucas, he lived in a big city, which is supposed to hold more dangers than being brought up in the country. They were both brought up in what could be described as respectable middleclass families. They were not the only child. I don't think that either of them could ever have been described as impoverished financially, and both seemed to have gone to reasonably good schools and had friends both in school and in the local community.

Lucas left school in his teens and became a career criminal virtually estranged from his family, James went to university and enjoys a fulfilling and quite lucrative career and is still close to his family. Oh, and Lucas is dead while my son is in Wester Ross in Scotland enjoying a few pints with some friends.

Did I see something of James in Lucas' face when I discovered him lying there under the tarpaulin? It was one of the things that had been nagging at me since that morning. If my son were to die it would probably happen in a distant, foreign land far from his family and most, if not all, of his friends. Lucas came home to die there almost as a lonely stranger.

I was dry and wrapped in my winter bathrobe when I heard the knock on the bathroom door. The water was draining noisily from the bath as I opened the door. Charli was still holding her album of photographs.

"I think I'll go to bed now." She said. It looked as if she had been crying but she seemed alright – as if the crying had helped her. "What time are you planning to go to Carcassonne?"

"I'm not sure, yet. The man from the consulate needs me to answer a few questions and sign a few forms but I don't know exactly when. I was thinking of getting there a little while before lunch and either seeing him before or after eating; probably before."

"I was thinking of spending a little time with Valerie in the morning. Is your car big enough to take her, too?"

"Of course." I said.

"What about little Sylvie?"

I smiled, "If Valerie has a car seat."

"I'll ask her in the morning. I think it would be fun. I've never been to the old city."

"That's fine. Before I go to Carcassonne, I've a couple of things to do, so that should leave the two of you time to make your plans." And I wiggled my eyebrows at her as I finished the sentence. I didn't mean to; it is the sort of thing I do mainly with my daughters. They usually either hit me or burst into fits of laughter. Luckily, Charli laughed quite unguardedly and said, "You are a strange man!"

As she was closing her bedroom door, I heard her call out good night and I returned the wish before closing the door and setting about cleaning the bath.

Redemption song

Later in the night, after finishing the book on the battle of Gettysburg, I got up to look out of the window. There seemed to be a strange light somewhere outside and when I looked it became obvious that it was just the moon. The sky was brilliantly clear, and the moon was almost immediately above the house beaming pale light down onto the ledge outside my window. I could see the garden quite clearly and understood why people prayed for clouds or avoided full moons when they were planning clandestine operations.

I was thinking of things pertaining to war and began to wonder more about how the war had affected the people in this little town. Obviously, this was in the Vichy half. What was called the unoccupied zone. I had read several accounts of events in war torn France. Some were factual and some were fiction, but they all seemed to focus on things like patriotism, betrayal, shame and vengeance. How can a people regain their pride and self-respect when their leaders have capitulated to the enemy without even much of a fight? That seemed to be the essence of it for the French, but it was not something I had explored with anyone who had lived through it. I wondered at how complex the whole thing must have been. And at how some people must have oversimplified things and caused huge problems for themselves and others.

It was too late to start thinking about where I should look for more information. I was sure that there would be lots of websites covering the history and personal experiences of people in

France during the war, but I was too tired to go and look at them now and, anyway, I was not sure if looking at any of it would help.

Back in bed I was just about sleep when Mary woke me.

"Jude's still not willing to talk." I said. I could see Mary's smile as she told me not to worry, that Jude needed to make her own path and would survive her current crisis.

I told her about my latest exploits and exchanged a few ideas about Limon.

"He's a very troubled person," Mary agreed. "It doesn't excuse his actions, but it might help explain other things."

"What do you mean?"

"Well, why pick on Lucas so much and not the other members of the family? And why did he act as if Lucas was a stranger when he encountered his dead body on the hill? Why go for the Pecheurs so aggressively, and why did he finally lose it all with you?"

"Lots of questions. What about some answers!" I pleaded. "My head hurts! I wish you could be here to smooth out some of my wrinkles!"

"I'm not sure of the answers. Do you know what sort of events led to the feud between the Limons and Pecheurs?"

"I am still not sure," I said whilst stifling a yawn. "Something to do with the war, I think. I suspect it's something bad. To do with the people who were shot, or might have been shot, at the Chateau."

"I'm sure it will all become clear to you in the end. Good night my love." And her voice was like a gentle kiss that guided me back into a deep, long needed sleep.

Chapter Nine

The morning was crisp and sunny, the birds were exultant in the gardens and I could hear someone downstairs opening and closing cupboards, turning on taps and playing music on the radio. It took me a couple of moments to sort out things in my mind. I almost expected Mary to open the door and exclaim that Jude had made coffee for us and could I come down and help her sweep up the mounds of spilled coffee grounds and pools of orange juice that seemed to be everywhere. I could almost hear the children laughing in the overgrown tangle of a garden. Then I re-focused my mind, brought it back to 'today' and started the process of getting up.

I was pretty sore across a range of muscles in my stomach, on my shoulder and on the front and back of my head. It hurt to brush my teeth! I took two painkillers out of the cabinet in the bathroom where I had put them the night before. I swallowed them with some of the water in the tooth mug. Then I dressed, huffing and puffing like an old man, thinking, 'so this is what it's going to be like not so long from now?' Then I shrugged the thought from my still aching head and walked down to greet the day. And Charli.

I asked her if she had gone for bread yet and she shook her head. She was drinking hot chocolate and scanning the local paper from yesterday.

"How are you feeling today?" she asked.

"I have felt better, but I could be feeling a lot worse. No dizziness, no nausea, just pain here and there."

"Take some painkillers." She said and I told her I had just done so. I hoped the pain would go soon. "Can I come with you?"

"Of course," I said, "Just remember that my son's name is James and he is a photographer."

"A photographer! Wow, you didn't say that before. Is he famous? Does he work for magazines like Vogue and Elle?"

"No, I said, "Come with me."

I showed her the landscape study of the Pyrenees that James had given us especially for this house, and the two dragonflies photographed when he was fifteen. I told her he was still selling copies of that all over the world. It was a classic image captured by him. Then I showed her the wildcat photos in the front room and the large print of a polar bear's face.

"Did he take that one in the zoo?" she asked?

"No, he was trying to get back to the vehicle he had been riding in. He was walking backwards, slowly. Each few steps he was taking off an item of clothing and dropping it in front of him, then he was walking slowly backwards again, taking photographs and trying to loosen the next bit of clothing. He got to the truck and was pulled in as he was still taking photos. I think that was the last one before they slammed the door on the bear's face."

"Why was he taking off his clothes?"

"James explained that a polar bear can run as fast as forty++ odd kilometres an hour. You can't outrun a polar bear, but you can distract them, and the easiest way is to keep offering items of clothing to them. They stop and pick each piece up, look at it, sniff it, perhaps even taste it then move on towards you again."

"And if you run out of clothing?"

"James explained that at least it would be quicker than hypothermia!"

"Oh!." She said as she studied the face. "What a big mouth. Look at those teeth!"

"Let's go and get some bread. Or would you prefer croissants?"

"Could we? Wow, today is going to be a good day! I can tell!"

I walked down the road hoping that her enthusiasm would rub off on me and gradually, as we walked through the centre of town, the pain started to drift away, and I began to feel more positive and a little bit more relaxed. People looked curiously at Charli as we walked together. Whenever I said good morning, she would join in like it was some game she had never played before, and I wondered if that was actually true. I wondered if she had ever been in quite such a relaxed and friendly place and been in a position to be accepted as part of it rather than as an outsider or troublemaker.

In the Boulangierie, Yvonne looked at Charli with a considerable amount of spite and turned to me with the comment, "Has this little wildcat been a bit too much for you, Monsieur?" She was looking at my cuts and bruises, but I got the point.

"Yvonne, this is Charli, a good friend of my son, James."

She started to edge towards a less hostile stance and then Charli leant over and took Yvonne's hand, "Hello. James is somewhere in the north of Scotland at the moment. I think he is photographing polar bears or some other ferocious animals!"

She said it with such conviction and reverence that I didn't know whether to laugh or pat her on the back.

Yvonne gave her a slightly pitying look and removed her hand from Charli's grip. "Have you known 'James' long?" And I could see that she was trying to pronounce his name in the same way that Charli had.

"More than a year. I met him when he came to photograph fish around the Iles d'Hyeres near where I live. Have you ever been there?"

"No. It's somewhere I've always wanted to go to, though."

"Let me know when you plan to go, and I'll tell you the best places!"

"Thank you." Said Yvonne, then she turned to me and said, "Are you really alright?"

"Fine, some bruises but no bones broken."

"You should come 'round and rub some salve on John's wounds, Yvonne. It would do him some good!"

I could have killed Charli, I felt like kicking her, there and then. Yvonne looked at my face and nearly burst out laughing.

"Let me know when you think he's ready, Charli, and I'll come 'round with my own bottle of oil."

The two of them found this very funny and Charli was still laughing as we emerged from the shop a few minutes later with some croissant and various pastries in a couple of bags.

"She is nice!" Charli said. "She really likes you! I thought she was going to rip my eyes out when she thought I was your girlfriend!"

I kept my silence until we were walking through the empty marketplace.

"Please don't do that again."

"You were embarrassed! I thought you were. At first, I thought you were angry because I had found you out, you know you and Yvonne, "and she moved her hands in front of her to indicate our relationship, "but you were embarrassed!"

"Just don't do that again, OK!"

"Alright! Sorry!" and she continued to giggle as she trotted beside me seeming to take two or three steps for every one that I took.

It was later than I had expected when we sat down to breakfast. I pulled out the details of Marc's wife as we ate our breakfast and thought about his actions over the past few days.

"Have you met Marc, Lucas' brother, yet?"

"No, only his mother and father. Philip seems nice. He looks like Lew's death has hurt him more than I would've expected."

"What do you mean?"

"Well, Lew was always telling me how his father, brother and sister all hated him and bullied him all the time. I used to have the impression that Philip hated Lew, but I don't think he did."

"People are just as capable of hurting the people they love as they are of hurting those they hate."

"I know what you mean. I think most people I've loved have hurt me. Even when they didn't mean to!"

I was not sure how to go on from that. It seemed like such a terrible statement, but she said it so lightly and in such a matter of fact way that it shook me a little.

"I think Philip completely misunderstood Lucas. Everything he did was the wrong thing, and I'm not sure that Lucas knew how to help his father do a better job. Not that it was up to Lucas, but you know what I mean?"

She nodded.

"Did Nathalie say anything about the family feud between the Limons and Pecheurs?"

"Nothing. She seemed to be deeply disturbed by what had happened to you and felt that it was all her fault. She said it several times – 'It's all my fault!' – like that, and there was nothing I could say to help her."

I had finished my breakfast and replenished my coffee.

"OK, well I am going to make a couple of phone calls, then I am going to be out for about an hour which means that I hope to be back here at about half ten. I'll use my mobile, so if you want to call anyone just use the phone there." And I pointed to the phone attached to our land-line.

I got up and walked through to the study, pulled the door to and sat down at my desk with the paper from Marc.

I listened to the sound of the computer, its cooling fan rumbling and blowing quietly in the background, the radio was now on again in the kitchen and there was a noise that sounded like Charli was clearing up the dishes. I wondered if she would clean them, too.

I thought about Mary and how good it was to hear her voice the night before and about Charli's banter with Yvonne. Then I picked up the phone.

"Hello, is that Madame Almoric?"

"Yes? Whose speaking?" She sounded very wary, so I gave her my name and asked her if she had heard of me. There are very few British ex-pats in the local area, and I thought she might have heard of me. I also thought that her daughter might have mentioned my name.

She repeated my name as if she was checking that she had heard it correctly, but I thought that she was also letting someone else near her know who was on the telephone.

"I live in Chabrassonne, Madame, and I'm calling you to ask you two questions. I'm sorry to be impertinent, but it is important that I find out the answer to these two questions. Do you understand?"

"Yes. Well, no. I understand what you are saying, but I don't know what your questions are, monsieur."

"Well Madame, they are quite simple. My first question is, 'Do you know where your daughter, Louise is?'"

"I see. You want to know where my daughter is."

"No, Madame. I don't want to know <u>where</u> she is. I want to know if <u>you</u> know where she is. It's very important, believe me, please."

"You want to know if I know where she is?"

"That is correct."

"And what is the second question, monsieur?"

"I want to know if you can assure me that she is alright."

"You want to know if I can assure you that she is alright?"

"Yes, Madame," This was becoming one of the most frustrating phone calls of my life, but I kept my patience and pushed on. "Can you answer these questions for me, please? I am sorry but what I'm asking is very important."

"Monsieur? Why is it so important?"

"This is a very delicate issue, Madame. I wonder, do you know that Lucas Pecheur, the brother of your daughter's husband, was murdered just a few days ago?"

"Why yes, of course! But what has this to do with my daughter?"

"Madame, A man publicly argues with his brother, who is then found brutally murdered. He has been stabbed and left on a remote country path. His wife, who also had a disagreement with him earlier, has also disappeared. Do you understand?"

"But that is ridiculous! Marc would never do such a thing!"

"Madame, I just want to clear the matter up quickly and without public embarrassment. Someone is out there, a savage murderer, and people are perhaps looking in the wrong direction. Can you please answer my questions?"

"Well Louise is not here."

"No, Madame and I do not wish to find her. Can you please help me by answering my two simple questions?"

After a pause filled with what seemed like a short, muffled conversation, she came back on the phone and said, "Yes, I know exactly where she is, and I can confirm that she is very well indeed."

"Thank you, Madame."

"Does Marc want to speak to Louise?"

"I can assure you that he does, but my mission was to assure him and other people, that she was alright. It has been a trying time for the whole family."

"If I give you a number, will you give it to Marc?"

"If that's Louise's wish, of course."

"Let me give it to you, now." And she dictated a number to me. I thanked her and eventually escaped her sudden flow of open chatter about 'young people and their problems'. It was as if the act of giving me Louise's number had validated me in her eyes, and I was now safe to talk to about private family matters.

It gave me one opportunity I was glad of. I was able to ask if Louise had sought professional help for her relationship with Marc. She had, and was seeing a counsellor from the Church's marriage counselling agency. I asked if she would want Marc to join her in counselling and when she hesitated, I said, "I would advise you to tell Louise that counselling was one of her conditions before she agreed to see Marc again. I can assure you that professional help will give them both a better chance." Finally, she agreed, and I was able to get off the phone.

I looked at the clock. It was getting late. I decided to postpone my visit to Charles Groussard until after the trip to Carcassonne. Instead, I telephoned Marc Pecheur on his mobile. It took only three rings before he answered.

After dealing with his questions about my time with Limon I said, "Marc, I called you to talk to you about Louise. Are you still wanting to know where she is and if she is alright?"

"Yes, yes." His voice suddenly took on a new urgency, "Is she alright? Where is she?"

"Slow down, Marc. I know that she is alright, but I don't know where she is."

"Thank God! At least she's alright! How do you know this?"

"Look Marc. I have a number. This will get you directly in touch with Louise. OK? But before you call her spend a bit of time thinking about what you plan to say. Don't just rush in after I give it to you. Give it some consideration, and if she wants a bit more time on her own and especially if she wants you both to get some professional help, make sure she knows that it's OK with you. Do you understand?"

He was quiet for a couple of seconds. It felt like everyone I spoke to these days wanted to take their time, humming and hawing on the phone with me on the other end. Still, I was acting pretty much like some old father figure and I was not sure how appropriate that was, except that I had the number and he didn't.

"Professional help? Is that really necessary?" I could hear the temper swelling in his voice.

"Marc? Is it necessary? You did hit her, didn't you?" More silence, "You're lucky she's prepared to talk to you, Marc. Don't throw away this chance. Think about it, OK?"

"Of course, "He said, more quietly than before. "I understand what you say, thank you, you're right." I breathed a quiet sigh of relief and gave him the number, then I wished him well and rang off.

I sipped the remains of my cold coffee and thought about things for a few minutes. For some reason, I was reluctant to call Charles Groussard and arrange to see him later in the day. Partly, it was because I was not sure when I would be back from Carcassonne, but I also felt uncertain of what I wanted to ask him.

I checked my emails as I considered what I should be doing next. I should really be 'phoning the other Charles, the very English Mr Patron. I was not even sure where his offices might be.

While I was thinking about this, I read an email from Jo telling me that she had spent the night at Jude's. She wanted me to know that Jude was alright, but still a bit low, and that they were going out with some mutual friends to a comedy gig in central London that night.

I smiled at the idea. Going to comedy shows of various sorts had become a family tradition over the years. Radio and TV shows tended to be relatively easy to obtain tickets for, and they were free, so while other families took their children to see expensive shows in the West End, we used to take them to see some of the biggest stars in comedy for next to nothing and then wander up to them for a chat after the performance. I dashed off a quick email to Jo asking if there were any spare tickets for shows in the coming week or two while I was around in London.

I was just finishing this message when Charli knocked on the door. I told her to come in and then my mobile rang. She waited as I answered the call.

Charles Patron was brisk but cheerful on the line. I told him I was going to be in Carcassone for around midday and wondered how long our meeting would take. No more than fifteen to twenty minutes was his judgement, and I could hear a slight hesitation in his voice just before I said, "I will be bringing a couple of people with me to the Cité. We will have lunch sometime after the meeting, would you like to join us?" He assured me that it sounded very tempting, but he didn't want to intrude. I made a short quip about having to look after both young ladies by myself and he wavered slightly, calling me a cruel old man, but remained certain that he could not spare the time. I was glad that he couldn't join us, but I was also glad that I had made the offer and had let him refuse me.

I turned my attention to Charli who said, "You have been busy! I've been going to knock on the door for some time, but you seem to have been on your phone forever. Are you still going out, too?"

"No. That will have to wait."

"OK! Valerie tells me that she has a child's seat and asks if we can pick her and Sylvie from their house."

"Sure, no problem. Do you know where she lives?"

"No, I thought you did. Well, I have to call her back now, so I'll ask her. When shall we go?"

"As soon as you're ready!"

I walked out of the study and into the kitchen with her. She went to the table and I crossed the room to the sink to rinse out my cup. There on the drainer were the dishes, cleaned and drying in the sun. I started towards the pot of soup and Charli said, "I have put the rest of the soup in the 'fridge, but I don't know where to put the pot."

Redemption song

I picked up the now clean and dry pot and examined it. It was not one of mine. Nathalie must have brought it with the soup already in it. I said to Charli that if Valerie lived anywhere near the Pecheurs' house we could take the pot back en route, then I trotted upstairs to go to the toilet and sort out a couple of things before it was time to leave.

I could hear Charli's voice as I walked up the stairs. Then, as I was drying my face in the bathroom, I heard her come up the stairs and enter her room, still talking on the phone. It was very strange having a young woman in the house like this. She certainly brought an added sense of life and vitality into the place, and acted as a sharp contrast to the events that had brought her here, and that had left me so bruised and troubled.

I was contemplating the enormous breadth of my ignorance about the people I was encountering, and the society I was living within, as I walked down the stairs. I almost didn't hear the knocking on the door. Perhaps I was too used to people bashing it angrily with their fists.

I walked down the hall and opened the door with only a slight flurry or reluctance and fear. On the step, looking just as reluctant and worried, stood Georges Dupont. I invited him in and walked ahead of him, talking loudly over my shoulder asking him if he wanted some coffee. He declined and I sat him down at the table opposite me and waited. Charli had obviously decided to remain upstairs and keep quiet while Georges was in the house.

"I came to apologise."

"No need to Georges, you warned me, but I could not leave soon enough to avoid them. Anyway, you had no control over what they were going to do. Not your fault."

"Still. They are policemen. There was a time when such things happened, but we do not allow such behaviour now. Well, you know what I mean."

"The marks and bruises are mainly superficial. My shoulder was nearly busted, and I think I suffered mild concussion, but I know it could have been a lot worse."

"It should not have happened!" I could see a mixture of feelings in his expression. Indignation and anger were there alongside an obvious frustration. "Almost everything we do as police officers is scrutinised these days, and investigations into major crimes are usually heavily supervised by our judiciary. Limon was given a level of autonomy that was ridiculous!"

"I'm sorry Georges. I don't think that Limon will continue with this case now. From what I understand, he overstepped the mark quite spectacularly with me and I think there will be some serious repercussions."

"I have just come from Lavelanet. They want me to take over the case, already. The details on the guy, Mitch, have come through and he seems like the sort of violent idiot who would have been capable of killing Lucas. I think the information we already have about parked cars and vans in town will show that he was here at the right time." He shook his head and it looked as if he was trying to disguise a shudder, "There are some things you just do not get used to, no matter how long you are on the force."

I nodded, "You know that the people at the British Consulate want me to press charges against Limon?"

It was Georges' turn to nod.

"Well, I really am reluctant to do that. The funny thing is that when I was being taken to Lavelanet I thought that Limon's actions were either personal – you know, he hated me and wanted to demonstrate what he could do to me, or something more sinister was going on, and Limon was covering up something about himself and his involvement in all of this."

Georges' eyebrows raised at that statement, and a dawning of possibilities in that area seemed to pass across him like a shadow.

"One of the things I discovered yesterday was that Limon was almost certainly not the killer, but he had played a major role in Lucas' life. And along with it I discovered that Limon was a very disturbed and unhappy man."

Georges snorted lightly at my statement, "So you feel sorry for him, even after what he did to you?"

"Not so much sorry, I think the man is sick and needs to be helped. Suspending him for a few months or sacking him will not solve the problem."

A wry smile emerged from Georges' troubled features. "Limon and therapy! I think he would prefer to be locked up or sacked!"

"Anyway, I have an appointment in Carcassonne and need to get going if I am to keep it. Limon threatened that he would arrange for me to be stopped and falsely accused of drink driving. Do you think that will happen to me if I drive into Carcassonne today?"

"No matter what you say, John, Limon is an arsehole! It won't happen because he has no power to make it happen. I'm sorry, just one of his many empty threats."

"Don't be sorry, I would like all the threats I receive to be empty!"

I walked him to the door, talking about how the weather seemed to be picking up again. It seemed to get warmer and drier for longer each year. Worry about global warming was just as pronounced here, in a small rural French town, as it was back in places like London. I couldn't understand why that surprised me and was still thinking about it when I little voice behind me caused me to jump. It was Charli wondering if it was time to go.

I closed the shutters and locked the front door before we left.

I took Charli out the back of the house, down the steps from the veranda and along the garden path to the ancient wall at the end. I unlocked a small wooden door that would have made any interior decorator still into "stressed" wood, salivate. Paint was peeling from it and the resin from the wood had bubbled in places as a result of too many years exposed to the hot sun.

Inside it was cool and dark. I fumbled for the light switch and walked down between my car and a series of shelves until I reached the garage doors.

My car was a larger than average French family hatchback. It was bright red and remarkably clean for a vehicle that was never washed or polished. I drove it out into the narrow, cobbled lane and closed and locked the garage door. It was not until we started moving that I realised that we had left the pot behind, but it was too late to go back for it now, so we drove through the town, heading for Valerie and JJ's house.

Then it occurred to me that Charli had been talking on the phone as she was walking up the stairs to her room.

I said to her, "So you got your phone to work?"

"Yeah!" she laughed, "You have more phone chargers in the study than anyone I have ever known."

I smiled, "My family and friends have all left chargers in the house so I just keep them all in that basket next to the fireplace."

"I can give you my number, if you want?" Her voice was a little reluctant but I thought that would be a good idea. In the end I dictated my number and she typed it into her phone and called me. It rang in the pocket of my jacket, which was somewhere on the rear seat and Charli laughed, thinking this was the funniest thing before cancelling her call.

As we drove past the garage that JJ worked in, I saw him waving at us, so I slowed and then pulled in, to the side of the road.

"I understand you are taking my wife and daughter into Carcassonne, today."

"I hope that's alright with you?"

"No problem! I wanted to say thank you. Valerie can drive, but she doesn't really like it, so she will do the shopping and visit people locally, but she would never willingly drive all the way there!"

He looked at me for a further few seconds and added, "I heard about what happened to you. They did a pretty good job on you, didn't they?"

"I'm lucky. It's all superficial." I smiled and he returned it with a huge grin and as he winked at Charli he said, "They're lucky you didn't hit back, eh?!"

I smiled again and said we would take care of his two girls, he thanked us again and thumped the top of the car as if to give us the all clear to go. I beeped my horn as we turned the corner and drove over the bridge out of the main part of town. I thought how strange it was for me to use my horn like that. In Britain I hate people beeping their horn, but here it is a natural part of the language of the road.

Valerie and Sylvie were waiting at the front window to their little house which was perched on a hillside looking down over Chabrassonne. It was one of a small development of houses spread out along a couple of roads which led over the hill and on towards a large lake, which was the main source of water for the area and was used by a small number of enthusiastic water sport fanatics. Sometimes, even this far away from the lake, you could hear the sound of motorboats charging noisily up and down the wide stretch of water.

Valerie and Charli seemed to be very relaxed in each other's company, and they didn't need me to help them fix the seat in the car and settle the little girl into it. She seemed a little shy, and I wondered if she was just tired. Far off, on the other side of the town rose the chateau, adopting a number of different architectural styles as it sprawled across the edge of the rocky outcrop before me. As I watched, a bright flash of light caught my eye, leaving one of those little spots of blindness imprinted on my retina. Someone had just opened a window and the sun's reflection had swept past me like a personal search light, seeking me out on the opposite hill.

Valerie and Charli opted to sit either side of little Sylvie. There was enough room for all three and the views in the back were OK. As I drove off, the girls opened the sliding window in the roof and started a conversation that only occasionally touched on me. So, apart from short asides to explain where we were, to Charli, or give them both little potted histories of the Cathars and local legends, I was left to my own thoughts as I manoeuvred my way through the winding roads over deep green hills and past great clumps of ancient woodland.

Eventually we passed through Limoux and drove down the river valley towards Carcassonne. Every kilometre took us lower and increased the temperature by another degree or so until we were driving along the hot flood plains of the river Aude, with the dramatic outline of the medieval Cité rising up before us.

When we first started coming to the area we were advised to keep away from Carcassonne because it was, on the one hand a terrible tourist trap and, on the other hand, a fairly grim and uninteresting small city. After spending time in the old Cité with our children, we began to wonder what the newer city on the other side of the river was like and took a day exploring it. To our amazement it was a much nicer, and older, place than people had suggested, and we began to realise that the advice had been coming from people who were, themselves, tourists. We discovered that the central part of Carcassone, called the Bastide St Louis, was a delightful place to spend some time and we also discovered a few very fine local restaurants that were well worth the trip.

Charles' offices were located in the heart of the Bastide and, as the girls wanted to take Sylvie to the old Cité I dropped them off at its main entrance then drove around the massive fortified structure and crossed the Pont Neuf, then turned left and followed the river to a large garden that looked out across the water and up to the old Cite. There always seemed to be parking spaces there, so I stopped, paid my ticket and walked through the town to meet Charles. I had agreed that I would phone the girls as soon as my meeting was over and that we would decide what to do, then.

Redemption song

The sixteenth and seventeenth century buildings held a sombre grace against the brilliantly blue sky, and their red tiled roofs seemed to be bleached into tones from pink to almost white from hundreds of years of burning light. Charles' offices were in a slightly more modern building put up during the nineteenth century and dressed up to look like something you would have expected on a Paris boulevard. A proud merchant's house, now holding the quiet snobbery and elegance of an outpost of the British Diplomatic Service. Perhaps I was being a bit unfair, but that was what was running through my mind as I stepped up and pressed the doorbell.

Above me, in the large arched porch, a video camera whirred lightly and focussed more intently on me as a precise, but slightly accented French voice asked me who I was and what I wanted. I waited as my answer was processed, and then I was buzzed in through two sets of doors. I emerged into a large reception hall with a young lady and a large, but neatly dressed young man standing behind a stylish, blond wood desk. Behind them a large, ornate polished wood and elegant cast iron staircase swept up to the first floor.

I was signing my name in a book and listening to the printer churn out my visitor's pass when I heard my name being called and Charles was bounding down the staircase to meet me. I took my pass and pinned it to my shirt as I followed Charles to one of the rooms on the ground floor, at the back of the building.

Painted wood panels and a dark polished wood floor were lit by three large windows looking out onto a beautiful garden surrounded by an ornate wall that looked older than the building we were in. We sat down in a couple of large armchairs in front of the elegant, marble fireplace and someone knocked on the door and brought in a large tray with a coffee jug, two china cups and saucers, sugar, cream and a plate of small pastries.

Charles poured out the tea and pulled a slim briefcase from the other side of his armchair. He started.

"Interesting legal system, the French have, you know?" I nodded but didn't say anything. "They have a mixture of different departments that carry out police work and a couple of different ways of managing the forces. Do you know much about the system?"

"Not really. Before this happened, I didn't even know the telephone number for emergency services in France."

"Really? Well, perhaps you don't want to be burdened with the details?"

"Didn't you tell me that a member of the judiciary is supposed to control investigations into important crimes and that the police basically do that person or that department's slog work for them. Is that right?"

"Well, sort of. In the Police Nationale you have a whole collection of different directorates and departments, but the ones you would be expected to encounter are the Direction Centrale de la

Redemption song

Police Judiciaire and the Direction Centrale de la Securite Publique. The judiciary are supposed to be responsible for the investigation of all crimes, and the police who make up the second directorate are there to assist the judiciary. Up until not that long ago your particular area used to have the Gendarmerie Nationale doing the police work. Now they are more your military types, and they would have made sure that at least a few of your bones were broken by the time you took your leave of their company! But, of course, I think they happen to be a bit more disciplined than chaps like Limon!"

I wondered where this was taking us. Was he going to tell me the police had beaten me up because they were confused or badly supervised? I didn't really care about the details, but I let him go on.

"Your local examining magistrates, well even your more powerful ones in big cities, too, can be either brilliant or dim-witted. They can try and control investigations to the point where the local police end up not being able to do anything but, quite often, they hand the task over to the police and wait to see what turns up. Word has it that your local chap spends a lot of his time indulging in private interests and leaves his trusted Limons, etc. to do all the leg work without them bothering him too much."

"So, Limon had a fee hand. He was not working under the close supervision of the magistrate."

"Spot on!" Charles gave me one of his best smiles, as if I had just been put to the top of the class. "The local chap seems to have a reputation. Started out as a highflier in Paris, then went back to restore the old family seat or something and treats the job like a part time thing that helps pay the gardener or something."

"What does this mean when we start looking at actions against Limon? Are you saying it was the Magistrate's fault?"

"Very good, very good! It is something like that."

I was about to say that I was not interested in taking action against Limon, anyway, when Charles just ploughed on. He had obviously been rehearsing this little chat.

"Britain and France are not so much "at one" with each other these days. Diplomatically speaking senior public figures on both sides grit their teeth very tightly as they put on their best smiles when they do the shaking of hands bits, but they are less inclined to co-operate than they have been for many years. We just sit in the middle, along with our French counterparts, and try to keep as many of the casters oiled and the button-holes buttoned, if you get my meaning?"

"I think I do."

"And since the election we've been busy basically trying to justify our existence. Places like this have been a bit of an anomaly for a while now and I think it won't be long before the axe falls, and this outpost will be no more.

He paused to look around the room then continued "but that is not your concern, is it? Now, we want to come down on old Limon like several hundredweight of old bricks, but we have to tread lightly and watch that our aim avoids unwanted collateral damage, as people say these days."

"Can I make a suggestion?" I was getting a bit fed up with all of this.

"By all means. Feel free."

"I didn't come here with the burning rage of a man who wants to see his attackers hanged, drawn and quartered."

"No, of course not. Punishment should fit the crime, etc etc."

"Well, something like that. I think I would like to insist that Limon takes a bit of time off and attends some therapy. He is a very unbalanced man."

Charles chuckled and said, "You mean like 'Anger Management' classes?"

"Well, I was thinking of something to sort out his own personal problems. Something from his past is tearing him apart. He needs to sort it out before he can ever stop being a liability to his department and colleagues."

"Interesting. You got all this from being abused and beaten up by him?"

"Hardly. I've learned quite a lot about him during the last couple of days. Things that relate to the Second World War and things to do with relationships and feuds between his family and the family of the murder victim."

"So, is that the sort of course of action you would like us to pursue?"

"Really, all I want is a proper apology, and for Limon to be out of circulation for a while, so that he can sort his own problems out – with proper professional help, of course. I don't want to encounter him six months down the line eager to harass me every chance he gets, and I don't want him sacked and privately going after some of my blood as recompense. Look at it as an optimum survival strategy."

"And the chap from the local judiciary?"

"Do you think he put Limon up to it?"

"No, I cannot imagine so."

"Do you think he is blocking the investigation?"

"Only through incompetence."

"And we are not going to be able to have him replaced?"

"You want him replaced?" He almost gasped.

"No, of course not. I'm just checking."

"Well, I think we might make this work. We put together a nice little complaint and then offer to let it fizzle out if they just apologize and sort out the problems of the person who did the dirty deed. That should work well all round. No lost face on both sides. Diplomacy at work in the modern world!"

I drank my coffee and agreed with him. It took a few more minutes to look over the documents Charles had organised during the morning. He made a few notes, including one regarding the photographs of me from the day before, then I signed and initialled my way through several bits of paper. I then stood up and shook his hand and he walked me back to the reception to hand in my badge and sign out. The door clunked with a dark sound of finality.

Redemption song

As we were dealing with the documentation, he had passed a comment which I had not thought about. It was a good job that the Consulate still had this outpost from Marseilles. Furthermore, if it had happened just about twenty odd kilometres further west the consulate office responsible would have been the one based in Bordeaux. I didn't really want to dwell on any of those sorts of observations. I picked my mobile phone out of my pocket and rang the Charli to say that I was out of the meeting now. It was just coming up to forty minutes past midday.

The girls had basically not moved since I had dropped them off. Just at the main gate they had encountered a small fair with several children's rides. Sylvie had ridden in two cars, a white swan and a very pretty horse and she was now driving a tank and shouting 'BANG' every time she passed them. I asked how crowded it was and they told me that they had both remarked at how quiet the whole place seemed to be.

I told them I would be there in about ten to fifteen minutes and they didn't seem to mind waiting.

"We've bought some sugar strands on a wooden stick. It is like pink cotton wool but very sticky and sweet!" said Charli, the laughter lighting up her voice.

I smiled at the idea of them eating candy floss. In France it is called Barbapapa, and there are a series of children's books about a family of characters with a father whose name is the same. He is a big pink blob and the family are all different shapes and are cheerful, happy creatures. My children used to love those books. They also used to love playing in exactly the same place at the entrance to the Cité when they were younger, and always wanted to have candy floss.

I walked quickly through the powerful sunlight, heading for my car, hoping the little bit of shade I had left it in was enough to keep it from being a complete furnace by the time I reached it.

Chapter Ten

Sylvie was beginning to show signs of boredom and tiredness as I arrived. She allowed me to pick her up from the princess' carriage as the carousel stopped, and I placed her in the three-wheeler buggy so that we could push her through the crowds to lunch. Even on a quiet day there are parts of the old Cité of Carcassonne that seem overflowing with people. The steep cobbled path took us through the thickest crowds, and then we turned left towards the Place Marcou, where a dozen cafes and restaurants crowd together offering everything from excellent cuisine to grimly presented, over-priced fast foods. I knew a really nice restaurant further along the Rue du Plo, on the other side of the square, but the consensus was that we should find something here.

It didn't take us long to agree on a small place where we could sit at a table in the courtyard behind the main restaurant, under the shade of a large umbrella. Despite (or perhaps because) we had been pushing our way through busy, noisy streets and into a crowded restaurant, little Sylvie was fast asleep in her buggy by the time we settled down at the table. Valerie and Charli debated whether to let her sleep or wake her up for some food. In the end, they decided to leave her, as Valerie had some food for Sylvie in a cool-bag, and they could feed her whenever she woke up.

The menu was typical of Carcassonne, with cassoulet and charcuterie featuring alongside a series of other popular dishes. Charli had never eaten cassoulet, so that was a simple choice. I kept her company by ordering the same and Valerie chose grilled lamb. We had some garlic bread while we waited for our main course, and large bowls of simple mixed salad, too. I ordered white wine and a couple of bottles of mineral water, and they had quite elaborate ice creams while I drank some strong black coffee to finish.

All the way through the meal I spent more time listening than talking. The conversation ranged around clothes, shoes, make up, shops, stars of TV, films and the music scene and experiences of different parts of the south of France. Neither had gone further north than Toulouse, they did not have passports, and had never visited another country, despite the fact that Spain was a just couple of hours away by car. Valerie admitted that she had crossed the border into Spain one summer when she went with the school on a field trip into the Pyrenees, but she had not known about the border crossing incident until they were back in the field study centre for the night.

They asked me about different places I had been to and I told them about Paris, Amsterdam, London, Edinburgh, Rome, New York and a few other places. They didn't want much detail. Just a couple of comparative questions about particular sites and scenes, or about particular shops.

A couple of times one or the other would admit that they had talked about going to some of those places with Lucas, or he had told them about what a place would be like, even when his experience outside France had been just as non-existent as theirs. He had been a dreamer and had read a lot compared to either of them. He was something, someone, an experience, that they both cherished in particular ways. I could see that they had both experienced something in their relationships with Lucas that had been special. They could share their memories and not feel jealous about what the other had experienced.

Their relationships and memories were coloured with a deep sadness that would have dragged them down if there had not been a lot of joy in the experiences, too. I suppose I had not expected that. Especially from the stories I had been told about what he was supposed to have been like, and the accounts of what people now call "antisocial behaviour". After all, he had been a thief and a con man who had stolen money from old people. Most of the time I just listened or responded to their questions, but I asked a couple of questions, too.

My first question was an attempt to find out what they specifically liked about Lucas and the way he acted around them.

They both agreed that Lucas had been a dreamer but, unlike people who just wanted to win the lottery or have some magic spell that would take them out of their present circumstances, Lucas worked hard at trying to find a route to the top. He didn't want to work in a boring business like his father's and spend his days trudging around doing the same things over and over and not get very far. He wanted to do exciting things that produced extraordinary results. His dreams of running his own night-club were not farfetched to them. He could have done it, and just needed the start-up money and the time to get it going. All of the criminal activities were just stop gap solutions to the problem of not having enough money to do what he really wanted to do.

Another thing about him was how he managed to share his dreams with you. You were part of the dream, he was doing them for you as much as for himself and you ended up sharing his dreams, too.

He was an artistic and sensitive person who was always trying to be tougher, braver and stronger than he needed to be. People showed him more respect than they did the bigger, tougher people in the gangs and groups he had been involved in. But he never seemed to notice just how well respected he was. He always felt that he was not doing enough or achieving enough. He never passed his own, tough measurements or assessments.

It was fascinating to see them build this image of Lucas.

I didn't want to burst any bubbles by asking why it was that he had left Valerie as soon as she became pregnant, or that he had stolen from those who had trusted him, regardless of the fact that they were criminals.

As it was, I didn't have to ask. Valerie actually volunteered an explanation for her situation. She said that she believed Lucas had left because she had already made up her mind to stay with JJ and pretend that Sylvie was his. JJ had a secure job and could provide the sort of stability that Lucas could never give. She knew that it had hurt him, but she also knew that she could not have tied him down and it would have been disastrous to have tried. Charli agreed and supported what Valerie was saying, telling me that she had got to know Lucas afterwards and he had spent a lot of time telling her about it.

Charli then told me about how depressed Lucas had become as he carried out his duties for the gang. It had started as something that would transform their prospects, but he had gradually felt more and more trapped. The compulsion to move on was growing greater inside him every day that they travelled along the coast and back. He would work really hard at making their life as good as possible, and she had a wonderful time, but then she would look into his eyes as they were sitting in a restaurant having a nice meal and she would see great sadness there.

So, she had talked to him about what was wrong. She had been worried that he was going to go back home and claim back his daughter and ex-girlfriend, but that had not been the problem. They were not managing to save much. No matter how much he made, they seemed to spend it just as quickly as he made it. He was becoming trapped in a system that was just as monotonous and soul destroying as his father's business and he was getting drawn deeper into things he did not want to be involved in. There seemed no way out until he realised that all he had to do was break the chain, take the money and run.

I had paid the bill and we were out of the restaurant, walking up towards the main chateau when this explanation finished.

My second question was really an extension of what Charli had told me. I wanted to know what Lucas had planned to do with the money. It turned out that there had been no great plan. What he wanted to do was go somewhere different with Charli and spend a little time thinking. He was seriously considering studying art and they had talked a lot about going to Paris where he could study and paint, and she would work in a beauty parlour to keep them going until he became a famous artist.

I was deeply surprised by this. I had expected him to have new plans for a night-club and I asked her why the change when both of them had said only a few minutes earlier that he could have run a really great night club and had always dreamed of doing something like that.

Redemption song

They both shared in providing the answer. His big dream; the dream at the top of all his dreams, had always been to become a world-famous artist. He had wanted this since he was a little boy. However, it was a secret he could only share with people he really trusted. He felt that if he could become really successful and wealthy, he could be free to realise his dream. No one would be able to criticise or ridicule him once he had proved himself better than the rest. So, he ended up tearing himself apart doing things he hated whilst holding that dream secretly in his heart. They both knew this, and they had known that he would not have forgiven them if they had told anyone else.

One of the tests they had set each other when Nathalie had first brought them together had been to see if the other had known of Lucas' real dream. It was proof that he had loved them both!

Standing on an empty beach late at night in the early summer, Lucas had looked up at the stars and had said to Charli that if he didn't start to do something soon about becoming an artist, he felt that he would die. She had been so concerned by his assertion that she had told him she would do anything to help them get away from there and start a new life. She would support him. She would help him make it happen. A few days later he told her that they were going to go away soon but she had to keep it a secret. When it happened, it had happened fast, and it had not turned out as either of them had expected.

There was a certain gloom drawing over the day as we walked down towards the Basilique St

222

Nazaire. I thought that a subject change was necessary and so I told Charli that I had noticed she had not smoked even one cigarette all day.

Charli let out a little groan and Valerie stopped the buggy to give her a hug.

"Nathalie and I have convinced Charli to try to stop smoking. Show him Charli!" and, to the surprise of a couple who were walking past, Charli lifted up her dress and showed me a semi-opaque patch on her upper thigh.

"Nathalie had a whole batch of them from when she gave up smoking a year or so, ago. She just brought them over and said the way to do it was to just stop! Don't think about it, she told me, just do it! Then she gave me the patches and said that I should put one of these on every day and they would help me not even think about it!"

"And it's worked." I said and when she gave me a slight sneer as if to say, "easy for you to say that!"

I continued, "Just take each day as a new day. Don't think about how many days it has been or when you might stop wanting a cigarette. Each day will be the first day, so spend your time concentrating on other things."

Valerie was giving Charli another hug when Sylvie roused herself from her sleep, so we got her out of the buggy to run around a little and then we sat in the shade next to the great old church, and the two young women took turns each to feed and play with Sylvie. I couldn't help but think about how my daughters used to play at being "mummy" to their dolls. I also thought about the different layers of truth that were emerging around Lucas. Even when you thought that someone had told you everything, they kept something back and, every time they answered a question, they left out information. Sometimes they lied and other times they just told you what they wanted you to know or what they thought you wanted to know.

The simple image of Lucas had become more complicated and less clear each time I had tried to make sense of it. I supposed that I had only known of Lucas for the last three days. It was not surprising to discover that it takes a lot longer than a few short days to begin to know and understand a person. I stopped thinking about this when I began to wonder whether it was ever possible to really know anyone. I was not even sure if I wanted to really know Lucas – dead or alive. It was as if the very act of discovering his dead body had tied me to his life. I was obliged to find out more about him and ponder on who had killed him and why.

We agreed to walk along the battlements for a short while and so we strolled along looking over the rest of the town and out to the surrounding hills as the afternoon took on a more golden and rested feel.

As Valerie pushed Sylvie along and chatted to her, Charli took my arm and walked closely with me. She pressed against my arm and thanked me for the lunch, and for the day, and I told her that it had been a pleasure. I also pointed out that she had spent more of the day with the other two, anyway. They were the ones to thank.

"I was speaking with Valerie earlier and she asked me why you seemed to be taking such an interest in Lucas' death."

I looked down at her and wondered what was coming.

"She told me that people in Chabrassonne think that you are a 'super detective' and even a 'retired secret agent'. Is that true?"

"No."

She shrugged and held onto my arm.

"So, never mind. I told her that you were just a good person and could see that Lucas had deserved better than he got."

"Thank you." I squeezed her arm a bit and added, "Lucas deserved more but he was lucky to have both your love, and Valerie's too." It didn't feel wrong or sentimental to say this to her. It was, as far as I could see, the truth, but to say it to such a young person made me feel a bit of an old charlatan. It felt a bit like I was trying to use my charm on someone younger and more easily influenced. Perhaps I was also trying to avoid answering the question. After all, why was I trying to make sense of the life and death of Lucas Pecheur?

On the way back down through the Cité I bought all three girls ice cream cornets and only made light reference to the fact that they had consumed large ice creams at lunch time. I bought a bottle of semi-cold water at the same shop and Valerie put some of it in Sylvie's cup for later.

The car park was a rutted and dusty wasteland filled with cars disappearing in a steady heat haze.

Redemption song

I had parked close to what had looked like a cliff when I had left it there. It was as if part of the car park had been created by someone who had carelessly ripped out the side of the low hill. There were a couple of scrubby little trees next to the car and, between the shadow of the cliff and the trees, the car had enjoyed a little shade. I put the air conditioning on before we tried to get Sylvie into her car seat and folded away the buggy. As Valerie fixed Sylvie in, Charli brought out a small bag from her backpack and said, "Look what I have!" and pulled a little doll in historic costume out of the bag. That made Valerie's job much easier, and soon we were on our way.

Somewhere nearby, there had been a medieval re-enactment group doing a show of some sort, and it took us a while to get out of the car park as a small troupe of horses and riders dressed in medieval costumes slowly plodded past. They were accompanied by others in costumes who were performing the occasional simple juggling trick or acrobatic feat to amuse those they passed.

At one point, Valerie cried out from the back of the car, "I know some of those boys! They do some work up at the chateau. Monsieur Groussard has done wonderful things since he came to revive the old family chateau."

Thoughts of the chateau and Charles Groussard lurked in the back of my mind as I drove along the main road out of town.

Sometime later, as we were passing through Limoux, I looked at my petrol gauge and thought about topping up my fuel tank. I would be driving a

226

long distance in a day or so, and the fuel here was a lot cheaper than it was in Chabrassonne.

I slowed down and started to indicate to turn off the road as we neared a petrol station. "Just going to stop here for a minute!" I called back to the girls then I began to guide the car to the only available pump. Late afternoon was obviously the time when people wanted to fill their tanks. It did not register at first, but as I stopped, I realised that the vehicle in the position in front of me was a VW minibus and that its colour was a dirty sort of cream with slightly faded green panels.

I turned to the girls and said, "Keep your heads down. You, especially, Charli. Check out the van in front of us. Is that like the van Mitch drives around in?"

"My God! It is! That's him at the petrol pump, now. Oh my God!"

She was almost on the floor by the time she finished speaking. Her face was very pale, and I could see that she was frightened and shaking.

"I can't just drive away. Keep down, Charli and everything will be alright."

I released the remote lock on the little door to my petrol cap and rummaged in the glove compartment of my car. I had my Blackberry phone in there. This has a camera, unlike my French Nokia phone.

I stepped out of the car and before dealing with the pump, I pulled out the phone from my pocket and held it as if I was reading a text message but what I did was use the video camera function to film the van, its number plate and the man who was just finishing pumping gas into his tank. Then I topped up my tank while watching the man lumber to the filling station shop to pay for his petrol. I preferred the French petrol stations where you filled up then drove to a little kiosk to pay for your petrol. This was more like a filling station in the UK. I told the girls to lock their doors and walked towards the shop.

The sun was lower in the sky now and long shadows were cutting across the petrol station. Passing from light to shade and back to light created a dream-like stroboscopic effect as I walked towards the building. I could see the man that was almost certainly Mitch waiting in the small queue to pay. I entered the shop and thought that I might delay queuing next to him by looking for some sweets to buy, but I changed my mind when I thought about him heading back to his van and glimpsing Charli in my car, so I stood behind him and waited. The people behind the counter seemed to be very slow and there was a quiet buzz of boredom and annoyance in the air.

Mitch waited in front of me with his shoulders hunched and his hands in his pockets. I was trying to think of what he smelled like. Some people just seem to have a distinctive smell. He emitted a mix of stale sweat and engine oil mixed with something else. As we neared the tills, I thought that it may have been the smell of fast foods. He smelled of sweat, motors cars engines and burger and fries. I looked out of the window and could see my car just behind his van. I was glad that I couldn't see anybody in the back seat.

"What happened to you? Your wife beat you up, eh?" Mitch had turned around and had noticed me. He had a slight wheeze to his laugh and his voice was softer than I had expected. He also had a more middle-class accent and form than I had expected.

"No. Just a few policemen." I shrugged.

"Wow, they are bastards, aren't they?" I nodded and he turned to go and pay at one of the tills. The other one became free almost immediately and I walked over and told the young man the number of my pump. Mitch paid by cash and was out of the door before I had finished my transaction. I watched him walk back to his van and climb in. He had not even bothered to look at any of the cars around him. He drove out and headed in the direction I was planning to take.

Before driving off, I took out my Blackberry again and looked at the short film I had taken. The number plate was clearly shown in the first sequence of the film. I turned to Charli and asked if it really had been Mitch. It had been, and she was still reluctant to get back onto her seat, so I moved the car out from the pumps and parked near the exit, then I phoned Georges Dupont.

He picked up almost immediately and barked a "Yes!" into it as if I was interrupting something important.

"Sorry to bother you Georges, but I've just encountered a cream and green VW minibus in Limoux."

"Really?"

"Yes, the number plate is…." And read out the number from the film on the other phone. "And the person driving it is about my height, long dark hair, unshaven, broad shoulders and not much neck, long arms, actually, very long arms. He has a square face with a squashed nose, thick lips and very heavy brow. He looks to be in his late twenties, early thirties."

"This was in a petrol station in Limoux?"

"Yes. He drove out and headed south along the Avenue Du Languedoc about two minutes ago. It looked to me as if he was heading either for Chabrassone or Quillan. They're the only two destinations of any note in that direction."

"It's the right number plate and description of the vehicle and the guy driving it sounds like the person we want to talk to."

"Good." I said. I wanted to stop talking to him and let him do something about it. "I took a short film of the man and his van with my mobile phone."

"How did you find him, John?"

"I didn't find him Georges. I almost tripped over him, but he has gone now, and he may be heading your way."

"OK, John. Thank you." His voice was cold, distant, slightly incredulous. It was as if he didn't know whether to trust me or not. I was certain that he really didn't know what to make of me. I had not been looking for Mitch or his van, but I suppose, to Georges at least, it looked like I'd just done a quick search, and both found him and shepherded him towards Chabrassonne.

I waited a little bit longer then said, "Does anyone want anything from the shop? Sweets, coffee?"

Valerie asked for some coffee and Charli half joked that I could buy her some cigarettes, then said that I could buy some chewing gum instead.

"Anyone want to come with me?"

Charli was wary of leaving the cover of the car but decided to brave it, anyway so we walked together towards the shop.

"He sounds less like a thug than he looks." I said.

"He comes from a very well-off family near Toulouse. Lew met him when he was buying drugs and selling them on to people in this area. Mitch was the dealer all of the posh kids on the south side of Toulouse went to. When the police started to take a lot of interest in Mitch, he just dropped out of the scene, then a few months later he turned up and invited Lew to join him and another guy on what Lew used to call the stupidest con game ever invented."

"Why stupid?"

"Because none of them really knew what they were doing, and they ended up stealing worthless jewellery and loose change. What they stole didn't even cover their costs half the time. If it hadn't been a break and escape from Chabrassonne, I don't think Lew would have stayed with them for more than a couple of days."

"But he stayed with them for a while?"

"Almost a year, in the end."

Redemption song

As we were walking back to the car I asked, "What happened to end the partnership?"

"The third person in the group, his name was Claude Dubost, was arrested in Lourdes, of all places. Lew and Mitch were site seeing and came back to the café where they had all agreed to meet up just in time to see Claude being pushed into the back of a police car."

"So they ran?"

"Didn't even wait to see what happened to Claude. Lew was all for hanging around just in case it was all just a mistake. He had this image of Claude being released and not knowing where they were, or what had happened to his belongings and money."

"It was all in the VW bus?"

"Most of it. Mitch argued that if Claude got out, he could phone them on his mobile."

"But he never did?"

"They got a call telling them where to send his belongings and share of the money."

"And they sent it?"

"They sent the belongings but, by then, they had already spent the money. As I said, they didn't really make that much, anyway."

I felt that it was safe to head back home now and so I started up the engine and joined the traffic through town. I think we all kept a close eye on the road ahead, and as we wound our way along the minor road to Chabrassone we also studied every little side road and small hamlet we passed, just in case a cream and green van was lying in wait for

232

us. Happily, there was nothing to worry about. We hardly saw another car on the road all the way.

After dropping off Valerie and Sylvie, we headed back into the centre of town and to the safety of my house. Charli sat in the front of the car with me, but she wore sunglasses and kept her elbow propped on the windowsill of the car so that she could cover her face with her hand. She stayed in the car until I had parked it back in the garage, then she trotted quickly to the back door and rushed into the quiet shade of the study. I made her some chocolate and took it through to her. She was sitting in one of the armchairs looking at a book titled, "Il était une fois....Chabrassonne" which basically means, once upon a time in Chabrassonne. It contained lots of old photographs of Chabrassone and told some of its history, mainly in the words of local inhabitants. The pictures started at the middle of the nineteenth century and ended just after World War Two. The book had been a present from James to Mary and I. He had found it in the local newspaper/tobacco shop. We had never even thought of looking there for local books!

I left her and returned to the kitchen thinking that I should have a look at the book, myself. I wondered if any of the pictures or information in the book would shed more light on the story that seemed to be threading its way through my life. I didn't feel like making much to eat, so I called through and asked if Charli would eat an omelette. I made hers with some local cheese, thinly sliced sausage and a bit of torn basil leaves. Mine had sausage, roasted peppers and some tomato inside it. I served them with salad, and we shared a bottle of very cold white wine.

I was surprised to see that it was nearly nine thirty by the time we had finished our meal and cleared the dishes away. I popped through to look at my emails and the telephone rang just as I sat down to my desk.

"John, its Nathalie Pecheur. I hope I am not disturbing you."

"Not at all."

"I just wanted to thank you. I seem to be doing nothing but thanking you these days, but I have to tell you how grateful I am." I was rummaging through my day, wondering what she could possibly thank me for when she continued, "Marc and Louise are talking again, and he admits that it was you that brought them together again. In the midst of everything you do this for us.. you also do this! I just wanted to say thank you. Marc and Louise are at their favourite restaurant in Camon."

"Yes, I know the place. It was always a favourite of ours, too."

"Marc says that you advised him to be patient and let Louise lead the way."

"Basically, yes. I hope I wasn't interfering!"

"Not at all. He won't listen to Philip or myself. Perhaps I can come and see you tomorrow?" She added the request as if it was related to her thanks, but it felt like she was using the thank you as an excuse. I didn't mind. I was happy to see Nathalie again, and I was keen to ask her some questions and hoped that her grateful mindset would encourage her to give me some answers.

We agreed to meet at eleven. I was to go to the Pecheurs' home rather than her coming to me. I put down the phone and Charli asked me who it had been. I told her about the call, and she sat down to look at the book again as I began to scroll through my emails. One of the cats, Rag this time, hopped onto the chair beside her, curled up and went to sleep.

There was a very long one from Jude, mainly telling me about work related things, but there was a thread through the narrative which seemed to me to be quite positive. She had always been better at telling me her troubles than she had been about telling me the good things.

I checked out the other emails before replying. James was still in Ullapool. He had been planning to leave for Edinburgh that day, but had met up with a gamekeeper who had been telling him about some otters in a river only a few miles from town, so now he was planning to stay up all night in order to catch the otters at play and possibly photograph them fishing in the river, too. I read out the email to Charli, translating it into French. She came up behind me and looked at the email. She pointed to the screen and read some of the sentences. She could understand quite a lot of it and her accent was reasonably good, too. I complimented her on her linguistic abilities, and she gave me a little curtsey before returning to her book.

Redemption song

I read a short email from Jo telling me that her and Jude had gone out with a group of people the night before and that Jude had spent quite a bit of time focussed on one particular young man. They were going to go out for a meal together in a couple of days. I sent her a quick note back saying well done, and that the date was a good sign. I then told James that he should remember to go home at some point, and that I wished him good luck with the otters. I thought that he was probably already bivouacked in amongst the bushes, fighting off the midges by now, but that didn't matter.

I then spent a while writing a positive and encouraging email to Jude under the guise of a set of notes and suggestions relating to her work.

There were a few chatty emails from other people and a couple of ex-colleagues wondering if I was going to be available for a spot of consultancy work in the very near future. I thought about it for a while but decided that I would answer people tomorrow.

I got up and stretched. I had not taken any pain killers since the morning and had been trying to ignore the various aches and pains that were clamouring for my attention.

"I'm thinking of going to bed." I said and Charli looked up at me with an expression that made me turn away. I was feeling myself drawn to her and she was looking at me as if to say, "Is that an invitation?" I felt myself flush and a thrill went through me which was difficult to suppress.

"Good night," I said, and my voice was slightly constrained, and my steps were unsteady and reluctant as I left the room and walked up the stairs.

That night I slept fitfully. I heard noises in the garden and got up to look out several times. I heard Charli move around her room a couple of times and I lay awake thinking about spring rain, and the sound of the sea, and the feeling of a hand turning lifeless as it slips out of your grip.

I woke up with a bad headache and stumbled into the bathroom for a couple of pills. I went back to bed and waited for the pain to subside. It didn't take too long, and it was good to feel the pain just gradually melt away. Then I noticed the smell of fresh coffee and heard movement in the kitchen. A French rapper was on the radio and the sky had small fluffy clouds racing across it.

I got up, dressed and headed downstairs, feeling older than I had done for some time.

Both cats were happily munching some food, fresh bread was on the table and the coffee was ready. Charli turned the radio down a bit and handed me a bowl of coffee. Outside, a strong breeze was stirring through the bushes and prodding at the trees.

"It almost feels like being next to the sea this morning."

"Thanks for getting the bread, and for the coffee."

"Yvonne sends her love. I think she's suspicious of me. She thinks I am your secret lover."

I drank my coffee and tried not to rise to her bait.

"We need to go shopping today." I said. "I have to go out a couple of times first, so I can't see us doing it until this afternoon. Do you have any plans for today?"

She shook her head. "Nathalie said I should go over some time and she would let me have a look in Lew's bedroom. She thought I might find something of his to keep as a memento. Do you think I could come with you when you see her this morning?"

"I don't see any problem with that." Then I thought about the incident yesterday afternoon and asked Charli, "Weren't you a little bit worried about going out for bread, this morning?"

"I thought about it last night. I thought, he isn't going to try to kidnap me on the streets of Chabrassonne, and there's no way that he can spot me without being spotted himself. And if he did follow me back here you could always bash him on the head with your rolling pin."

I laughed and drank more of my coffee, "You're quite amazing." I said without thinking.

"You are quite amazing, yourself!" and she got up and kissed me on both cheeks before kissing my bruised forehead. "Let's have something to eat."

I asked he if she had found anything interesting in the book she had been reading the night before.

"Not really. Did you know they used to make hats here?"

I said I had known. A number of places around here had specialised in them. I told her about the hat factory next to the Pecheur's offices and she go up saying that there were a couple of photos in the book showing what was probably the factory.

She was flicking through the book as she came back into the kitchen and said she had also seen a couple of pictures that might have been Lucas and someone that looked a bit like his brother or father. First, she showed me the factory. It was a strange building, like a vast shed. There was a picture of people in the factory working on different stages of making hats. Everyone was very sombre looking and dressed like nineteenth century peasants. However, the date on the caption showed that it was taken in the middle of the nineteen thirties. I looked more closely at the faces. You could easily fall into the trap of matching the faces of people you knew to the ones in the photograph, regardless of the facts. I saw a man very similar to Georges Dupont, but Georges was not from this area, and so it could not have been a relative of his. I saw a young woman that looked quite like Yvonne. She was sitting very erect and proper with a very stern expression on her face. But beneath the hard look there seemed to be a great sense of mischief ready to bubble through at any minute. Of course, I could just be ascribing my own knowledge of Yvonne onto this stern young woman's image. Charli leaned over me and pointed the same woman out saying, "It looks like she was about to burst out laughing, don't you think?"

Redemption song

Just at that point Charli leaned on my shoulder and I let out a little involuntary grunt as the pain drove through me. "I'm sorry," she said and moved to lean on my other shoulder. She spoke into my right ear that she would rub some pain killing gel into that shoulder after breakfast then she leant over me again and turned the pages of the book until she found a picture of the chateau.

"That's the building on the top of the hill above the town. Something happened there during the war." She said.

"Does it say anything about it?" I wondered.

"Not really. Look."

There was a picture of a very erect looking, woman wearing what looked like a tweed jacket and a long tweed skirt. She had a bunch of flowers held casually in one hand and a pair of secateurs in the other. She was standing by the French windows that looked out onto the patio and gardens that I had sat in earlier in the week. The caption said it was Madame Clotilde Groussard. The photo was from around the late thirties. It had a very potted history of the chateau and then a few enigmatic sentences about a trial that had taken place soon after the Second World War regarding the belief that some Resistants had been murdered by the Milice in the grounds of the chateaux. Madame Clotilde Groussard had died shortly before the trial was due to start, and as she was a key witness, the case had been very unsatisfactory. It did not mention names or anything useful. Over the page was what looked like a reproduction of a postcard of the town with the chateau towering over it. I pointed to it and Charli said, "Yes, the picture must have been taken near where Valerie now lives."

Charli then showed me a picture of the village football team from the early nineteen twenties and pointed out two boys that could have been Lucas and Marc. No names were given, but the picture really emphasised the differences between the two brothers. I didn't say this to Charli, but I thought the picture very strange.

Firstly, Nathalie did not come from Chabrassone. Secondly, both boys seemed to be of about the same age. Of course, they might not have been relatives of Lucas and Marc. We might have been looking at poorly produced, indistinct black and white images and using them to create a fiction.

Charli said, "They have got to be related to Lew and Marc, don't you think?"

"Could be." I said and closed the book, "Is there any more coffee?"

I looked at the clock and debated whether it would be discourteous to phone Charles at a quarter to nine in the morning. Just a few days ago I would not have worried about such niceties but today I was thinking of the sorts of things I wanted to ask Charles and I wanted him to be as open as possible when I started asking the questions.

I looked around for my mobile and remembered that I had connected it to its charger the night before, so I went through to the study to get it. In passing I moved the computer's mouse and scanned my emails. There was one from Charles

Patron, which surprised me. I clicked on it and it informed me that he had intended to give me a copy of the article he had mentioned the other day but had left it in his brief case by mistake. So, here was a copy in the attached file. I double clicked the attachment and printed it out as I disconnected my phone and put the charger back in my desk drawer. I took one look at the picture in the article and folded the two sheets of paper in half before placing them in the drawer with my charger.

Back in the kitchen I sat down and called Charles Groussard's number. I got his answer machine and left a short message telling him that I would like to pop 'round and see him sometime today. Then I phoned Nathalie's home number. She picked it up almost immediately and when I asked her if she minded Charli coming along with me there was only a little pause before she said, "Of course, that would be lovely. She can spend some time in Lucas' room while we talk." I told her that I thought that was a good idea and put the phone down.

"Thank you, "said Charli, "Now let's see what we can do about your shoulder."

There were a few items of medication that the doctor had left with me after his examination the other evening. I had studiously ignored them all, just bundling them into the medicine cupboard in the bathroom, but Charli had obviously been studying them carefully. One was a tube of clear ibuprofen gel. When she started to unbutton my shirt, I stopped her, telling her that I still knew how to take my own shirt off. What I did not say was how unsettling it was to have a young woman unbutton my shirt for me. I think she could tell, or at least that is how I interpreted her smile as she stood back to watch.

She made quite a bit of comment about my various bruises and insisted on prodding every one of them. Some hurt and some were just blotches of colour, but I felt every single touch as if they were little electric shocks. She stroked my stomach, where the bruising was still pretty bad and not at all superficial. "Perhaps I should rub some of this on here too," she said, and I had to take a deep breath before insisting that the shoulder was the place she should focus on.

The swelling in my shoulder was very pronounced and the whole area from the shoulder down to almost my elbow on my left side was tender. The gel was cold, and her touch was incredibly gentle with just enough firmness behind it to make sure the gel was absorbed in my skin. I tingled and ached, and a considerable amount of pleasure washed over me as she massaged and rubbed my shoulder and arm. It was hypnotic and electrifying and when she had finished, she massaged my neck saying she still had a little gel on her hands and that it shouldn't go to waste. Close to my ear she said gently, "Are you sure you don't want me to rub your stomach, too?" and I almost lost the will to resist.

"Thanks, that was wonderful." I said and fumbled for my shirt. "I think I need to go out and buy some meat. Do you want to come out with me?"

Redemption song

"Sure," she said, and then she kissed me on the top of my head before crossing to the kitchen sink to wash her hands.

I watched her silhouetted against the window. The sun was still strong, but the white fluffy clouds seemed to be gathering together. They would soon crowd out the warmth, the wind was building, and it looked like a storm was heading our way.

Chapter Eleven

It was cold enough for us to need jackets. Charli borrowed one from the hat stand. It seemed to engulf her, but she still managed to make it look stylish. I was worrying that I might be growing just a bit too biased as we walked through the streets towards the market square.

I had forgotten that it was a market day. Small stalls and odd people with bits of jumble and junk littered the side streets leading to the main market square. Old books and redundant light fittings vied for attention with a rack of antique dresses and a homemade display of knives, saws and blades. I said hello to a variety of people both on the streets and behind stalls and jumble. It was one of the things that helped make this place special for me, and I could see by Charli's expression that she loved the atmosphere and rich chaos of it all.

It gave me a chance to buy some locally produced cheeses and various dried meats and sausages. I was tempted by a couple of rabbits until I saw Charli's face. We moved on and she pointed out a fruit stall where we bought peaches and plums and some big green apples. Eventually, we reached the butcher's shop. Walking through the doorway took us from noisy bustle to quiet calm sealed by the closing of the door. I had been coming to Monsieur Gilles Deloffre's shop for almost ten years, but he still treated me very formally every time I went to buy some of his excellent meat. I had been planning to buy a mixture of things, mainly to freeze, but the ideas were vague in my mind and I had been waiting to see what he had on offer before I made my decision.

"Good morning Monsieur, what do you have for me today?"

"Good morning monsieur, Mademoiselle. I have some mouton you might like, and I've kept back some wild boar because I know you like it so much."

We entered into a discussion about meat and Charli left us to wander around the shop. Eventually, she stood by the window, looking out into the crowd as I watched Monsieur Deloffre bone the mouton for me. He wrapped everything in white paper with his shop's name printed in one corner and put them all in a plastic bag. I thanked him and turned to leave. Charli was still standing by the window. "He's just across there, John. I think he's waiting for me to come out of the shop. Look."

I followed the direction of her gaze and there was Mitch, hunched against one of the pillars holding up the roof of the old market. He was watching people go by, but his gaze casually kept returning to the door of the butcher's shop. I pulled out my phone and called Georges Dupont.

"Hello Georges. I'm sorry to be disturbing you like this, but I wonder if you are still looking for the chap who drives the VW van?"

"It's you, John. Good morning. Don't tell me you have found him again!"

"I'm afraid so. He's standing in the market square. He seems to be following me. What would you like me to do? Let him sneak up on me as I carry my shopping home?"

"Where exactly are you, John?"

"I'm standing in M. Deloffre's shop, looking out of his window straight into the gaze of someone who might know something about Lucas Pecheur's death. M. Deloffre is a very kind and patient man but I'm sure he doesn't want me cluttering up his shop."

"Perhaps you should just leave the shop and let him follow you?"

"Well, Georges, I have a guest with me. A young lady who's a good friend of my son and I don't want her involved in any of this." It seemed strange negotiating with Georges like this. I wondered what was going on.

"OK John. I have a couple of my colleagues with me and we're quite close to the market. If you and your friend could leave the shop and walk towards Rue St Francois."

"Towards the hotel?"

"Yes. We'll be walking towards you. What is he wearing? That little bit of information might help."

Redemption song

"He has on a brown jacket over a deep blue shirt. He has no hat, is wearing jeans and cowboy boots, dark hair, two-day growth of stubble, long arms with his hands currently stuffed into the jacket pockets." He repeated this to his colleagues as I dictated it to him, then he rang off with the promise that they would see me soon.

I apologised to M. Deloffre and we walked out of the shop. Charli held onto my arm with one hand and carried a bag of fruit with the other. I was laden down with the other bags. "Don't look in his direction." I told her. "Smile at me and tell me about the best meal you have ever eaten."

"What?" she looked up at me, "Why?"

"M. Deloffre's meat is outstanding. Tonight, I'm going to cook some of it and show you that I'm telling the truth."

We were near the corner of the market, pushing our way through the crowds with Mitch trying to keep up. I didn't want to look back but there were enough windows to give me little glimpses of him shouldering his way towards us. I thought that he was probably aiming to reach us just after we moved into the relative quiet of the little side street Georges had asked us to head for.

There were a smaller number of ad hoc peddlers on this side of the market, and as we started past them into the Rue St Francois, I noticed Georges walking towards us with two other men. One of them was a policeman I recognised from my little trip to Lavelanet. He had been the driver. I saw the recognition in his face as we approached them. Behind me I heard a voice calling out something that could have been Charli and I glimpsed her face. It was white and rigid with fear.

Georges and one policeman passed to our right and the other policeman went to our left. It was as if we had just passed through a small group of friends walking together. Casually they headed for Mitch and then there was a muffled grunt and we turned to see Georges standing in front of Mitch who was being held by the other two policemen. Georges nodded at me and I took Charli to one side as the four men walked past us, heading for the police station. Mitch didn't even look at us and Georges paused just long enough to say, "See, it was simple, after all. I might call you later. OK?"

"Sure." Then they were away, and we were heading back through the market towards the house.

"Are you alright?" I asked as we entered the house.

"Yes. How do you think he found me? Do you think he saw me when I went to buy bread?" She was shivering and hugging herself as she stood in the middle of the kitchen.

"I think he was hanging around in the market, hoping to see you. If he'd seen you earlier, I think he might have tried to intercept you. He was prepared to try to talk to you, even with me around, so if he had seen you earlier, he wouldn't have hesitated."

She still looked pretty shaky as I walked around the kitchen putting things in the 'fridge, freezer and cupboards. I looked at the clock on the wall and realised that it was ten thirty. We had half an hour to get ourselves to Nathalie's. I asked Charli if she still wanted to go and she said of course, then left the room saying she needed to go to the toilet. I could hear her being sick in the toilet as I stood at the bottom of the stairs and I wondered at the fear Mitch had been able to generate in her. Then I walked through to the study and fished out the printout of the article sent to me by Charles Patron. I looked it over briefly, then I folded it up again and stuffed it in my jacket pocket.

The wind was dying down as I looked out of the window. Trees that had been waving over the tops of the roofline had calmed to an occasional shake, but the clouds seemed to be growing deeper and darker at a steady rate. I heard Charli come down the stairs behind me and before I could turn, I heard her say that she was sorry. "It's like a knot that keeps tightening in my stomach. The tension was becoming greater and greater. I kept thinking about what Mitch must have done to poor Lew and when I saw him out there in the marketplace, waiting for me, I could have died!"

"Do you mind walking? I think it won't rain until later today and it seems silly to take the car." I turned and she was standing in the doorway still looking pale and very vulnerable, but I could see a defiant spirit displayed in her body language. It was clear in the way she stood and the way she turned her head to look from me to the sky outside.

"I think the walk would do us both good." I walked towards her, "But I'll take an umbrella, anyway."

"Very English." She said in an attempt to sound English, but it sounded quite strained, as if she was trying to force herself to be more light-hearted. As I was locking the front door, I heard the telephone ring, but I decided to leave it. They would either leave a message or call my mobile.

We walked up towards the chateau at the top of the town and crossed over the bridge where I had intercepted Nathalie only a couple of days before. Charli and I talked a little about the chateau and the church we passed, then I pointed up to the Chapel of Calvary and we talked about the path on the other side of the hill. I said that if we had time before I had to leave for London, I would take her up and show her where I had found Lucas. It was while I was saying this that I realised that I had very little time left before I was due to go back to see my son and daughters.

"One of these days, perhaps I can come with you to London and meet your family." She said. I agreed that one day she would do that.

As we reached the Pecheur residence, a strong gust of wind brought with it a feeling of light drizzle, but it passed without turning into rain. It was as if the spray from a garden sprinkler had been blown across us.

By the time we reached the front door Nathalie was opening it and welcoming us in.

Although the house was quite new, probably less than ten years old, the interior had an old-fashioned feel. Perhaps it was more rustic, I thought, but certainly not cheap. The house was clean and very tidy, the carpets were thick and there was a quietness that always seemed to me to come with expensive furniture and the smell of polish. We were ushered into the living room and Nathalie brought in a large tray with coffee and a plate full of very nice pastries. I thought that they probably came from one of the more refined patisseries in one of the larger of the local towns such as Mirepoix, Quillan or Lavelanet.

I asked where Philip was, and she explained that this was one of the business' busiest days. Of course, it was Saturday and the Pecheur business sold to co-operatives and individual farmers, many of whom made a great deal of the fact that farming was a seven-day, twenty-four hour a day job. If you were selling to the farming community, you visited them at their convenience, showed that you, too, worked longer hours than those outside the community, and you showed them sympathy and respect. So, Saturday was naturally Philip and Marc's busiest day of the week. On Sunday, for some, you needed to be seen at Mass.

Nathalie asked me how I felt and if I was recovering well. Charli told her about how badly swollen my shoulder was, but refrained from talking about my stomach, and we had a brief conversation about Marc and his wife. I then told her that I thought that the police might have the prime suspect for Lucas' murder in custody.

She was shocked and asked me how I knew. I explained what had happened on the way back from Carcassonne and told her about earlier this morning. Then I suggested that it would probably be best to keep this knowledge to herself for the moment, as I was not sure what the outcome would be.

Charli said, "But they have him now. Surely that's the end of it?"

"I think they have proof that Mitch was here at the time of Lucas' death. They have information from other police sources to link the two of them together, and I think that there will be information from the police on the coast indicating that Lucas was being sought by a gang they were both connected to. But those things do not make much of a case for the prosecution."

There was a silence, then Nathalie asked, "Do you think it was this man Mitch?"

"There's a good likelihood that he's the one," I said. "If they can find evidence connecting Lucas with Mitch it may swing the whole thing."

"Evidence? Such as what?" Nathalie persisted.

"Well, Lucas must've been in Mitch's van. Perhaps Lucas was not killed at the scene. I think he didn't die there, but I'm no expert in these matters. I think that if Mitch is involved, his van will be full of evidence and Lucas's clothes and hair will also provide links." They both looked at me for more. "You know, blood traces, fibres, oil, dirt, fingerprints, that sort of thing."

We finished our coffee and Nathalie poured some more for myself and Charli, then showed her up to Lucas' bedroom. It was where he had stayed just before it had all happened. He had taken a small bag of things with him when he went to the house in town, but everything from his most recent visit back through to his early life was contained in that room. I stayed in my seat and waited. When Nathalie came downstairs again, she closed the living-room door behind her.

"She seems like quite a resilient girl. When I first met her, I thought that she was quite frail and frightened, but she's stronger than she looks."

I agreed and sipped my coffee. Nathalie took a little pastry and put it on her plate. Despite its size, she proceeded to cut it into smaller pieces with a suitably small dessert fork.

"Did you want to tell me about Lucas?" I asked. I was beginning to feel an urgent need to get all of this over and done with.

"Yes. It's been hard for us all. You can hardly imagine what has been going through everyone's minds and yet, I have had so many different emotions pushing and pulling at me, ever since… well since a long time."

She poured herself some more coffee and nibbled a fragment of pastry.

"You seem to have realised that Lucas was different to my other children." I knew what she meant by different, but I didn't want to prompt her anymore. "He was not Philip's. There, I've said it! You are the only one I've ever told, apart from his father, and that was a disaster!"

"And his father?" I had to prompt. She was struggling to tell me, but she needed some sort of encouragement.

"Lucas is Charles' son."

"Charles?"

"Charles Limon. Lucas was his son." I had felt that this was the case for a while, but I was so glad to hear it being said by Natalie.

"When Philip was really struggling to get the business going, he would spend days virtually sleeping in the old offices he had inherited from his father. I had two children to look after and was struggling, too. We had arguments and said and did terrible things to each other. Then one day someone crashed into the back of my car as I was driving back from my parent's home in Ax les Thermes. The swine just took off after knocking me into the stone cliff at the side of the road. I had the two children in the back, Lucas and Diane, it was raining. Everyone was just driving past, ignoring me. Then Charles came on the scene. He was polite and charming, he took care of everything, and brought us home safely. It turned out he was stationed here, and he visited me a few times to make sure I was all right, and to tell me how he'd tried to find out the culprit.

It seemed so natural. During one of his visits he commented on a small bruise here," She pointed to her left temple just behind her eye, "I admitted that Philip had hit me, and before we knew what we were doing we were making love! The affair lasted for several months. It was a very intense time. Then, Charles was temporarily posted to Toulouse, and when he came back, he just seemed to ignore me completely. That was the end! I felt so bad about the whole thing that it drove me very close to suicide. If I'd not been pregnant, I think I probably would have done it."

"Did you ever tell Philip?"

"Absolutely not! It would have destroyed our marriage. It did not take much to encourage him to believe that Lucas was his son."

"And did you tell Limon. I mean Charles?"

"Not then."

"When did you tell him?"

"I decided to tell him when I met him one day, when Lucas had just started collège. He walked into the bank when I was queuing up with Lucas. Charles bumped his briefcase into Lucas' back and apologised. I was standing with my back to them both and didn't want to turn around when I heard Charles' voice. They seemed to be getting on OK, so I continued to look in the other direction and hoped that I wouldn't be noticed.

When it was my turn to go to the till I just walked over and hoped that Lucas would follow, but he just kept on chatting with Charles. Then, when I was finished with the teller, I turned and saw the expression on Charles' face change. I said hello to him then walked past, telling Lucas to hurry up."

"Is that when he began to bully Lucas?"

"No, I really do think that was my all fault. I began to worry that I'd made a grave mistake by not telling Charles about Lucas. The way his expression changed when he realised he was chatting with my son had frightened me. I thought that it would better if Charles understood."

"So, you told him?"

"I tried." she continued, becoming more and more upset as she told the story, "It was late autumn, the trees were almost bare, and it was raining. I called up Charles and told him that we had to meet. He just did not want to see me at all, but I insisted. So, he told me to wait up by St Joseph's church and I walked up there and stood by the door waiting for almost an hour watching the rain just drop. It was cold, too. I was worried that it was getting late and I needed to get back to prepare for the children coming home from school. Lucas and his sister were now studying on the same school site, although she was in the lycée by then, and the bus back to Chabrassonne arrived promptly at five thirty every day.

Then Charles arrived and told me to get into his car and he drove us off at high speed. I was frightened, but he wouldn't stop. He drove until we were just beyond a place called Bouriege."

"Yes, I know the place. I walked through there earlier this summer on my way to Alet les Bain. It's quite a way from here. Further by road, too."

"At least twenty kilometres over small, country roads. He stopped and I started to tell him that he was Lucas' father. That I had not told him before because he had been so cold and dismissive at the end of our affair. He jumped to the wrong conclusion and started saying that I could not threaten him. The only person I would hurt, if I told about our affair, would be me. He called me some terrible names. He was nothing like the person I'd known all those years before! He was sneering at me when I repeated that Lucas was his son, not

Philip's, and that I'd seen the strong resemblance when I saw the two of them together at the bank.

I tried to explain my fears and worries, I was not going to tell anyone about the affair but I wanted him to know the truth. Then, when I finished telling him all of this, his face grew wilder and uglier, like a madness was overtaking him. He then started to shout at me telling me to get out, get out. It was pouring with rain and I did not want to leave the car. I wanted to go home.

Then he just leaned over me and opened the door and simply pushed me out. One minute I was sitting on the car seat, the next I was on the gravel by the side of the road. Then he just drove off!" She was just controlling her sobs, but it was getting harder for her. I walked over and sat next to her with my arm on her shoulder.

"There I was in the pouring rain in the middle of nowhere, and my children would be home from school at any minute. I stood up and watched as his car disappeared over the brow of a hill, then I turned towards Chabrassonne and started walking. After a couple of kilometres, I entered Bouriege. I was soaked to the skin and shivering, and an old lady called to me from one of the houses. She took me in and got her son to take me back home in an old Renault van that must have been with the family since before the war. I was so grateful I didn't know what to say. After dropping me off outside my gate, he wound his window down and said to me that if my old man ever did that again to me, I should tell him, and he would come around and knock his block off! I so wanted him to do that to Charles, but it would not have done any good. Charles had the upper hand."

"That was a terrible thing to do!" I said, "it was monstrous! And Charles began harassing Lucas after this happened?"

"Soon after. And It got worse, and I was powerless to do anything to help. I just watched my husband, my children and my ex-lover gang up to try to destroy my youngest son."

She cried for a short while on my shoulder, then went away to the kitchen to sort herself out. I stood up and looked around the room. I studied some of the photographs and looked at a couple of the paintings. One above the fireplace was a pretty good, modern painting, which I realised must have been of Nathalie. It had strong lines counterbalanced by a lightness in tone. I thought it most resembled something by Hockney, of all people, and I looked closely at the bottom where I found a thin black set of curled letters, it said 'Lucas P'.

From behind me Nathalie said, "He was good, wasn't he?"

"Very." I said, "I spoke to my son a couple of days ago and he said he remembered Lucas. He told me that Lucas had been a very talented artist, and that he'd been deeply impressed with him when they were both at that special art course up at the chateau. Do you remember?"

"Of course! That was the summer just before all of the bad business really started. I think it was the happiest summer of Lucas' life."

We then heard some footsteps coming down the stairs and Charli came into the room. Her eyes were rimmed with red and she had a slightly sheepish look on her face.

"Nathalie. I just want to say thank you." And then she walked over and held onto Nathalie as both of them began to cry.

I waited. There were still things I wanted to ask, but I'd lost my chance for the time being. I wanted to sort out so many things in my mind and I had so little time left to do it all. It was already twenty to one and I had not seen Charles Groussard, yet. I walked out into the hall and took my mobile out of my jacket pocket to see if I'd missed any calls. I must have switched it off at some point, so I pressed the button and put in my code and the phone told me I had missed three calls. Two from Charles and one from Georges.

I called Charles back and found that he was available. He sounded a bit fraught, which was quite unusual for him, but I didn't try to find out anything on the phone. I wanted to wait and see him face to face.

I walked back to the two women and told them I had to go. Charli used that as an excuse to leave, too and we hugged and kissed Nathalie, pulled our jackets on and I picked up my umbrella and looked out of the door.

"The wind has picked up again." I said and Nathalie commented that it might become too windy to use the umbrella. I looked down at it and said, "If it can survive the sort of weather you get in the north of Scotland, it will be OK here. We walked up the path with me unconsciously using it like a walking stick and I heard Nathalie comment to Charli that I looked "very English", and I shook my head which made her laugh.

"Where are we going now?" Charli asked as we headed back towards town.

"I'm going up there," I said, using the umbrella to point out the chateau.

"Can I come with you?"

"All right," I said, "but I have a couple of private matters to discuss with Monsieur Groussard. Perhaps we can arrange for you to take a little wander around the chateau while Charles and I talk?"

"Sounds wonderful!" and she really sounded quite enthusiastic.

We walked up the shorter, steeper path to the front of the chateau, rather than winding our way along the route that cars now take. That route leads first to the old stables and then past some of the old fortified thirteenth century remains. From this path we emerged onto a wide platform of garden framing the "improved frontage" built during the eighteenth and early nineteenth centuries. Looking back, you had a wonderful view of the town and the hills beyond. The dark clouds seemed to be crowding lower over the whole place, but there was still no rain.

I used the umbrella to point out the place where Valerie's house was and then we turned back towards the chateau and walked along the path to the great front doors. As we reached the steps, Limon slipped out of the door and turned towards us. His face took on a strangely hungry look, as if he had just finished his starters and was ready for the main course, and he walked purposefully towards us. I noticed that he was not in his usual formal grey clothes. He had a pair of jeans with paint splatters of different colours on the legs and his t-shirt under his jacket was dark blue and marked with paint, too.

He walked straight up to me and, without speaking, he feigned a left jab at my face. Without thinking I moved my right arm up to block it and swung the handle of the umbrella into his face. It was completely unintentional and a reaction to his move, but he leapt back as if I had clubbed him viciously with the handle. In surprise, I walked towards him as he stumbled backwards holding his cheek, then he recovered enough to stop and pushed passed me muttering something under his breath that I just couldn't catch.

I looked from the retreating figure to the surprised look on Charli's face and then to the front door, which was now standing open. Charles Groussard was staring at me with a terribly shocked expression on his face.

"Hello Charles," I said, "You have some strange guests today! How are you?" I transferred the umbrella to my left hand and walked up to shake his hand.

His gaze moved from Limon, as he disappeared around the corner of the house, to Charli, and then to me. His hand automatically raised to mine, and I introduced him to Charli. He nodded and greeted her almost absent-mindedly, then let us into the house.

As we walked across the great, bare entrance hall, which always reminded me more of a large stone porch, than of anything else, I noticed that Charles was smelling distinctly of wood smoke, as if he had just been lighting a BBQ or bonfire. We walked in, went through another doorway and crossed the large, dark room feeling the benefit of its thick carpeting, and the large fire in the hearth below a great gilded mirror. This was a more comfortable, warmer room to be in. We were offered coffee and both of us declined, and we stood in front of the fire looking into the flames. Everyone seemed to be waiting for me to decide how the meeting was going to develop.

"I said to Charli that we would need a few minutes talking on some private matters, and that she might be allowed to look at part of the house."

"Of course," Charles shook himself out of his vague uncertainty and said, "Let me show you where you might go, my dear. I had some guidebooks printed a couple of years ago, let me see." And they walked over to a large sideboard where Charles pulled open a drawer and I saw him opening a booklet, pointing to a couple of things in it and then pointing her towards the door opposite the fireplace. He was talking quite softly to her and I could not make out what he was saying. She seemed to wait patiently until he was finished, then she walked away, out of the room.

We sat on two chairs close to the fire and I asked him why Limon had been to see him.

"It was a private matter." He tried to brush the subject to one side.

"Was it to do with his actions as a police officer, or the feud between the Limons and the Pecheurs?"

As he hesitated, I pulled the printout of the article from my jacket pocket and opened it in front of Charles.

"It seems like quite a family affair, Charles. Doesn't it?" He looked at the article, and I could see some of the pompous front deflate. "This trial. It involves Limon's father or his uncle? And was it Philip's father or uncle? And the judge, Charles? How close a relation was he to you?"

"Limon's father, Pecheur's uncle and my father." He pointed to each name on the printout.

"And of course, there's this house, your great aunt and the possibility of a few murders, too."

"It was a long time ago, John, and France was a place tearing itself apart. It should have stayed as history. Arguing about it now is pointless. It makes a mockery of what happened."

"And what exactly did happen?"

"I'm not sure anyone alive really knows." Charles got up and poked the fire with a beautiful, wrought iron poker. I watched as the sparks floated up the chimney and realised that the smoke smell on his clothes had nothing to do with this fire.

"That article is a complete nonsense, really. It tries to sensationalise and trivialise things. Limon and Pecheur were part of the acting administration during the war. They were both involved in resistance work, but there were a lot of rivalries. A lot of conflicts brought on by ideologies and personality cults. Leaders of small groups tried to dictate everything, creating major problems for others. Limon and Pecheur were not in the Milice. The Milice was a militia set up mainly by the pro-nazis and fascists after the Allied Forces invaded Algeria. That action caused great confusion, brought about the downfall of Maréchal Pétain's government and turned some Frenchmen to the idea that perhaps the Americans and English really were the enemy after all.

The two men, Pecheur and Limon, were on the borderline, and sadly in Chabrassonne, a small faction of the resistance pushed their hand at the wrong time."

"They shot the resistance members up here, at the chateau." I said it as a fact, and he shook his head.

"That's just it. It really isn't clear what happened. Remember, they were both patriots. My great aunt never liked either of them. Pecheur had been the deputy head of the police when the war broke out, and he was moved up to the top position when the authorities didn't like what his boss was saying and doing. His boss was my great aunt's best friend. I don't know, but I think that they had been lovers and had gradually settled into a deep friendship, but he was a 'gentleman' and Pecheur was a 'brute'. You can see what it was like. Limon had been the mayor and, as such, was a key member of the local administration. She didn't like either of them.

Redemption song

There was an incident and shots were fired. One of the people was hit and blood was spilled, but the records all say that the three members of the resistance were arrested and deported to a camp in Germany. My aunt made the claims and built up such a hatred and anger towards the two men that when the war ended, they were nearly lynched. You know, such things happened in a number of places! My aunt was dead by the time it went to court, and no one really wanted to look at the records in detail for the truth. Even the priest had believed old Clotilde! He had even arranged a requiem Mass for them shortly after the incident."

"But there was a trial and they were acquitted."

"Again, that was a mess. There was an official enquiry first of all, and, once they looked at them, it was shown that the records were clear – there seemed to be no doubt about what had happened. Local opinion tried to force a trial, but there were all sorts of more important things going on for the authorities to want to be side-tracked by something like this. Then Pecheur, I think his name was Jules," I nodded that it had been Jules, "Yes, Jules had been suffering from depression. You have to understand that he had been keeping the police together during a very difficult time, and he'd suffered horrendous abuse from those around him. He committed suicide, and his note claimed that he had been 'responsible' for the deaths of the three men. Of course, he was referring to the fact that they had all died in a Nazi concentration camp, and that he had put them there. But that was enough to cause the whole thing to explode again. The idiot who was in charge of the suicide investigation made the note public, and there had to be a trial. My father was the presiding judge, it was a media fest, but it ended by clearing both men – Limon and, posthumously, Pecheur."

"So, what about the painting?" I waved the printout of the article at him.

He pushed the paper back down onto the low table with his finger pointing to the image. "That was nobody's fault, really."

"It destroyed Lucas."

"You think so?"

"Yes. So much of the story of Lucas stems from that conflict, and probably from that painting, too."

"Well, Lucas was a very bright young lad with a wonderful talent. He could draw whatever he saw or imagined. Such a waste!"

"But why did he paint the thing?"

Charles sighed and sat back in his chair. It took him a minute to answer my question.

"It was rumour that drove it. One of the kids in his class cut out a small article in a local paper about the trial and accused him of being one of a family of cowards. Fights were started and most of them ended with Lucas as the looser. He grew very bitter about the whole thing. Then, at a special summer course we had here with a couple of local artists, he painted this damn thing. The two artists were thrilled. It was like Goya's picture of a firing squad, you know, the one called 'The Third of May'? I was not around that day and the finished work was taken away and the two artists wanted to display it in their gallery and drum up interest for this new, bright young artist.

What they didn't know was that they were stirring up a hornets' nest. There, clearly in the painting, are the faces of Philip as one of the gunmen shooting the resistance fighters, and Charles Limon giving the order to fire! You know what the press can do to something like that! A local police inspector and a local prominent businessman, and there is the businessman's son pointing the finger at them!"

"Why did he do it?"

"Lucas?" Charles spluttered, "He didn't even think about what he was doing. He was working out his own personal problems in the way he knew best. You or I might run it through in our mind, over and over again until we had pushed it through our systems, or we might have written about it our diaries. Lucas painted and sketched his problems away. Only this time he was catapulted into the air like a clay pigeon and everyone took pot shots at him. The artists dropped him like he had the plague; his father and brother had always been ambivalent towards him and now they just turned on him; and then, Limon turned his full fury on the boy, too. Nothing could stop him!"

"Weren't you in a position to stop him?"

"Me? No! How could I have done anything?"

"Have you no position of authority here?" I had come here to find out more about Charles and had learned about everyone but him, to this point.

"Me? I know what you are getting at. I just happened to have inherited this house. I was a solicitor in Paris, nothing more, and people here have nicknamed me the 'Judge' because I look quite a lot like my father, who was one, but I am no more a judge than you are. I've done some legal consultancy work for various people over the years, but I have no authority here! I'm not one of your landed aristocracy such as you have in England."

I didn't labour the point, instead I asked about Limon, again. I wanted to know why he had been here.

"He knew that I still had the original of the painting. He thought that I had shown it to the paper, the one that produced this garbled nonsense. I had kept the painting because I felt responsible for it when the artists returned it, but I didn't want to destroy it. The idiot had not worked out that several newspapers in the area must have photographic negatives of the painting. I dare say that could phone up any local paper tomorrow and order a dozen copies of it and they would be on my desk by the next day, with an invoice for a few Euros per print. He just couldn't understand."

"So, he came here and bullied you until you destroyed the painting?"

Charles looked both tired and exasperated. "I had no choice! The man is absolute poison! It broke my heart, but I let him do it. I lit a fire in the garden," He pointed out of the window, "and he smashed up the original and fed it to the flames. I felt like pushing him in after it, but I am not like you, John."

"What do you mean?"

269

"I have no physical courage. I just crumpled under the pressure."

I didn't want to argue, but I didn't feel any courage inside me. Just a deep sadness as I put some more of the story together.

"Thank you, Charles. You've explained a lot. I wish I'd come to you earlier."

"Don't thank me John. I may not have told you this a few days ago. Lucas' death shook me. It hurt me, you know. I really liked the young man. I just wanted to help him in some way, but he never really trusted me. Not after the painting incident. He occasionally accepted my help or hospitality, but I was never more than a convenient dupe to him. I think he stopped liking or trusting anyone after that summer."

I stood up and shook his hand. "Let's go and see where Charli is." I pulled out my mobile and scrolled through the numbers until I found hers and pressed the call button. She answered as we walked out of the room that we had been sitting in. "Charli? We've done our talking. Where are you?"

She was in a front room on the first floor looking out over the town and agreed to come down the main staircase and meet us in the hall.

We said thank you, and I told Charles that I would be away for a few days as I had to see my family and sort out some things in London. I told him I would call him on my return and would invite him around for a meal. We walked out the big front door and began our descent to the town with a gusty wind tugging and pushing at us all the way.

Ian Smith

Once through the door Charli trotted upstairs and I walked into the kitchen. There were two messages on the answer machine. Both were from Georges wanting me to call him. I called him on the home phone, and it took a few rings before he answered.

"Ah, John, thank goodness you returned my call. Is that young lady still with you?"

"What do you mean, with me?"

"Is she still in your home?"

"I think so, Georges. I have just returned from visiting Charles Groussard. Do you want me to see if she is around so you can speak to her?"

"No! No! Just keep her there. Don't let her leave. I'll be around in a minute and I'll explain everything."

He seemed quite excited, and more than a little triumphant. I pulled out some note paper and a pen from the drawer and put it on the table then I trotted up and knocked on Charli's door. She opened it and I said, "Grab your things and come downstairs, quickly!" and turned to go back down.

"What? Everything?"

"Yes, everything!" I put as much urgency into my voice as I could. She was down in the kitchen very shortly after me.

"Here, write me a note to me saying that you are sorry, but you have to go away for a while. Say thank you and sign your name. Quickly!"

She looked at me and scribbled the note. I folded it and said, "Write John here."

She did and I put it on the table. I unlocked the door to the garden and gave her the key to the garage. Go and unlock the garage door but leave the key in the lock. Just inside the door there are two light switches. Put on the one furthest from the door then go to the work benches on the other side of the garage. On the floor you will see a small trap door. Use the little handle on it to lift the door up and go down the steps. OK? Close the door behind you and keep quiet."

"Why? What's going on?"

"Do you want the police to take you in for questioning?"

Her face turned pale. "I've got to go." Her voice was very strained and low, and she tried to push past me to go out of the front door.

"No time. This is the only chance you've got."

She couldn't even look at my face. She looked at the kitchen floor, then out to the garden, then she ran.

I pushed the kitchen door but didn't close it properly, then I put the kettle on and walked through to the study to have a look at my emails. I was just about to start checking them when a gentle knocking began on my front door.

I went down and opened the door and let Georges and his colleague in.

"Come in Georges. Charli does not seem to be around at the moment. Must have popped out for something. I've just put the kettle on, would you like some coffee?"

"Later, John. Are you sure she's not here?"

"Well I looked around the house and called out to her, but she doesn't seem to be here. What's going on Georges?"

"In a minute," He said again. "Which room is she in?"

"She's in the one to the left at the top of the first set of stairs."

Georges nodded to his colleague who trotted up and took a look at the room.

"Not here, sir. Looks like she took everything with her."

I looked at Georges, "That's strange? She knew I was only going to be out for a short while!"

"Let's go and sit down," Georges said. "I need to explain. In the meantime, I think my colleague should just do a quick check around, just in case she's somewhere in the house."

I looked at Georges with what I hoped would appear to be a vaguely confused expression on my face and said that by all means they should do what they thought was best.

I followed him into the kitchen and sat down facing him. He picked up the folded piece of note paper and said, "Is this from her?"

"I don't know. It must be as its not in any handwriting I recognise." I read it and passed it over to him telling him how strange this all was.

"John. I must tell you. The young lady you may think of as Lucas' girlfriend is a very dangerous young woman."

"What? Charli?"

"Yes, Charli. Charline Jacqin is wanted for a whole string of different offences from straightforward theft to con tricks, and from prostitution to drug dealing."

"Wow!"

Redemption song

"And she was involved in Lucas' murder."

"How? She was the one who pointed us towards that young thug, Mitch."

"I think she was planning to have put a great deal of distance between herself and this place before we caught Mitch! She's apparently been looking for a large stash of money and jewellery which Lucas appears to have been hiding from them."

"So, Mitch was trying to find out where the loot was when he killed Lucas?" I asked.

"Mitch claims that it was Charli that killed Lucas, not him. John, we need to find her, and we need to do it fast!"

I looked from the note to the kitchen door and said, "Good heavens! She might have stolen my car!"

We both rushed down and opened the garage door. There was my car, untouched. I pointed to the key in the small garage door. "She must have come through here and gone out through the main garage door. She could be anywhere, now!"

We walked back towards the house and Georges was on his phone telling people to start the search. He asked me how long a head start she might have had, and I told him not more than an hour. After a series of short questions and a brief discussion about some nicotine patches which she appeared to have left behind, the two policemen began to take their leave of me.

"I want you to stay around here until we find that young lady. OK, John. She might come back. You never know."

"That's a damn nuisance," I said, "I have to get back to London by Monday evening."

"You're flying?"

"No. I was going to drive!"

"Well you will have to postpone your trip." Georges said as he left the house.

I walked back to the kitchen and opened the freezer door. Inside were some frozen leftovers of a beef stew I had made more than a month ago. I took them out and placed the containers in the microwave oven and set them to defrost. I took out some small potatoes, cleaned them, put them in a saucepan of water and lit the gas under them. I took out another saucepan and emptied the partially frozen stew into it, placed it over a low flame and walked back to the freezer. I then took out some frozen French green beans, put them in a plastic dish and placed them in the microwave. The potatoes came to the boil and I adjusted the heat so that they would boil gently as I fished out a couple of plates, cutlery, glasses and condiments. I turned the stew down to low as it began to bubble and stirred it.

Once the potatoes were cooked, I drained them, put them back in the pot, dropped a large knob of butter on them along with a small handful of chopped parsley, then covered them with the lid. I switched on the microwave and walked down to the garage.

"Come up. I know it's a bit late, but lunch is ready." I called down into the cellar and left the trap door open.

Redemption song

When she was sitting in front of me with a plateful of food and a glass of red wine, I said to her, "Now tell me, Charli. How did you end up killing poor Lucas?"

Chapter Twelve

Charli hardly hesitated between plate and mouth. She chewed her food, swallowed and said, "Is that what you believe? That I actually killed Lew?"

There was not much time left, so I answered quickly, instead.

"Don't make any mistakes here. Don't mix up facts and emotional games. I just want some truth, Charli."

"But you know I loved Lew. I couldn't have killed him."

I did pause to chew some food before I moved on.

"Charli, I have just had the police here, searching the house for you. I've hidden you and am now harbouring a wanted criminal suspected of murder. Please stop playing your games and start telling me what happened."

"You know what happened. Lew stole some money from Les Gamins and Mitch has been after him and the money ever since."

Redemption song

I sat there looking at her. She did look quite frail at this particular moment, and she seemed to resonate with a form of vulnerability that drew you in.

"It's a good story, but it won't hold up when they get you in for questioning."

"You wouldn't do that to me, would you? Don't hand me over to them!" Her eyes had grown larger and there was a look of panic and fear in her face and radiating from her body language.

"Charli, please. Talk to me. Lucas didn't steal anything from a gang. Tell me what really happened." I was beginning to feel frustrated by the silliness of this.

"What do you want me to say?"

"I told you. Just tell me the truth." She looked at me with wondering eyes as if asking me how I could do this to her and I continued, "Let's start at the time when Lucas and Mitch were travelling around conning old ladies out of their savings."

"All I know about that is what they told me afterwards."

"You know more than that." I looked at her, studying her now guarded eyes.

"Perhaps the guy they left behind is after them. Maybe he killed Lucas!"

"Charli!" I shouted, "Enough!"

Then I calmed my voice, "The neighbours will phone the police if I start shouting. Stop these stories. The gang, the gang of you three that is, was the main story. I think you made up the other one as a fallback position. Which is fine, but not here. Not now."

"It's true!"

"Everything you have told me is full of the truth, but not all of the truth, and not in the right order." She looked down and ate some more food as I continued, "One of the three of you was arrested. I am sure of that. Mitch is too thick to affect his escape from even the dumbest police, and Lucas was clever, but not the most cunning or devious of people. I vote you in as the candidate. You were picked up by the police and had to chase after them once you'd escaped."

There was more silence. She drank her wine and tried to avoid looking directly at me. So I said.

"How did the re-union work out? Was it at that point that things fell apart, or did something else cause it to end up like this?"

She let out a very deep sigh that seemed to shudder right through her whole body. She put her fork down and looked at me.

"Mitch isn't quite as stupid as he looks, but you're right. Lew could not have escaped from a school playground without help. You don't know the half of it."

"Tell me."

"We were in a small bar in a village deep in the mountains. Lew was off buying fuel and we were sitting having a beer when Mitch said he was going for a piss. I sat there looking at a magazine, he had been staring out of the window. I should have realised!"

"He'd seen the policemen and had left without warning you?"

"Like I said," her eyes were not focussed on me, anymore, "Mitch is not as stupid as he looks. I found out later that he went out into the back yard where the toilets were and climbed over a wall onto a back road then called Lew. I was left as the decoy."

She paused, so I prompted her. "You were arrested?"

"You could call it that. They started by wanting to know where the others were but then they lost interest in Lew and Mitch."

"It was like a small, concentrated drop of my life. One and a half days I was there. I let them use me like a doll. They became so excited by it all that they stopped caring about what they did. When I escaped, I left them all asleep and drunk, and I tried to set the fucking place on fire, but it didn't work. I just managed to burn out one of their cars instead!"

"This is the police?"

"They were just men. OK they had uniforms and official papers, but they did what all men want to do!"

I waited. I felt her beginning to want to tell me. She had probably never talked to anyone honestly before. Perhaps this was her chance? Then I gently prompted, "Was it hard to find Lucas and Mitch?"

She sneered, "We'd agreed on a rendezvous point; Le Lavendou. Partly because we all knew it, and partly because it was outside the areas we had been working in. They were so frightened, so worried that they might be followed, that I actually got there before them! I was waiting in the café we had agreed to meet in when they first arrived. They were so relieved and pleased they didn't even consider what I'd gone through to escape! Not one minute, not even one second!"

I poured out a little more wine for her and she gulped it down.

"Mitch wanted us to go to another area and try the same game. It had been going well before the bastards had picked me up, and they hadn't considered what it would be like if they had been caught instead of me. I mean, they had thought about it as they'd driven down to the coast, but once I was there everything was back to being OK again, and Mitch wanted more for the stash."

"I wanted a rest and he couldn't see why I needed one – after all, he was fine!"

"Lew just wanted to take the money and run, but he could see that one third of what we had was not enough. He wanted to do what I wanted and what Mitch wanted. Always trying to please everyone. It was pathetic to watch, really. They were both still boys. Anyway, I got a couple of days grace, a chance to really clean up and sleep. God, I needed the sleep!"

"Then Mitch screwed things up by trying to fence a few of our things, and a local gang took a very close interest in us. He was so fucking stupid. I could have told him what to do, but he just went out and acted as if he was in some big city where a little bit of stolen property here and there is hardly noticeable within the flood of other stuff."

"So, we got out fast and ended up in a little shit hole near Perpignan. Mitch kept running on and on about how Burgundy was ripe for the picking, and that we could catch the end of the tourist trade up there, too. He had all these stupid schemes! Lew was scared, as always, and was talking about stupid things like running a nightclub – he found a derelict building in this place and started measuring it up for his dream. Everywhere we went he would do that. One minute we were all agreeing it was another dead hole, the next he was saying we could turn this place or that place into a major night-spot."

She sat quietly for a minute. I think she was just realising that she had opened up a little, and I didn't want her to stop. She needed to keep up the momentum, so I quietly asked.

"Did you have a big argument? Was that how it happened?"

"God, no! We were always arguing! Lew suddenly got this idea that he wanted to 'take me away from all of this'. You see, I had been with both of them, off and on, you know, just casual nights for company and a bit of sex. Then before the arrest Mitch had been sort of madly in love with me, which had been a bit of a laugh, really. Then I think he sort of clammed up afterwards. He felt guilty, I thought at first, but then I became to think that he now saw me as damaged goods. I mean, you know, I did what I had to do to get out and it was somehow me to blame? Anyway, he was getting over that, but we were in this place with two bedrooms and Lew ended up sharing one

Ian Smith

with me, and he went a bit crazy for me. That was when he told me all that stuff that he always kept secret, and, of course, he made me swear never to tell anyone."

"Suddenly, he sat up in bed the night before we were due to head off to Burgundy to try our luck there and said he had had enough. He didn't want to go. He pleaded with me to come with him. He even wanted us to leave the stash behind! All of it! Get a fresh start, you know?"

I nodded and gave her just a bit more wine, and pulled the fruit bowl between us. I used a small sharp knife to cut slices of peach as I listened.

"He was so desperate to do it that I didn't know what to do. He wanted us to leave and get on the first bus that came. I mean, it was just after midnight in a shitty dump on the coast where nothing happened! I said, steal a car and we can drive it until the petrol runs out, then make a choice from there. It was the first thing that came into my head, but it caught his imagination and he was up, pulling on his trousers. 'Give me ten minutes,' he said, 'and I'll be back with a car. Pack our things and I'll see you outside. Ten minutes.' He kept repeating it as he dressed, as if it was some sort of magical formula."

"How did you feel about doing it?"

"Oh, I didn't mind, really. I was getting fed up with the game we were playing. It was only a matter of time before we got caught properly, and Mitch was even more of a liability than Lew."

283

I poured out the last of the wine as I said, "So, there you were with your bags outside, waiting for Lucas and Mitch fast asleep in the flat - is that what happened?"

"Exactly. We drove in a sort of loop. First we headed back the way we'd come earlier; Perpignan, Narbonne, Montpellier, and as he headed to Nîmes, I said, 'Hold on, I do not want us to even go past that place', so we turned off and somehow ended up in a place called Aigues-Mortes, which was even more in the middle of nowhere than we had been before! So, we went back 'round to Montpellier and eventually started driving north. We had no idea where we were going and ended up in the Cevenne, which is very beautiful, but what do you do there, diving along in a stolen car, wondering where to stop and rest?"

"Did he know that you had taken the stash of money and things?"

"Funny you should ask that. He didn't and he felt so guilty because we were stuck in the middle of nowhere, and he had no money for petrol, food or a place to stay. He was devastated! You know, he felt like he had failed me completely. And then, when we stopped the car I took out the rucksack that we used for the main stash and he was furious! We ended up having a blazing row at this stupid picnic site, with families who were just sitting down to eat their food and look at the pretty scenery. I think we must have looked a sight, too. Tired, unwashed, untidy, noisy, swearing and shouting!"

She gave out a little chuckle as if it was some sort of family reminiscence, and carried on, "It was crazy. I think we said about everything and anything we could possibly say to hurt each other, but we never got to the point of hitting out with our fists. I tell you, it came close for me!"

"Then, one minute we were standing facing each other across a picnic table shouting in each other's faces and the next he was in the car, turning it in a swerving circle with the little stones flying around like bullets. He stopped and threw my bag at me from the car and drove off! Just like that."

"I seem to be hearing lots of stories of people being abandoned in lonely places. That was a terrible thing to do!"

She looked up at me curiously, as if it was strange to think of such acts of cruelty and uncaring as anything other than the norm.

"I was furious, but it turned out that it wasn't as bad as all that. You know, I'd already put some of the stash in my bag, just as an insurance policy – I'd been let down by people before, you know. Amazingly, some people took pity on me almost immediately, and drove me first to a place called le Vigan and then, after feeding me, drove me on to a town called Millau. They even gave me some money! Of course, I didn't tell them that I actually had some cash of my own. At the time I thought that every little helped. Well, I still do! From there it was easy to get to Narbonne, then Carcassonne and on to here."

"Did you meet up with Mitch on the way?"

"At first I thought about doing that. Then I thought that it would just be silly. What did I want Mitch for, anyway?"

"What made you come here?"

"I just knew that this was where he would go."

"And the sketch map? That was not from Lucas, was it?"

"How did you know that?"

"Lucas wouldn't have done such a messy map, and I suspect his handwriting is a bit better than that, too."

Again, there was another little hesitation, as if she was wondering whether to tell me something or not. She shrugged and said, "Mitch drew it a while back when we were thinking of using this as a place to rendezvous. He had spent quite a bit of time here selling drugs to local kids, messing about, using it as a place to hide from people he'd crossed in Toulouse. But Lucas had a kind of love/hate feel for the place and ended up insisting that it was too close to the area we had been working to be a clever place to rendezvous."

I could feel us losing the momentum as we came closer to the story of Lucas' death, so I tried a different tack.

"Where were you in the week before Lucas' death? It didn't take a week to get here from Millau?"

"I had to spend a bit of time working out what to do?"

"What do you mean?"

"I didn't want to just wander in there without a plan of action!"

I was feeling we were losing it completely, now. I wanted to press on that but decided that I couldn't afford to lose the information she might give me about Lucas' death.

"Who got here first? Mitch or you?"

"We got here almost at the same time. Mitch is not the most subtle of people, but once I'd gotten through to him, I was able to convince him that we were both on the same side. Lew had double-crossed both of us, after all! We found out where Lew was, and waited until it was dark. The house is similar to this actually, but a bit bigger. We went through a garage similar to yours and up to the back door. Mitch had been there before, when Lew had been living in Chabrassonne. He didn't even have to break into the house! Nothing was locked! We walked in and there was Lew sitting on a settee with the TV on and several bottles of beer on the floor all around him. He looked terrible!

Mitch just went to work on him. He grabbed him and simply threw him on the floor, he put one foot on Lew's back and used some wire to tightly tie Lew's wrists behind his back.

Lew was drunk and half asleep and didn't know what was going on. When he saw Mitch and me, he actually grinned at us as if we were playing some game; old friends coming 'round for a bit of fun after not seeing each other for a while! It just made Mitch furious, and I had to quieten him down. He was going to wake up the whole street.

Mitch picked Lew up and tried to make him stand, but he was all over the place. I told him to leave Lew alone. It was all very well getting revenge, but we wanted the money. We searched the place from the very top of the house to the cupboards under the stairs. It's funny 'cause, I wondered about there not being a cellar. I just couldn't figure it out. You see with such a big house it stands to reason that it should have had a cellar!"

"There's a ridge of rock running along one side of Chabrassonne. It's the continuation of the volcanic outcrop that gives you the chateau and the Chapel hills. The original builders used the outcrop to build part of the wall around the town. Then, when the people of the town finally demolished that, they used the solid rock as foundations for these houses. They added to the slope at the back to build up a decent bit of ground for growing things behind the houses and then built small coach-houses or stables at the end of the gardens with cellars below them - . beyond the road, the land finally slopes down to the river."

She nodded as if that made as much sense to her as it did to me, and carried on, "So we found nothing. Not a single trace of the stash. Again, Mitch was almost off his head with anger. Lew was asleep on the floor next to the settee and Mitch went over and kicked him in the stomach which only served to make Lew sick!"

"I got a basin of water and some cleaning stuff and made Mitch undo Lew so that he could clear up the mess.

Mitch insisted on tying Lew up again afterwards, and eventually we started to get through to Lew that we were not playing games. I could see that he was starting to get quite frightened – which is not difficult for Lew, he just had to think of something, and his imagination did the rest.

I went over and sat with him for a while, leaving Mitch to through the house again He was desperately trying to find the stash hidden somewhere. Lew was sitting there not saying anything, and I tried my little girl act, telling him that I'd been given no choice. Mitch was very angry and dangerous. All he had to do was tell Mitch where the money was, and he would go. Then we would be OK and happy again. I tried to get Lew to see that giving Mitch the money was the answer to all his dreams."

"It didn't work?" I asked.

"Nope. It seems that having your hands tied behind you and being pushed around can stop you from being seduced!"

"Well, I can see that it might be a barrier. What happened, then?"

She shook her head and I could see her struggling with what she wanted to say. "Mitch came in even angrier than before. He was holding this knife in his hand, and he was saying things like, 'I'll cut you up, you little piece of shit,' and, 'I'm going to skin you alive until you tell me where the fucking money is!' Things like that, and it didn't just scare Lew. It scared me too. The whole thing was completely out of hand. I was beginning to wonder how I was going to get out of this."

"It was all just to scare Lucas, though, wasn't it?" I asked.

"I don't know. Mitch is not the sort to do things like that. He had to have worked himself up to it. I thought that he had pushed himself further than he should have, and was out of control."

"So, you took the knife away from him." I said it as a fact rather than as a question.

She nodded, "Not immediately. He was waving it about, too much and he got Lew to kneel down in the middle of the floor on a big rug. I could see that Lew was about to piss himself. He was shaking and then he suddenly stopped and looked around at me. There was a sort of look of surprise in his face. As if he had just woken up from a dream. He looked up at Mitch and shouted, 'Vive La France!' and I thought then that Lew had gone completely mad, and that Mitch was going to cut his face off. So, I leapt up and went to Mitch."

"It took me everything I could think of to get that knife from him, and then I stood there wondering what to do. I mean, what can you do in a situation like that? I almost walked out, but I realised that I was in too deep for that. It was well after midnight and where was I going to go to in order to escape from these mad people?"

"I knelt down to face Lew and showed him the knife, and he spat in my face. I was so shocked, I didn't know what to do, so I pointed the knife right at his throat with my arms stretched out like that." She reached halfway across the table, holding her fork towards me like it was the knife. "I could see the point of the knife make a little dent in his skin, but it didn't cut into the surface. Then with the knife there, I demanded that he tell us where the stash was. I said that we would find it sooner or later, so there was no point in making it harder for us and for himself."

"I was talking to him, quite quietly when he just smiled at me as if I was quite far away, even though I was closer to him that I am to you, and he said a really weird thing. He said, 'It should really be a gun, you know?' and then he just thrust himself forward onto the knife. I was so surprise that I didn't even have time to react and pull the knife back, and he almost took me with him as he jerked further forward and started to convulse violently in front of me."

"Mitch grabbed me, lifted me up and started shaking me saying, 'What have you done, what have you done?' and Lew was dying on the floor at our feet! I was so completely shocked! I didn't know what was going on. Then a sort of automatic pilot took over and I began to take control of the situation again. Lew was lying silently on the floor, and Mitch was quietly sobbing in front of me. Two completely useless figures! I Got Mitch to just wrap Lew in the carpet, and then made him drag the package out of the back door. Then I told him to bring the van closer to the back of the house. We had parked it quite a distance away – there is nowhere easy to park in this place!"

"While he was away, I did a bit of tidying up. Despite our searches, we had done very little to mess the place up. It's just a holiday home and when no one is living in a place like that it's just like a series of empty hotel rooms. There's nothing much to mess up, just doors and drawers to close.

I even remembered to check the floor to see if I could see any blood stains. I thought that knife wounds produced huge amounts of blood! I went out and touched Lew just in case we had made a mistake. Just in case he was still alive. Have you ever touched a dead body? Oh, of course, you found Lew, didn't you? Well you'll know. There is no mistake. There is no life left in the body. Whatever had been there, had now gone, and you can tell."

She was silent for a while and I poured her out some iced water and pushed the glass towards her. She nodded her thanks and sipped some of it.

"When Mitch came back, I thought we would awaken the whole neighbourhood. It was dark, and we tripped over and bumped into things as we carried Lew to the van. That's the other thing they don't ever tell you about dead bodies. They are bloody heavy to carry! Lew was such a small, light guy when he was alive, but his dead body weighed a ton! I have been thinking about this a lot since then. Do you think that somehow, life makes your body actually lighter, like life has some sort of anti-gravity property we have never really explored before?"

I shook my head and said, perhaps, it sounded like it could be true. She nodded at me again, and at that point she really did look like a little girl. I saw a glimpse of the real little girl inside, as if I was catching a private glimpse of someone through a briefly opened door. Then she was back to the final part of her story.

"Mitch and I took Lew away. We argued about where to put him. Mitch said that we should have left him where he was, but I just knew that we should take him somewhere else. I kept thinking about things like fingerprints and other stuff that we must have left behind. Then Mitch said he knew a place where they used to go as teenagers – somewhere you could go to smoke dope while looking at the stars. 'No one goes there,' he said, 'and we can drive all the way up to it, too.' So, we went up that scary track in the dark and rolled him out of the van onto the path."

"Then we had another argument about the rug. I eventually won that one and we took the rug away, leaving Lew covered in a couple of plastic sacks we found nearby. The rest of the night we couldn't sleep. I was thinking about all sorts of things. The fingerprints really worried me, and I wanted to go back to the house, but Mitch refused point blank and would not let me go there.

Eventually, it dawned on me that we had not even looked through Lew's pockets. After a lot more argument, Mitch agreed that we should go back to Lew's body, but only on condition that, once we had searched Lew's pockets, we would leave Chabrassonne. I agreed. It was well into the beginnings of morning by then, and I was frightened that people would notice us, so I was glad when we drove up the hill and reached the Lew. In the daylight Mitch didn't want us to park next to the body, so we went along the track, turned at the junction and drove back towards the way out, on the lower road. We had no idea there was a church up there! We had thought it was just a looped path up and down the hill."

"It took me quite a while to get Mitch out of the van. He didn't want to go and do it, but he didn't want me to go on my own. Eventually, we got out and retraced the route of the van by foot. I took the wire off Lew's wrists. It didn't seem right, somehow, to leave him with that wire, but we found it difficult to get his arms to move, so we left him almost as he had been before the wire.

"Hold on. When I found him he had…"

"A plastic tag on his wrists?" She interrupted, "Yeh, I had thrown the wire into the bushes, but his arms were sort of stuck behind him, and it sort of freaked out Mitch, so he put that tag on Lew's writs instead. He has all sorts of crap in the pockets of his jacket!"

"Poor Lew had nothing in his pockets except the keys to the house. I put them in the pocket of my jeans, and we were just about to leave when we heard someone singing."

"That was me." I said.

"Yes, well we didn't know which direction the singing was coming from. It could have been from either end of the path. Mitch was panicking, so I just grabbed his arm and forced him to go through the undergrowth towards the van. I insisted that we get the VW moving before we started it up. We were pointing downhill, so I thought it wouldn't be that difficult. Mitch didn't start the motor until we had rolled to the junction with the main branch of the path again and then we were away."

"So, you came back to cover your tracks and look for the stash?" I could see that she was completely drained by the story. I just wanted some confirmation.

"I suppose you could say that. I am not good at going away and leaving things undone or leaving other people to rummage around in my things."

I looked up at the clock and saw that it was now just after four in the afternoon. We had been so intent on the story that I, at least, had not noticed how dark it had become, and that the first wave of rain was now beginning to fall.

"Well, you have a choice to make, Charli. Decision time."

The rain grew louder as it built up force, and gusts of wind were beginning to sweep it across the windows like wild waves cutting across a fast boat.

"The police will be back. They will not just sit around twiddling their thumbs waiting for you to turn up. You need to leave here as soon as possible and disappear."

"Will you drive me down to Carcassone? Perhaps you can take me with you on your way to England. We could travel together and spend a couple of nights in hotels on the way." She was starting to get back on track, her thinking was clearing, and she was putting everything behind her.

I shook my head. "I can't. I won't do it."

"It wouldn't be difficult. No-one would know and I would make it really good fun. I would like that."

"Charli, you are not listening. That has never been on the cards."

"That's not true. We've come close to it. I know!"

"But it's never going to happen. It's not just that I'm still a married man and won't betray that, no matter how tempting it is, I don't want to. The price is too high."

She looked at me in disbelief.

"The fact is, if you want to get away, you have only one chance and it does not involve me driving you anywhere."

She sat there with a hardened look on her face and said, "OK, I'm waiting."

"Take a raincoat and one of the hats from the coat rack and wrap yourself in them, I will give you a hundred Euros, which is all I have in cash, and go to the bus stop down next to the hotel. At quarter past four there is the local bus for Carcassonne. It is remarkably punctual. No one will take notice, keep your collar up and your hat down and sit at the back. Once you are in Carcassonne you can go where you like. They either think that you are hiding out somewhere else in town, or that you have already gone."

"That's crazy!"

"It's not. You have five minutes to get there. Wait on the side road leading from the market square to the hotel. It's the road they arrested Mitch on, but you will be OK. You can see the main road from there and can see some distance down the road that the bus comes along, before it turns past the hotel and reaches the stop. If you see no one watching the stop dash over when you see the bus arriving, and go."

"And if I see the police waiting for me?"

"I will be here, but I can give you no more guarantees."

"Why should I trust you? Once I leave the house you could phone your policeman friend and tell him where to get me."

"I promise you that I will not tell them about the bus. Climb on that bus and that's the end of the whole thing as far as I'm concerned. Too many people have been hurt already. These people are friends, and I've done enough messing about. I promise I will not warn the police either that you are going for the bus or that you have left on it. It's my solemn promise to you."

She shook her head and stood up as I fumbled in my wallet and passed her the money. With her bag on her shoulder, she walked quickly through to the coat rack. She chose my wife's best raincoat and a hat that matched. With them on she managed to look very stylish, despite the fact that the coat and hat were a little too big for her. There was a small telescopic umbrella hanging up there, too. She picked it up and waived it at me. I nodded and she slipped the loop handle over her wrist. She walked to me, kissed me gently on both cheeks and turned away from me.

"Here's looking at you." She said in a pretty lousy American accent, giggled and went out, leaving the door open and the rain swishing in, first on the floor, then on the wall and so on.

Redemption song

I closed the door without looking and walked back to the kitchen. I was about to pick up the phone when I heard a loud click behind me. I stopped and waited for a second.

Then I remembered and walked over to the CD/radio/cassette player and pressed the eject button.

Our whole conversation had been recorded on that one little tape.

Chapter Thirteen

I thought about the telephone as I collected the dishes and took them to the sink. As I ran the water, waiting for it to get hot, I put the cassette back in the machine and rewound it. I then played it back and fiddled with it until I heard Charli's voice say, "I am not good at going away and leaving things undone or leaving other people to rummage around in my things."

There was quite a long pause after those sentences. I rewound and listened to them again then I stopped the tape. I switched on the CD player and saw that a CD was already in the machine. I started the CD and pressed 'record' on the tape machine and started the process of cleaning the dishes. A song started up that I recognised as an early Belle and Sebastian song called, "Get me away from here I'm dying."

I thought about the song and the last words said by Charli that I had left on the tape.

I finished washing everything and dried my hands. The machine was now playing a song by

Redemption song

Nick Drake called "Northern Sky". It was obviously one of my mixed selection CDs. I turned the volume down and called Georges using the home phone.

"Georges, Have, you found the VW van, yet?"

"Here we go again, John. What little secret have you been hiding from me now?"

I told him it was not quite like that. I felt that everything had come to a head. It was all reaching some sort of conclusion. The rain was battering at my windows and I needed to get back to my own family. I also needed to go to church before I could go away. The Saturday Vigil Mass was in the little church of St Mary's in the centre of town, and I was not certain of being able to go to Mass during the next twenty-four hours.

I didn't say all of that to Georges. Instead, I told him where I suspected the Van might be, and he complained bitterly at me for telling him. He did not like the idea at all. So, I told him the simple solution was to go and wait for it to come to him. He could then sort out the implications afterwards. I told him it was all up to him.

I then told him that I was leaving for England that night and that I would send him something to help him through the coming days while I was away.

He didn't know what to make of all I had just said to him. His last words were, "OK John. But I want one last word with you before you go." and I told him that I would be at Mass and then I would be on my way.

I did a little bit more tidying up. Some things went from the 'fridge to the freezer and other bits went from the 'fridge to the bin, then I took the rubbish out and put new bags in the empty bins. I walked around the house and thought about how I had not been able to speak with Mary for a while. I missed her so much it hurt, but I knew that I could wait.

I checked my emails quickly and saw that there was little to worry about. James was on his way south from Edinburgh now, and I emailed Jude and Jo to say that I would be home some time on Monday.

I then walked up and looked around my room, put some things on the bed for packing and went into the bathroom. I took a couple of painkillers washed down with some cold water from the tap. I splashed my face in the cold water, too and dried myself facing the mirror. It was a surprise to look at the face in front of me. The bruising was lighter and more colourful. The swelling was down. I looked at that face as I rotated my shoulder and felt the way that it hurt, and how it affected my movements. I wondered if what I felt to be true really was true. I wondered what all these different layers of truth really meant.

When I was standing at the door putting on my coat and an old floppy hat, I thought about why people stayed in a place like Chabrassonne. I thought about how people stayed in places like this all of their lives without once picking up their things and leaving to get away from the lives they had ploughed out for themselves. I felt that this was quite an extraordinary thing, and yet it was no different from the small world I had grown up in, and the place that my parents had lived and died in. I shuddered and felt profoundly grateful that I would soon be on the move for a while.

On my way to church I stopped at a neighbour's long enough to hand over a set of keys and ask them to pop in and feed the cats. An occasional flash of lightning illuminated odd parts of buildings as I walked through the streets. The thunder told me that the lightning was quite some way off, but I was still glad that I had not taken my big umbrella. Somehow the thing felt soiled by its brief involvement with violence. I didn't want it with me in church.

At the entrance I met a couple of people I knew and walked into the poorly lit space as if I was submerging myself further in a shared mystery, which I suppose I was. I looked around me as the people I had walked in with moved on up to the pews at the front, genuflected and slid into their places.

The priest approached and greeted me. Commented on the weather and talked a little about a social event he had been planning for the parish for some time in the autumn. I agreed to give him some help, and he held my arm briefly to tell me how sad he had been to discover that I had been so badly treated by the police. I told him it was nothing, a silly mistake, and he patted my arm in a conciliating way and moved on to greet someone else. I heard a voice say hello and I turned around to see Yvonne.

Ian Smith

"You seem lonely without your little friend." She
said.

I smiled, "Not so much a friend as someone I
was keeping an eye on for a while."

"So, has she gone?"

"In a manner of speaking." I looked at my watch
and thought for a second and then said, "You'll
probably see and hear a bit more about her before
long. It looks like she was one of the people who
killed poor Lucas. I'll be away for a few days
visiting my family. Perhaps when I get back, I
might tell you the whole story?"

"I think I'll look forward to that," she said and
then, as the bell for Mass rang she added,
"Although I'm not sure I want to hear about that
girl."

I stood in a pew near the back, and Yvonne
walked up quickly to join her friend. The younger
priest was actually taking the Mass, and I listened
very carefully as he gave a homily on the
Transfiguration of Christ. The Gospel had told of
how Christ had basically gone for a walk with two
of his disciples and at the top of a hill Christ had
been transformed. Light had shone from him and
two of the greatest prophets had come down from
heaven to talk with him. The young priest talked
about how we all had something of God in us and
could be changed in unexpected ways. He told us
that we were never what we seemed to be, and
were not as dull, as weak or as frightened as
people thought we were. One day we would
surprise other people and surprise ourselves, too.
The light would, in some way, shine from us.

Redemption song

I thought about poor young Lucas, and I prayed for him, but I was still feeling strangely numb. It all felt a bit like one of my dreams. Tragedy had scrawled its graffiti across this place for the last few days, and I had followed it around, watching the images appear, watching it deface peoples' lives. I knew that I was being affected by it all, but the hurt had not reached the surface yet!

Then, as I continued to wonder about it all, tears simply flooded my eyes and I walked up to receive communion half blinded by them. The tears ran down my cheeks and joined the rainwater on my collar as I walked back to my place.

After Mass Yvonne walked quickly up to me and kissed my cheeks saying, "Take care on your journey. Come and see me as soon as you come back."

I walked out with the small group of parishioners and a figure in a dark raincoat slick with water joined me, matching my steady stride.

"Good evening, John. How was Mass?"

"Enlightening," I replied.

"So, young Father Giles was taking the vigil Mass, then?"

I smiled and told him that Giles had been the priest.

"We have a new visitor, John. I thought you should know."

"Did she arrive with a useful van and a little collection of valuables?"

"There seems to be no surprising you! I was hoping for at least one little trick up my sleeve."

"Never mind, Georges. I'm sure Charles wll have some good explanation why the van was on his property but let me suggest one little thing. Something that I wouldn't suggest unless I had good reason."

I walked for a couple of seconds, thinking about it again before speaking. Georges said, "Come on John, out with it."

"I suppose it is more of a question. You see I know some of the reasons why you could have been expected to find the van where you did, but I think it is a little bit more complicated."

"It always is."

"Well ask yourself why Limon would want a painting to be burned and ask yourself what else was burned at the same time."

"Limon?" George paused and I turned to face him.

"I know he is a little bit mad, but he is also a shitty policeman, and I now think he has been a pretty corrupt one, too. I kept thinking to myself what link there could have been between Lucas' death and Limon, and it kept moving back to old stories, old feuds, old pains. But it was not the old things that were the only connection. This afternoon, Limon forced Charles to burn a painting done by Lucas when he was a teenager. What else did they burn together? You might ask your two young visitors what they think was in that fire, too."

Georges was slightly confused by my advice, but he accepted it anyway and as we stopped on the corner of my street, he turned towards me and

I could see that he was looking quite worried. "You look very sad and tired, my friend." He said as he took my hand.

"Some stories seem designed to break your heart, Georges. Keep strong and have faith."

I turned and walked away.

In the house I finished my packing and looked out a few essentials such as passport and maps. The lightning was now closer, and the periods between the flashes and the booms seemed like unnecessary hesitations in a conversation.

I gave up just as I was gathering everything in the kitchen. I had to make the call.

She answered after the second ring. I told Nathalie some of the story, warned her that all hell was about to break loose, and that I had to go as my family needed me. I said her I would be back in a week or so, and I would then try and fill in any gaps the police were reluctant to tell her or felt she shouldn't know.

I ended by saying that her son had been a victim, but that I had found out that he had also been a very special person whose passing was something we should all mourn. "I have no doubt he is with Christ this very night." I said and felt that I sounded more like a priest than most priests. She thanked me and I was glad to know that she really did understand that I was telling her what I believed to be the whole truth.

I turned off the lights, locked the final locks, and left the house.

As I was driving down the narrow road from my garage, I saw a figure stumble out from the shadows. He didn't even register the car as he stomped his way along the narrow road, and it took me all my skill to avoid hitting him with the car. It was Limon, heading towards my house. I stopped the car and considered getting out and speaking to him, then I thought, "what the hell!" and phoned Georges instead, telling him what I had just seen. He wished me goodbye and I drove out of Chabrassonne, and into the stormy night.

As I crossed the bridge on my way out of town, I began to run through everything I had done during the day, and an image of a cassette tape lying on the kitchen table leapt into my mind. I'd left it there with the intention of putting it in an envelope and posting it to Georges. At a junction just out of town I stopped and turned the car. This was deeply frustrating!

The wipers swept across the windscreen admonishing me with every slick arc as I threaded my way back to the house. I drove to the front of the house and parked on the narrow street – only intending to stay for a couple of minutes. I switched off the engine but left the lights on and dashed out of the car into the heavy rain.

As I opened the door, I thought of the shambling figure of Limon heading down the back road and put on the light in the hallway. Picking up a walking stick, I felt its light hardness and the smoothness of the varnish over the gnarled, knotted wood. It seemed logical to take the precaution, but I still felt foolish as I walked warily into my own home.

Redemption song

In the kitchen, without the light on, I could see that the back door was closed, and a stroboscopic flickering of lightning illuminated the garden and the kitchen, revealing the tape on the table. Despite this illusion of safety, I turned on the light before walking into the room. It felt colder than it had seemed only a few moments before and as I turned to look further into the room, I saw the dishevelled figure of Limon sitting at my kitchen table. He had a glass at his hand which looked like it was half full of spirit. A brief glance to the dresser showed that he had helped himself to my best malt whisky.

"That was quick work." I said as I walked over to the table and picked up the tape. "I saw you only a few minutes ago on the back road and here you are drinking my whisky."

He raised the glass and saluted me before gulping most of it.

"I got the taste for this muck when I was sent on a training course to your country more than fifteen years ago."

"Why are you in my house, Limon? Looking for me, or for something else?"

When he put the glass down on the table it betrayed the unsteadiness he was trying to hide. The glass rattled and clumped on the surface and he withdrew his hand. I noticed that a bruise glowed like a dull bluish light under the skin of his cheek, and his eye above it was slightly puffy and narrower than its counterpart.

"There isn't any evidence here for you to take away and burn." I looked at him as I said this and an empty grin appeared on his face. It emphasised the lack of any apparent life behind his eyes, and I felt a small shudder pass through me. His voice was like thin gravel.

"I learned a long time ago that evidence is a relative concept. It only has meaning in the proper context. It seldom gives you the truth, often obscures it. We use it all the time to help us hide the truth from ourselves."

"So, 'What is truth?' is that what you are going to say next?" I snorted.

"I don't care about the truth! Truth is a crock of shit. Truth is a hole in the ground!" He slid the glass violently over the surface of the table towards me as he said this and I managed to stop it from going over the edge whilst still looking at him carefully.

"Why are you here, monsieur Limon?" I emphasised the monsieur and kept on trying to engage him by looking straight into his eyes. He seemed to be looking back at me, but I just could not engage with anything there. I wondered if he was perhaps on some sort of drug. There was an emptiness there; a disengagement that frightened me.

He slowly nodded and I thought that he might have been acknowledging the formality in my voice. This seemed to be reflected in what he started saying. I realised almost immediately what he was quoting from.

"The victim was subjected to a considerable degree of systematic physical abuse prior to his death. The single knife wound to the oesophagus displayed no signs of hesitation cuts and appears to have been inflicted with considerable force and confidence; perhaps utilising professional knowledge gained in the armed forces. The body was removed from the scene of death and was deposited several hours later in the location where it was finally discovered. Bonds, most likely heavy-duty electrical cable, had been used to restrain the victim and were removed some time after death occurred.

No evidence of sexual abuse was evident although the victim showed signs of having been either regularly abused in the recent past, or of having taken part in sado-masochistic activities relatively recently. Perhaps within the last two weeks. "

"Can they tell that much?" I asked when I realised he had finished quoting from Lucas' autopsy report.

"Oh yes! And a lot more!"

"It just adds to the picture of abuse suffered by Lucas. Your son had a hard life." I said quietly.

"My son!" He stood up suddenly and the chair banged away from behind his legs and into the 'fridge. "My son?" He looked around the kitchen as if he had just arrived. "What do you know about my son?" and then he slumped forward, leaning on the table for support.

"When did you realise that Charles Groussard was involved?"

"That man started sniffing around Lucas almost as soon as he was eleven. He took a 'personal interest' and drove a wedge between the boy and the rest of the family. He fed him full of shit about the war and used it to manipulate him."

I almost made some comment asking if that is why Limon joined in on the persecution of Lucas, but I bit the jibe back.

"I used to stop him from making rendezvous with Groussard! The lad was not a homosexual!"

"Why didn't you do something legally? You were a police officer, after all?"

"That man has more influence than you can imagine! Anyway, you need the young person's co-operation for it to work, and Lucas was doing it to spite those around him. There was nothing I could do."

"So, you blamed other people. You blamed your son. Did you also blame his mother?"

"That stupid bitch let it happen! She was as much to blame as the rest of that family!"

I heard a rustle in the hall, but it was obvious that Limon was oblivious to everything. He was talking to me, but he was hardly conscious that it was me he was speaking to. Perhaps he was really just speaking to himself.

"When I discovered that Lucas was still visiting Groussard from time to time I went to the guy and told him that enough was enough. His arrogance was so huge I couldn't believe it! He even showed me pictures of Lucas, pictures that made me shrivel up inside. The boy was trussed up like some pathetic animal and people were doing things to him! It was too much to take. Groussard showed me that the boy had more to lose than anyone. That I stood more to lose than to gain by exposing it all."

He paused and I said, "Perhaps it would have been better if it had been exposed. Lucas would have been able to escape the cycle of abuse. By doing nothing you just left him to keep on suffering it."

"You don't understand! Lucas wanted it that way. He didn't want my help!"

I shrugged. This man's perspective was completely out of my field of vision. I asked the only obvious question, "So when I saw you coming out of Groussard's, what had you achieved? What had you got him to burn?"

"I made him burn everything! The painting, the photographs, letters and video recordings. Everything! I pointed my gun in his face and said, 'This is my authority! This is my evidence!' I should have shot him, then! The snivelling coward could hardly stand whenever I pointed the gun at him. His knees kept buckling under him. It was pathetic! No more 'Mr Arrogant'!" He stood and thrust his hands into his pockets. I wondered if he had his gun with him and considered what I would do if he drew it from his pocket and pointed it at me. Would my knees buckle, too? Probably.

"So, Lucas and his little gang used to go and take part in little S&M romps up at the chateau with Groussard? That's what you got him to destroy evidence of?" I was still processing this new information.

"What do you think I have been saying? Yes! You know, I'm not even sure if Groussard took part in those. It was Lucas' friends that did it. The boy couldn't even choose friends that he could trust. They took on Groussard's role for him while that slimy bastard just sat back and filmed it all!"

"And the girl I was with today. Was she part of that, too?"

"What girl?" Limon looked at me like I was trying to trick him.

"When I met you coming out of the chateau? That girl."

"I never saw anyone but you. I just saw you there and thought – you are part of it too. You must be. So, I wanted to hit you – see you fall back down those stairs, but you were too quick for me then. Neat trick! Afterwards I realised that you are just an ignorant foreigner stumbling around in the dark. You would never have found out about all of this if I had not told you. Never!"

"But I think I would have found out, eventually." Georges emerged from the hall and turned to me, "You've left your lights on in your car."

Two policemen walked into the room and stepped to either side of Limon. He looked so lost and betrayed that I felt more sorry for him than he possibly deserved. It seemed like there were too many victims in this whole sorry mess for me to count. Were we all just victims, I began to wonder, but I knew that that was just so much nonsense! An easy trick we can play on ourselves to allow self-delusion and fear to cloud our judgement. Is it easier to be a coward or is the word coward the derogatory term people who are safe use for those who are abandoned and oppressed beyond hope?

Georges was talking to me and I had to say, sorry and ask him to repeat it.

"Why did you come back?" He asked. "I thought you were already on your way?"

"I was, but I forgot this." I said and I produced the cassette tape from my pocket. "I was going to send it to you, but I can give it to you, now."

"What is it?"

"I recorded Charli as she told me her version of Lucas' death. How much of it is true you will have to judge for yourself. No doubt she will produce a dozen versions before the end of this is reached. I don't know why I took so long to see her role in all of this. She's a very convincing liar, but I think it was more to do with the fact that she's so obviously one of the victims, too. So often it seems that the greatest victims can only escape from their abuse by becoming the abusers."

"I had hoped that there would be some element of the story that would point the way forward for Lucas' family. Something more than the simple facts that Lucas had been a victim, and that his death had been a senseless waste. Anyway, put the tape on your machine, I presume you still have cassette machines? Good, just rewind then listen to what she has to say."

I looked across at Limon and he was just standing there with his head bowed and the life in him barely detectable. I turned and walked down the hall with Georges, pulled a set of keys from the coat stand and handed them to him.

"I want to go now, Georges. Here are a set of my keys. Can you lock up when you leave?"

On the doorstep he hugged me like an old friend and told me to take care. He said that I should not drive for very long. I should find a hotel and order some food and a bottle of wine and stare at the TV for a while.

I hugged him and walked out to my car. Behind it a police car with a flashing light was parked closer into the narrow gutter that served as the pavement in the street. The rain was still pounding everything, so I didn't wait around.

As I drove over the bridge for the second time, I felt a certain amount of weight slide from me and as I pushed the car up through the rolling hills, I began to feel easier and easier. All those silly pieces of philosophical thought that pass through your mind as you encounter big problems melted away, and all of the heavy feelings of responsibility seemed to move back into some sort of perspective.

I drove past the small fortified village of Camon and thought of the fine restaurant there. Was Marc there again with Louise? Perhaps JJ was there with Valerie and Sylvie, treating them to a special Saturday night meal? So many other friends could be there.

I thought of the last time Mary and I had been there. I could see her struggling to eat some token bits of food. I sat there worried that I was making her do this, and she looked up at me with that wonderful smile she has and told me that she was having a lovely time. She didn't need to eat more than a tiny amount of anything. A small taste was enough. And we sat there, looking out over the darkening valley with the sun catching the tops of the trees, turning them red, making them look as if they were all bursting into flame. Then she had taken my hand and told me that she loved me.

I drove for some time with that memory tucked into my tired mind.

Up through Mirepoix the rain seemed to be following me but as I dropped into the open land and joined wider, straighter roads I felt the rain lighten and the storm seemed to be dropping further behind me. It didn't seem long before I was driving through the edge of the city of Toulouse. I could see its cathedral like some brilliantly lit ornament jutting up through the rainy haze and then I was driving through the more run down, semi-industrial ribbon of development stretching out to the north.

I kept to the N20, shunning the toll motorways, as always, thinking about the way the road allowed you to pass through so many peoples' lives. Little glimpses of families sitting together in brightly lit rooms; someone looking out at your car as they begin to close the shutters; people going into shops and cafes, running out of the rain. I passed busses full of people huddled in their seats watching the rain as the dampness slowly spread through their rain-filled clothes.

After a while the N20 turned into the A20 but I didn't mind. I accelerated and soon passed Montauban where I remembered sitting in a small restaurant with Jude on her own seat, propped up with two cushions provided by the waitress, and James in a buggy holding a spoon and looking expectantly at me as I scooped up the next portion of the meal I was feeding him. I remembered it because of the kindness of the people in the restaurant and because the food had been so good. It was around the first time we discovered Chabrassonne. We had stopped in that same restaurant every year for the next few years until one summer we turned up and discovered the place had been boarded up; they were going to redevelop the site. We never stopped there again.

It took me a few short minutes to pass around the town. I felt as if I was rushing faster and faster away from something and began to panic. What was I doing? Where was I going?

As I passed Caussade, I saw a sign for Cahors and considered getting off the A20. The next exit at Lalbenque tugged at me and I began to feel tired. I thought of Cahors and the temptation grew. But along with the temptation came memories. The road seemed to be disappearing into a lost, dark landscape and I thought about more than one breakfast in Cahors, of a candlelit meal there where Mary had held my hand and told me that she loved me. I wondered when I had last done that to her; told her I loved her; and realised that I had done it so many times over the years that it was silly of me to even think of worrying about it. It was a daily statement that did not diminish through repetition. I knew how we both felt and left it at that.

I kept on past Cahors and the light rain began to build into a deep, rolling set of cascades, which seemed to fill the windscreen faster than the wipers could push the water off. I switched the wipers to a quicker and even quicker speed and felt their hypnotic effects as my tired eyes struggled to keep their focus. Lightning began to play across the completely black sky. Sheets of brilliant light, jagged nets of lightning and an occasional rip, like the heavens had split open, appeared before me. I am not sure that I have ever seen such a light show, with the different types of electrical activity playing across my windscreen. It was like an academic demonstration or an over-the-top Hollywood production. Few cars were sharing the road with me now, and they all seemed to be crawling along through the night. I just kept passing these solitary vehicles as they huddled to my extreme right.

I put on a CD at random (in the dark) and found I was listening to another one of my mixed music compilations. The Stone's "Wild Horses" was followed by "Life on Mars" by Bowie, and I began to feel slightly more awake. Then Nick Drake's sombre "River Man" was followed by "Boys Don't Cry" and then Bob Marley with "No Woman, No Cry"

I saw signs for Rocamadour and knew that it must be looming up somewhere to my right and noted that Souillac was not that far ahead when Cold Play began to sing "Spies". As I was leaving Souillac behind I had listened to a song by a group whose name had escaped me but whose song was part of my life despite that, then Dylan sang two songs to me, one which kept saying to me "Turn, turn to the rain and the wind" and the other constantly referring back to these visions of Johanna. The music had kept me going, but I knew it was time to stop when that old favourite from Belle and Sebastian rose out of the speakers and gently prodded me. It pleaded, "Get me away from here, I'm dying." And I began to look for a place to stop.

On the edge of Brive-la-Gaillarde, I saw signs for the usual small hotels and slipped out of the sparse traffic and the slick new road. Along a street badly in need of repair, just past a huge but closed Géant superstore, I found a little French Motel where I could stop.

They had no food to offer as the restaurant was closed, but I suppose that I looked so tired and hungry they decided to take pity on me. After signing the register and a little credit card slip, I struggled to my room with my overnight bag on my shoulder carrying a tray holding a selection of cheeses, some bread, a small block of butter and a bottle of red wine.

I sat in my fleece waiting for the heater to warm up the room with the late news on the TV and an array of cheeses before me. Mary would love this, I thought, and poured out the wine. "Here's to you, my love. See you soon!"

I called James before turning in and told him that I would be home by Monday morning. I was thinking that I might arrive at the coast in time for a ferry on Sunday night, but that I might not go over until the following day. I had also been toying with the idea of stopping off briefly in Paris at lunch time, but I wasn't sure.

Redemption song

Before going to sleep I also had a talk with Mary.

I told her all about the things that had happened. I felt like I had been hollowed out with a sharp paring knife, and that everything I had wanted to keep of myself had been left on a shelf, but I had not found the time, yet, to put it all back inside me. She was very comforting. No sharp comments pointing out what I had done wrong, no subtle reminders of my foibles and weaknesses. She reassured me that I had done as much as I could do. There was a point where other people needed to take responsibility, too.

But it was hard, thinking about the mess I had walked away from. I had lifted up the stones and looked at the uncomfortable and shameful things underneath. I had not helped or healed.

She told me again that I could not be held responsible. She said, when people ask you for the truth, it is sometimes the hardest thing to give them. They ask for something they don't really want. What they want is reassurance, comfort, forgiveness, a passing on of blame, an easy solution. The truth is sometimes too painful to bear. And who are we to give out truth or dish out judgement? All you can do is be as honest you possibly can.

I understood what she was saying, but it was not easy. I knew that what she was saying referred to me, and our life together, as much as it referred to the things that had just taken place, or been revealed, in Chabrassonne.

Ian Smith

I closed my eyes and felt myself falling into an emptiness that I was convinced I would never climb out of... ever again.

Chapter Fourteen

I woke up with a church bell ringing somewhere. It was nothing like waking up in England, the bell was a dull, monotone clang, which rang out its repeated note every second, without any pretence at musical design or skill.

I refreshed myself and took some pain killers before getting dressed. Then I packed my small bag and left the room looking for breakfast and a quick exit. There was nothing I wanted from the meagre breakfast on offer at the hotel, so I just paid up, thanked the people for their kindness the night before and left.

The Geant was closed as it was Sunday, and I drove through the quiet streets thinking about food and looking at the occasional pedestrian as if they might have been old friends – all I needed to do was look at them more closely to discover their identity.

As I drove through the centre of the town, I saw more and more people. They were heading for the large church in the very centre of the town.

Sometime during the night the rain had stopped, and the honey coloured stone buildings of the town looked bright and clean as they lined up along the wet roads. The sky was clearing, too and a vague mist of evaporation clung to the pavements as I drove along.

By the time I started to see places where I might stop and have something to eat, the feeling of hunger had gone.

I drove north out of the town crossing over a river and passing a strange tower that looked almost like a sandstone light house, or perhaps a stone telescope standing on its end. I drove through peaceful rolling countryside until I eventually found my way back onto the A20.

I decided against playing music this morning and occasionally dipped into the various passing radio stations as I made my way through familiar towns and place names. We had travelled up and down these roads often as a family and I could not get out of my head the various jokes and arguments we encountered as we passed through this corridor of France.

These memories had been part of the reason why Mary and I had decided to go down to Chabrassonne when she became ill. We had not been "escaping to the country" although there had been a strong need to find a period of peace and quiet. Her illness, and the medication she had been given, had made her deeply sensitive to certain types of noise, and the busy life of the city which she loved so much had been too much for her to bear at that time. It had also been a chance for us to spend time together undisturbed and free of other distractions.

Like most things, the idea had only partially worked. The need to see other places and do other things had driven us to spend a little time on the Mediterranean coast, and then we had visited the woman she had shared her first time in France with when she had gone on her school exchange. That had been a special meeting for both Mary, and for me. It had been over forty years since they had last met, but they had unexpectedly been like sisters together. She had never imagined that such a thing would have been possible. Mary was so pleased with the meeting it had given her a new energy and we had headed up this road together, planning a bit more time in London.

Early summer along roads like these it had been quite different from today. It had been hotter then and the green had been of a different shade. It had been younger and lighter with a lot more yellow in the colour mix. Now the summer had left everything tinged in a redness that had pushed the greens towards browns and the yellows to orange or ochre.

As I neared Chateauroux, I felt an overwhelming need for some coffee and found a motorway services where I could stop and feed that need. It was a fairly grim place trying to entice tourists off the road, and into the countryside around it. I felt the place deserved better than this scrappy effort, but was too preoccupied to give it more thought. I took some coffee in a big paper cup and walked over to the newsstand where I bought myself a paper, then I sat down and skimmed through the stories hardly noticing when I had stopped reading about corruption in local government and started reading about a footballer's indiscretions with a famous French actor's wife. Economies and policies passed me by, and I ended up reading the cartoons and scanning the job advertisements despite the fact that neither were of any interest to me.

I finished my coffee and folded up the paper. I thought that people would like to read it when I got home. Mary had always followed French politics more avidly than she had looked at the British kind. As I walked through the little shop, I noticed that they were selling bags of croissants and I bought a bag of them on impulse.

I ate one of the croissants as I continued the journey, but felt no desire to eat the rest. I was beginning to feel hungry in a way that croissants could not address. An emptiness in my stomach tugged at me like the stitches in a wound, and I began to look for somewhere else to stop; somewhere real.

As I passed the outskirts of Orleans, I saw a sign for Chartres and that set my mind thinking about other times, other holidays, and I looked for the exit to the town. Along the N154, I looked ahead and remembered how we had all agreed that this was a bit like driving towards Ely in England. The cathedral seemed to tower above the wide, flat land like a single beacon, and the longer you journeyed along the road, the more you began to feel that you would never get there. Then, suddenly, the place was there in front of you, and it was time to stop.

I parked at the bottom of the town by the river and wandered up through the steep streets to the cathedral. Mass was just starting, and I stepped into the ritual like a person walking into a welcome pool of clear water. Everything seemed right and as it should be. The music was perfect, despite the fact that it was the sort I usually hate, the sermon was a fumbled and clumsy affair, but it was just as it should have been. I took communion and felt whole with all those around me, and it felt as if there was nothing else I needed. After the final hymn had finished, I sat down again, and the tune of a different song rose in my mind and grew so strong I had to get out.

Down the hill from the Cathedral I walked into a café that I had been in a couple of times before. I walked through the ground floor and started walking up to the first-floor dining room. I saw some of the local men look at me strangely, but I just smiled and wished them good day.

The waitress came up and asked me if I was going to be all right up here. There was no one else around. I had not noticed. I asked her if it would be OK to be served up here and she shrugged, "Why not." She said, "The rush is over. I don't mind." She smiled at me and I knew that she could see my sadness. She could see that I had an emptiness that was greater than simple hunger. I told her what I would like to eat, and she went away.

The windows looked out over a narrow road that led back up to the cathedral and I remembered our first visit here, when we had noticed that although we were on the first floor, we could actually look up the road from the window to people climbing further up the hill. For some reason it had captured the whole family's imagination.

The waitress came up with a glass of wine and a dark, rich beef stew accompanied with simple vegetables and deep yellow noodles. I thanked her and she went away to leave me to my food.

Mary said, "It's time to let go, you know." And I looked up into her face. She looked very pale, but so beautiful to me that I took in a short gasp of breath. She put her hand out and touched my arm saying, "I love you, you know." And her voice pierced me so deeply, I couldn't hold my knife and fork. I put them down and tears were welling up in my eyes.

"But I miss you so much." I said. "I can't live without you."

"You are doing well enough," she said. "It takes time."

I watched her fade away for the last time, and then I started to cry.

In the empty dining room, with a low sun cutting along the steep narrow street, highlighting the still wet cobblestones, I bowed my head and cried.

As the song inside me kept on saying over and over again: "I always cry at endings." I could also hear my voice call out to her, "I love you, too."

Redemption song

Mary had died earlier in the summer. I had driven her back to London slowly after our trip to the coast. We had stopped at various places on the way. She was becoming very ill, despite the brief feeling of renewal from her visit with her old friend. I was almost out of my head with worry as we drove on, but she became calmer and calmer as we travelled further north.

She died two days after we returned to London. James missed her death by one day but seemed to handle it well. Josephine had been there and had helped keep things together. Jude had been, at first, overwhelmed with grief but had remained solid, too; both were a great help to me, but I had been left stunned.

I discovered that I didn't want any sort of life without her. It didn't matter what happened next. I had lived more of my life with her than without her, and I didn't really want to live long enough to reverse that balance in my life.

Then, the one I loved the most rescued me. Mary came to me and we talked.

She comforted me and had been with me for the whole of the rest of the summer. I had moved back to Chabrassonne because it was easier to live there and spend time with Mary, than it had been to allow my family and friends to intrude on this new-found stage in our relationship. I had begun to believe that all I needed to do now was to join her. I was going to end my life and become one with her forever.

It was a madness that I'd allowed myself to believe. A crazy self-indulgence that ignored everyone including, Mary, my family and even my own soul!

Discovering Lucas' body had been a blow to me.

As this new reality began intruding in on my quiet life, Mary began to recede. When Jude started to have problems again, and I knew I was losing Mary. I discovered that I was having to deal with greater and greater intrusions into my life, and I also discovered that I needed to go back to my family. My selfish time had finally come to an end.

When I told Nathalie that I believed Lucas was now with Christ in heaven, what had I really been saying? I was talking about Mary, too. I was realising what my selfishness had been doing to me. I'd been so selfish that I had tried to deny the person I loved the most; her "Greatest Reward"! As a Christian, that had been my guilty secret, and something I'd tried to avoid admitting.

But Mary and I had been together for so long she understood me better than I did myself. I still didn't know how to go on without her, but the last few months had shown me that I would never really be without her - so what happens now?

I had been sitting staring intently at the empty chair in front of me for a long time. My eyes were dry, and my food was cold.

"Monsieur? Are you all right?" The waitress was standing by the stairs watching me.

"I am fine, Madame. Just fine."

I paid the bill and walked down the hill towards my car thinking how the problem had been partly solved for me. I had been pulled from the brink by

Mary, herself and then I had been forced to confront the pain and confusion when you lose a loved one. Not from the inside. Not as a grieving partner, but as the person asked to make sense of it all on behalf of other people.

If I had killed myself, what sort of solution would that have been?

I had appeared to be a quiet, happy-ish man on the day that I'd found Lucas. I had been operating as a rational, solid person. But I had been like that because I'd made the decision to end of my own life.

I climbed into my car. It was time to head for home and tell everyone that I, at least, was back from the brink.

Time to find out how to start living again.

As I headed out of Chartres, I decided to put some music on. Without looking I ejected the disc I had played the night before and fumbled a new one into the slot. A guitar started playing and I instantly knew what it was. Bob Marley was playing an acoustic version of the song I had been singing as I had climbed the hill the day I had found Lucas. I found myself joining in as Bob sang and played. I had not realised at the time just how appropriate the song was going to be, but I suppose everything seems clearer when we are given the chance to look back.

Going north to Dreux, heading for the coast on the D154, I joined the great Bob Marley as he sang his "Redemption Song".

The sun turned the long avenue of trees along the sides of the road a deep golden, and the clouds raced silently across the sky as if they were all late for the same appointment.

I knew that feeling well.

Printed in Great Britain
by Amazon